Evil Turn

Douglas Watkinson

First published in Great Britain

All paper used in the printing of this book has been made from wood grown in managed, sustainable forests.

ISBN: 978-1-78003-850-6

Printed and bound in the UK

Pen Press is an imprint of
Author Essentials
4 The Courtyard
South Street
Falmer
East Sussex
BN1 9PQ

A catalogue record of this book is available from the British Library

Evil Turn is the fourth novel in the Nathan Hawk series.
Other titles are:

Haggard Hawk
Easy Prey
Scattered Remains

www.douglaswatkinson.com

I used to be a high-ranking English copper until my temper got the better of me and I broke a fellow officer's jaw. I was 'required to retire' as the British police so delicately put it.

I should've learned from the experience but no, I still blow the odd fuse or ten. When my wife was alive she used to rein me in, but since her death there's been no one to do that. My good friend, my more than good friend, the elegant Doctor Laura Peterson, tries her best but it's a tough call.

I've got four grown-up kids, by the way, who live thousands of miles away – Nepal, Japan, Haiti and Los Angeles. They're all impetuous by nature and they worry me, usually with good reason. Thanks to e-mail and Skype it often feels like they're in the same room with me. Is that good or bad? I'm not sure...

When I first came to live in this truly beautiful English village I thought early retirement would be a breeze. Wrong! But just as I was about to go mad with boredom a neighbour did me the courtesy of being murdered and suddenly it was ... like the old days. Without the paperwork. Without a boss telling me to be careful.

The local police didn't like me poking my nose in and made that pretty clear, but they got over it once I'd solved their crime. It also gave me a reputation which brought other people to my door with crimes the police couldn't solve. Nice to be wanted.

Nathan Hawk

Before I became involved...

Joe Flaxman had seen the man three times now. It hadn't bothered him to begin with, since over the years several down-and-outs had used the barns and outbuildings to doss in and so long as they didn't mess up the place, steal things or stay too long, they were welcome. There was something disturbing about this man, however, and Joe couldn't quite put his finger on it...

The first time he saw him Joe was out in the yard at dusk watching the bats wheel and swoop on their insect prey, which meant he was standing in the shadows, perfectly still. The man emerged from the old grain store on the other side of the yard and was clearly annoyed about something, mouthing and muttering his complaints. He was better-dressed than most of them were: anorak over a jumper, jeans and boots. Hair tied back in a ponytail. He wasn't carrying a bag, though, the usual rucksack or Tesco carrier, so maybe he'd already settled in...

Joe stepped forward into the half-light; the man saw him, turned and fled, off into Speaker's Wood. Fast on his feet for a dosser, Joe thought, as he went over to the grain store. It was now a place for storing long-dead machinery, mementoes of the past when his father and grandfather farmed the land: old tractors, ploughs, rollers. He found no evidence that the man had bedded down there and assumed he must have been checking the building out as a possible home for the coming winter.

About a week later, Joe saw him for the second time. Again it was dusk and this time the man was up on the roof of the grading shed where, thirty years ago, small potatoes were separated from large ones; cabbages, sprouts and cauliflowers were trimmed, then packed into sacks and boxes. Joe used it as a garage these days. His own Chevy Silverado was there, alongside his wife's runaround Peugeot, so it wouldn't have been a safe place to bed down in anyway, but the man seemed to be examining the ventilation turret.

Joe called out to him and the stranger grabbed at the weather vane which for the last twelve years had pointed north towards the prevailing wind. It creaked and gave way, causing him to lose his footing momentarily. A slate came away, rattled down the roof and broke into several pieces where it fell. For a few seconds the man was outlined against the fading sky, arms outstretched, the unfastened anorak like the wings of a bird waiting for the wind to lift it into the air. There was no wind. The man turned, slithered down the other side of the roof and disappeared. But why the hell had he been up there in the first place?

The third time they crossed each other's paths was inside the house, and that gave Joe cause for concern. Carrie spent most of her time at home on her own and if the man was getting bolder and hungrier, where might it end?

It was six o'clock in the morning; Joe had been up for half an hour and was eating a bowl of cereal, thumbing through *Farmer's Weekly*, a ritual, not a pleasure, these days. Bella, an elderly German Shepherd, always at his feet, suddenly sat up and growled, her nose pointed at the door through to the rest of the house. Joe didn't question her. He hurried to the door, out into the corridor and followed Bella down to the middle back room, as they called it. He entered in time to see the man exiting through the French windows. He turned to Joe, their eyes met for a split second, Bella ran at him as he side-stepped between the long glass doors and slammed them behind him. Joe didn't think it worth pursuing him for the very good reason that he had youth on his side.

He talked it over with Carrie when she came downstairs in response to the hullabaloo. He hadn't bothered her with the first two sightings; she would've brushed the incidents aside and continued with whatever she was knitting at the time. But the man had been inside the house on this occasion. That was different. Carrie still seemed fairly relaxed about it, though.

"He's come in for food," she said, as if that were all the explanation needed. Joe wouldn't have been surprised if she'd suggested they leave some out for him.

"If it's for food, why the middle back?" he said. "Why not the kitchen?"

She shrugged. "French windows, easy to open. How old is he?"

"Young. Thirty. Something mean about him."

"What d'you mean, 'mean'?"

"A look in his eyes."

3

She laid both hands on the table and tapped out a rhythm with her splayed fingers. It was a sign that she was thinking and about to come up with a suggestion. When it came, Joe didn't like it.

"Why don't you go see the doctor?"

He hadn't seen a doctor for ten years or more. He didn't trust them. "What for?"

"Check-up. You're nearly sixty. Things happen. They can nip them in the bud these days..."

"Hang on a sec," he said, rising from the table. "What things, what bloody bud...?"

He suddenly realised what she'd been referring to. Her Aunt Jane had died a couple of months ago from the effects of dementia. The last few years of her life she'd 'seen things'. People.

"Jane was ninety-two," he whispered, fiercely.

"It's no respecter of age."

"What isn't?" he demanded.

"Well, nothing is..."

The conversation was about to spiral into him pushing, her side-stepping, the pair of them ending up not speaking for a week. The dog had already recognised the signs and slunk away under the table.

Joe knew what he'd seen: an intruder he didn't like the look of, but to keep the peace he made an appointment at the Health Centre for a consultation with Doctor Harris.

When his name was called by the terrifying receptionist, Joe made his way nervously down the passage to Doctor Harris's office. The door was slightly ajar from the last patient and he knocked on it.

"Come in," said a bright voice from the other side.

He stalled. It was bad enough that he'd come to see a doctor. But a woman doctor? He entered; she smiled and gestured for him to take the chair beside her desk while she finished off notes from the previous appointment, then brought up Joe's records on her screen.

"My word, Mr Flaxman, the last time we saw you was twelve years ago for a cut on your arm." She turned and smiled at him. "It seems redundant to ask you how it is."

Harris was short, overweight and bossy. They were the three characteristics her patients took away with them, but, as any of her colleagues would have testified, she was a fine doctor. Even so, she threw Joe immediately.

"How would you like me to address you, by the way? As Mr Flaxman or Joseph?"

"I answer to both. Mainly Joe."

"Right, Joe, my name is Clare. How can I help you today?"

Because of how the chair was placed he was facing slightly away from her. She leaned forward to correct that.

"My wife wanted me to see you," he said.

It won't have been about sexual problems or difficulties with conception, Harris thought, but she checked all the same. "How old is your wife?"

"Same as me. Fifty-nine."

"And why did she want me to see you?"

5

"She's worried that I'll turn into Aunt Jane. She died recently..."

He wound his finger round, close to his right temple, to indicate Jane's loopiness in the months leading up to her demise. This wasn't going to be the quick in-and-outer Clare had hoped for. It was her last appointment of the morning and she'd promised to go riding with a friend that afternoon.

"Is Aunt Jane your mother's sister, or your father's?" she asked.

"Neither. She's Carrie's aunt. My wife's."

Clare nodded and tried to explain that, though it might be genetic, you couldn't catch dementia like a cold. Joe either didn't understand or didn't believe.

"Is there a history of mental illness in your side of the family?"

"No!" he snapped.

"Joe, I'm going to take your blood pressure. No one has done that for twelve years and we do like to have a record. Would you take off your jacket, roll up your sleeve for me?"

The need to stand up, to move, to do something with his hands loosened him a little, and as Clare took the reading she recalled another patient whose wife had sent him to see her. He had turned out to have bowel cancer which he'd been too embarrassed to seek help about and had died, unnecessarily, a year later. For all his apparent fitness, Joe Flaxman needed careful handling.

"Your blood pressure is 130 over 82," she said.

"Is that good?" he asked.

"Put it this way: I wish mine was and I'm half your age."
He blurted it out. "She thinks I'm seeing things. I know I'm not. Well, I am, but they're real."

His directness caught Clare on the hop. She wasn't overly keen on being the referee in a who-saw-what contest. She asked him to explain and he told her about the young down-and-out. She listened with care and his account sounded remarkably feasible. Nevertheless, she was aware that farmers had their own particular problems, especially in the current economic climate. She referred back to his notes on her computer screen.

"Speaker's Farm. Yes, I've ridden through the wood once or twice. Yours will be the large house..."

He nodded.

"Is business going well?"

"Business is fine," he said.

He gave her a compelling résumé of how he'd turned from Brussels, cabbages and cauliflowers to egg farming, fifteen years ago. She seemed fascinated so he went into detail. 'Free-range eggs from birds who live happy lives' was the company slogan. The birds were housed in high-tech sheds, went outside in the day, came in at night, everything automated: feed, water, droppings, egg collection, grading. She asked how many birds he had, expecting the answer to run into hundreds.

"Sixteen thousand," he said.

"Good God! That's an awful lot of breakfasts."

She still hadn't worked out why his wife had sent him to her, if indeed there was a medical reason. She turned to the ever-reliable subject of stress. The business must put a strain on him, she said. When did he and Carrie last take a holiday? That was thirty-two years ago, their honeymoon. Since when, Clare discovered, Joe had worked seven days a week, rising at six in the morning, rarely finishing until five in the evening. And as she began to express her concern at the relentless nature of his lifestyle, her patient cracked, quite unexpectedly, and revealed the possible underlying explanation for his visit.

"What's it all been for?" he said. "Money? We got piles of that, we don't spend any. It was all meant for my son, Aaron, but he doesn't want it either. He'd rather go killing people."

"I beg your pardon?" said Clare.

"He shot two men he'd been in business with. Shot them dead. He's on remand in Stamford. Carrie says he couldn't have done it. I know he did. I also know you can't run a business from a prison cell."

Clare was shocked. She'd heard about the two bodies found on the edge of Speaker's Wood and she couldn't deny that since then she hadn't fancied riding near there. But at least she now understood why Joe's wife had wanted her to see him. She feared the repercussions from her son's horrendous crime.

"That is a dreadful thing to have happened to you, Joe. The effect of it will run deeper than you know and Carrie, being a woman – your wife of ... thirty-two years, did you say? – can see the toll it's taking."

He looked at her and she passed him a box of tissues. He pulled out a couple and dabbed his eyes, then turned away to blow his nose.

"I don't think there's anything physically wrong with you, Joe, but I would like to see you again in, say, two weeks' time."

She was the first person he'd ever revealed his true feelings about Aaron to, and even then he hadn't said much. He hadn't needed to. The story, from his side anyway, was in the tissues Clare Harris had handed him and he'd used.

"So, I'm not seeing things, then, Doctor ... Clare?"

"You may well be seeing things, but I'd bet money they aren't a figment of your imagination. You should tell the police."

When he arrived home, Carrie was anxious to hear how he'd got on with Clare Harris.

"You never told me she was a woman," he said.

"I thought it'd be a nice surprise for you. Did she give you anything?"

"To stop me seeing things, you mean? No need."

She nodded. The doctor was always right in Carrie's world, which raised the question: who was the man Joe had seen in the grain store, on the garage roof and in the middle back room? Joe had no idea, but he'd be ready for him next time. If there was a next time.

Carrie prodded him. It used to be her invitation to whisk her upstairs for an hour or two's love-making. These days it usually conveyed her delight at what was on television that evening.

"It's *Strictly Come Dancing*. Only two more weeks to go!" she said. "We'll have supper on our knees, shall we?"

For some reason he suddenly felt very old, as if time had passed him by on so many things while he'd been building up the business.

"Nice idea, love," he said.

They sat watching *Strictly*, seated on the new sofa. It was the size of a double bed. Joe preferred the old one they'd had, the big leather Chesterfield he and Carrie had picked up for a fiver when they were first married. It had been black with grease, worn through in some places, but at least it fought back when you sat in it. This one swallowed you whole the moment your backside touched it and it carried on digesting you throughout the evening. You had to rock back and forth to get on your feet again. But Aaron had thought it was high time his mother had a new sofa and bought her one, so Joe reckoned it was here to stay.

As *Strictly* started, they tucked into the steak and kidney pie which Carrie had bought from Newitt's specially that afternoon. There were four couples left and, as usual, Joe fancied the girl with the best figure while Carrie rooted for the lame dog, some old lady politician who could hardly move, let alone tango. As she came on to do her bit, Bella raised her head from the flat-out position she'd been in at Joe's feet and growled. She'd heard something in the distance, beyond the house, out in the yard or in the woods.

"Steady, girl," said Joe.

He handed Carrie his plate and stood up.

"You think that's him?" she asked. "Talk about picking his moment."

"I'll go see. You carry on watching and keep the dog from barking."

He went through to the kitchen without turning the light on and at the back door slipped into his wellingtons. His work jacket was hanging on a hook in the alcove. He put that on and checked the pockets for cartridges. Then he reached back into the alcove for the Purdey, loaded both chambers and stepped out into the yard, the shotgun broken over the crook of his arm.

There'd been no rain for a couple of days, so it was firm underfoot. He paused and looked round and just as he was about to blame Bella for her wonky hearing he saw a flash of white, up by the attic window of the old barn where his grandfather used to stable the horses. He knew immediately what it was. It was one of the barn owls that returned most years to raise a family and live off the rats. He wasn't sure if it was the male or the female but the flight was silent, not panicky like other birds. Then he saw its mate follow. Something had disturbed them.

He made his way over to the barn, staying close to the side of the house, then using the cover of the old grain store. He trod the last twenty feet across to the open barn doors, in open moonlight, as if he were ... walking on eggshells.

He entered and enough light followed him to see the inside of the building. Like everywhere else it was full of old machinery, old tools, old tackle corroding away rather than being scrapped. He stepped into the shadow cast by an old digger and looked round. Nothing was out of place and he knew these relics like the back of his hand, each piece a memorial to his family's past. Whoever had disturbed the owls, if indeed anyone had, they were up in the attic, and as he started towards the stone steps on the far wall he heard something in the boarded loft above: creaking rather than a regular tread as somebody moved towards the stairwell. Joe retreated into the shadow and waited. Whoever it was took their time, moved cautiously as if feeling their way as well as seeing it. Eventually the feet appeared at the top, the legs appeared, the body appeared as the man he'd cast as a dosser descended the narrow steps, hugging the wall. Joe stepped into what light there was, closed the shotgun and called out.

"Hold it!"

The intruder flattened himself back against the side wall, eyes wide with shock, arms raised. Joe approached him and was about to issue another instruction when the man jumped, down off the side of the steps, and ran towards the door. Joe raised the Purdey and fired, aiming wide, and caught the man in his leg. It brought him down, screaming, cursing then pleading.

"No, don't ... please, don't shoot..."

Joe walked over to the man as he got to his feet, hopping on one leg while trying to nurse the other. It was bleeding, having taken five or six pellets, but he wasn't mortally wounded and made a feeble grab for the shotgun. In response Joe whipped the butt of it across his face and felled him like a skittle, rolling and turning before he passed out. Joe took out his phone and called the police.

- 1 -

I never cared much for Tom Blackwell but at least I knew why, and that can't be said of most people I've taken against down the years.

I certainly never expected to see him again, but there he was strolling down Morton Lane towards my house on a cold August morning. It was unlikely to be a social call, an old colleague seeking me out for a chat about the past, and in hindsight I should've pretended not to be in. Like a fool, I went out to meet him at the five-bar gate.

He was dressed against the British summer, quilted anorak zipped up to the throat in armorial fashion so I couldn't see what he was wearing underneath. I reckoned it would be tweedy jacket over a crisp shirt and Police Federation tie. The grey flannels, which I could see, had turn-ups and knife-like creases. The shine on the shoes would have dazzled had there been any sunlight to bounce off them. It all meant that he was probably still married to the plain and pernickety Karen.

Our opening conversation had the sparkle of a spent match.

"Nathan Hawk, my dear friend!" Typical copper. Two lies in one sentence. 'Dear' and 'friend'. "Keeping well?"

"Can't grumble. Yourself?"

13

"Likewise, likewise."

That was another of his peculiarities that had always annoyed me: his habit of repeating words or phrases. I leaned over the gate and we shook hands. His was warm, mine was cold: his high-tech anorak versus my jeans and T-shirt and a belief in weather forecasts. Warm, sunny with a light breeze from the south, the girl had said...

"Nice place you've got," he said. "Quiet lane, no through traffic..."

"That's the way it is with dead ends."

"Right, right." He looked away as he recalled my late wife. "I was sorry to hear about Maggie, Nathan. I kept meaning to drop you a line, but you know how it is, you wonder if people would rather be left alone. But I am sorry."

"It was nine years ago, Tom."

"Jesus, was it really?"

He held the sympathetic frown for a moment or two, then gazed past me to the house, wondering perhaps if I was going to invite him in or just carry on leaning. As it was, my curiosity to know why he'd suddenly appeared in my life got the better of me.

"Fancy a drink?" I said.

He glanced at his watch as if lightning might strike at the mention of alcohol before lunch.

"Yours was always a single," I said, lifting the metal loop which held the gate. "And you could make the bloody thing last all night."

He smiled. "Yours was a double, ice to the brim. And it lasted the best part of five minutes."

I pulled the gate open a yard or so and in he came.

Once Blackwell had finished pretending that he liked dogs and had spoken kind but nervous words to my own drug squad reject, I pushed her out into the garden and invited him to sit at the kitchen table. He took off the anorak, hung it fussily over a chair and proved that I was still a master at judging people by their appearance. There was the tweed jacket, the immaculate white shirt and a tie you could turn a fried egg with.

From an ever-ready bottle of Bell's I poured a single into a tumbler where it looked ridiculous. I went to the freezer for ice, added a few chunks to my own double, took my place at the other end of the table and waited.

After a series of nods and smiles he made a show of looking back on our brief working relationship with that wry amusement time uses to soften hostilities of the past. His memory was surprisingly detailed, which made me suspect he'd done some research. We'd first met eleven years and three months ago, he informed me, when I was a Detective Chief Inspector in Hamford and he was a young Detective Constable. I was leading the inquiry into a stomach-churning murder, the kind which had me phoning my daughters throughout the day to make sure they were still alive. A woman in her early twenties had been raped, strangled and cut into chunks so that her killer, an old boyfriend, could get her out of his flat more easily. Six bin bags in all.

Blackwell tried to skip over the occasion when I'd given him a verbal hammering followed by an ultimatum. He pretended to have forgotten the reasons for it, so I reminded him. I'd noticed, early on in the inquiry, that he was one of those people with a talent for getting others to do their work for them, clean or dirty. At first I'd thought it was laziness on his part, but if so why did he spend more time and effort getting the rest of the squad to carry his load than it would've taken to do the job himself? Something far more subtle than indolence was driving him. The skill, the finesse with which he operated, without his victims realising, was impressive. 'Impressive' is the wrong word, I know, but I can't bring to mind its pejorative equivalent...

It was in the days before open plan and way, way before standing up became the new sitting down, so middle ranks and above still had their own offices. With chairs. I always left my door open but suggested that he close it behind him on this occasion unless he wanted the others to hear our one-sided discussion. Hands in his pockets, he hooked it shut with his foot, then stood looking down at me while I effed and feffed my way through a series of accusations, finally asking if he'd always been a lazy bastard or had somebody taught him. He didn't so much as blink. Was he happy at home? Did he owe money? Was he ill? Had there been a death in the family? All the usual and necessary stuff. No to everything, so I asked if it went deeper. Was he maybe scared of turning over the stones in this murder? Frightened of the details chiming with his own darker side?

By then, in his shoes, I would have picked up the desk and thrown it at me, but all I got from Blackwell when I finally allowed him to speak was sweet reason, so elegantly expressed that it nearly had me wondering if I'd read him all wrong. And just as I was about to ask him to have a seat, maybe a whisky, talk things over reasonably, I put a name to his behaviour. Manipulative. It may be common currency these days, but in those days the word, the concept itself, hadn't long been in fashion. I challenged him with my thought and he shook his head in bewildered innocence.

"Guvnor, I haven't the faintest idea..."

"I mean whatever job I give you, making coffee, counting body parts, you persuade some other poor sod to do it for you! And all for the pleasure of watching them jump through hoops that you're spinning."

Control freak. I'm not sure how popular that phrase was then, or I'd have tossed it into my crude assessment of him. I gave him a week to change his work ethic (another modernism), or I'd have him reassigned. He stared at me, part respect, part defiance.

"All I can say is I'll try. Can I go now? Shall I leave the door or close it behind me?"

I toyed with the idea of leaping across the desk and ripping his trouser pockets from their seams, given that his hands were still firmly in them. Instead, I said quietly, "There'll always be a place for men like you in today's police service, Tom, specially at the top."

Subsequently, he had gone up the career ladder like a window cleaner possessed and had reached the dizzy heights of Commander.

I rattled the ice in my drink and he smiled again.

"We had a theory as to why you took it with all that ice," he said. "It made you drink it more quickly, before the ice melted and diluted it." He raised his glass. "Absent friends."

He took the smallest sip I've ever seen qualify as one.

"And a few enemies," I added.

He didn't quite know how to take my acknowledging the humanity of some of our old adversaries and it may sound pious that I did, but a fair few of the villains I'd nicked in my thirty years weren't evil men; they were just wrong. Not half as wrong as some of the coppers I'd known.

Blackwell gazed round the kitchen, as if trying to see beyond the walls.

"Big house," he said. "I mean beautiful, but big. For just you."

I put the question he was trying to ask into a sentence for him. "You mean do I live here on my own?"

He smiled. "The vase of roses on the window sill isn't your style, Nathan, so I assume a woman's hand."

"Her name is Laura Peterson and she's a local GP. She doesn't live here."

He badly wanted to know the reason for that but hadn't the nerve to ask, so I indulged him. If Laura and I moved in together, I said, it would close a door on a crucial part of my life, one that I feared would never open again. He assumed I was talking about my days in the police service. I corrected him. My professional past, though unforgotten, wasn't a place I was keen to revisit. My family, on the other hand, my four children who had flung themselves all over the world, were a different matter. I nodded to where my favourite photos of them stood out from plates, bowls, cups, saucers and everything else the kitchen dresser was designed to hold. Setting up house with Laura, I summarised, might finally cut the cord which I fondly imagined still held us all together.

"And what about Laura?"

"What about her?"

"Does she have a past she wants to revisit or ... or is happy to keep secret?" In response to my off-key look he quickly added, "Sorry, sorry, I'm prying."

He certainly was and there was bound to be a reason for it. I explained that Laura didn't have a past in the sense he'd meant, that her life as a GP meant almost everything to her, that her frustration with a National Health Service she both loved and hated never once made her forget why she'd taken up medicine in the first place. It went straight back to the Hippocratic oath. She had other interests, naturally, and that's where I came in. Not as an interest in my own right, but as someone she could share hers with. A willing and responsive listener.

"What are those interests?"

"Poetry, mainly, but you know, painting, opera..."

He was wise enough not to question me further about them. He took another sip which was hardly worth swallowing. I countered with a swig.

"How are the kids doing?" he asked.

He stood up and went over to the dresser, the better to see a photo of my daughters, Fee before she went off to Japan, Ellie a year into her course at the Sorbonne.

"Good-looking girls," he said.

Something happens when a middle-aged man makes a remark like that about your daughters, no matter how innocently it's meant. I guess I'd whiplashed back to the squad room mentality where similar words would have been followed by declarations of intent, who would fancy doing what to the girl being ogled.

I went straight from there to wondering if there'd ever been another woman in Blackwell's life, before or during Karen. I doubted it, even though for all his cramped personal style he was a good-looking man. First impressions for me always involve the other bloke's hair, comparing it to my own diminishing head of the stuff. Blackwell's was an upturned white scrubbing brush, at odds with dark eyebrows but enviable all the same. A closer look gave you the chiselled face and skin which looked a good deal younger than the man wearing it.

I was still no nearer to knowing why he was here, but assumed he hadn't sought me out only to leave without telling me.

"Connor and Jaikie well?" he asked.

He spoke as if he knew them. He'd certainly met them when they were in their teens and I shouldn't have been surprised that he remembered their names. I remembered his two. Georgina and Graham. Their mother brought them to the office one day and they made absolutely no impression whatsoever.

"Jaikie seems to live a charmed life..." I began.

He pointed, to interrupt me. "We saw that film, *All Good Men and True*. Christ, he was good in that!"

"So people keep telling me."

He frowned. "You didn't think so?"

"I thought he was bloody marvellous. It's just that to me he's still Jaikie, the kid who's always late for school."

He pretended that he knew what I meant, even though I wasn't entirely sure myself.

"Can't be all roses, though," he said. "I mean America's no place to live."

"He would disagree. Besides, he's also got a flat in Chiswick, the Beverly Hills of Britain. Shares it with an old schoolfriend. Female."

"Ah, well, at least you see him...?"

"Occasionally."

The conversation was beginning to rile me. There'd been too many questions, him to me, which I'd tried passing off as me being interesting, him being boring, wanting to hear all about my vibrant family.

He smiled. "Does Connor still have you spitting feathers?"

Con didn't so much hack me off these days as worry me, serious middle-of-the-night stuff, bolt upright in bed, full sweat. Blackwell nodded as if, again, he knew what I meant, but I reckoned his kids were as prim and proper as their mother.

"Connor's his own man," I said, struggling to say it with pride. "Christmas, for example. The rest of us were here, no one had heard a word for over a month and, just as I started to worry, the bugger walked in Christmas Eve, asked if we were all going up to the carol service."

"Where'd he been?"

"Haiti."

"He works there?"

I laughed. "Generous of you to assume that he works, but Con has turned the gap year into a gap decade. God knows what he does for money. I've stopped giving it, he's stopped asking for it."

He sighed as if, on my behalf, he was juggling the pros and cons of having such interesting children. He nodded back at the dresser. "And the girls have both gone, by the sound of it?"

"Fee works in Tokyo, Ellie works in Nepal. You don't get more gone than that."

I thought it was high time I asked about his two.

"Georgina married three years ago." He shook his head. "Nice enough lad, got his own business, something to do with pest control. At least he isn't a copper."

"Similar line of work, I suppose. More sociable hours."

He lowered his voice as if to confide a shameful secret. "The police service you and I grew up with is dead and gone. It's now the National Crime Authority, as I'm sure you know. In the reorganisation I found myself washed up in the OCC."

There's a whole list of character traits I can't stand, but phoney self-effacement is right at the top. It's as bad as full-blown self-importance. People didn't find themselves 'washed up' in the Organised Crime Command. They were a chosen few, picked for their skill, knowledge and effectiveness. Tom Blackwell had all three attributes in spades and was exercising them right now on me.

"Trouble is I've come in halfway through this particular caper ... near the end, really. My predecessor keeled over, couple of months ago. I'm the new boy." He jumped sideways, an old-fashioned device for securing the listener's attention. "Your office was always a jungle, Nathan. Who keeps this place so spick and span?"

I told him that a lady in the village came once a week to do stuff around the house.

"A cleaner, you mean?"

"My father's ghost won't allow me to call her that. What caper?"

He sat down at the end of the table again and nursed his drink. After a moment or two's heavy thought, as if wondering whether to proceed or call the whole thing off, he asked me to picture the fishing port of Grimsby, in particular two trawlermen who had battled the North Sea, the cod wars, falling prices, quotas, Greenpeace forever on their backs. They were running out of money. They were married to a couple of sisters who wanted families but were forced back to work, one of them as a nursery nurse, the other as a barmaid.

Two years ago, a local man walked into the pub, sat at the bar and struck up a conversation with the wife serving him. His name was Aaron Flaxman and he told her he was looking for a boat to import 'an assortment of stuff, mainly from Europe and North Africa'. Verbatim. The wife put the idea to her sister and within a month they and their husbands were smuggling cigarettes, booze, perfume, designer clothes, car parts – you name it, they carried it, all under cover of the family business, all on a small scale, while they learned the trade. Then one of them got greedy.

"One of the men, we think. The women would've kept it

as a perfect business partnership, everyone with a theoretical say..."

"Like John Lewis, you mean?"

He gave that a moment before nodding. "Anyway, into the partnership hustles a man, late twenties, Liam Kinsella. The kind of man other men don't want hanging round their wives, especially if they work away from home. Handsome, polite but not quite sure of himself, according to the wives. Looking for excitement. And he'd just inherited a pot of money which he couldn't wait to invest. So, cut a long story short, three months later an OCC crime analyst reported that an English firm had blipped onto her screen and was due to bring in a job lot of heroin from Liepaja, a town on the coast of Latvia."

I shrugged my ignorance of both town and country.

"Baltic Sea, once a fishing port, now a mixture of everything. Very Russian, very windy, very dirty. The heroin was worth 15 million quid on the street and weighed in at 220 pounds. That's the size of an unfit copper."

There was a pause as we both thought back to colleagues of that size we'd have cheerfully seen ground into powder and sold for profit.

Blackwell picked up his thread. If an English team was handling this haul, the analyst wondered, how would they get it back to Blighty? Charter or cargo flight, heavy goods vehicles, container ship, overland by horse and cart?

"You smile, but it's been done," he said. "This stuff hailed from Afghanistan, came up through Russia wrapped in a consignment of handwoven rugs supposedly bound for some poncy furniture store in Oslo. And, as the rugs arrived in Liepaja, so did our Grimsby trawler, ostensibly to refuel before heading home. Question then for OCC was how to elbow aside the Humberside Crime Squad, and when and how to intercept the target."

I couldn't let 'intercept' go unchallenged. It was another of those handy euphemisms, a word with a fatter meaning now than it had twenty-five years ago. Back then, 'to intercept' meant to nick a letter or get the ball off an opposing player; now it meant to shoot down enemy aircraft or catch a serial killer.

Blackwell smiled and gestured for me to say it my way.

"When to jump in and nail the bastards."

He nodded. "And OCC spent far too long faffing around, afraid of offending colleagues in Humberside, which meant the trawlermen sailed into Grimsby mid-November, unloaded a meagre catch and feigned disappointment. Later the same night somebody went back to the boat for the heroin, took it to Aaron Flaxman's father's farm."

"Two hundred and twenty pounds of heroin's a lot to sell," I said. "How did they plan to get rid of it?"

"In one fell swoop and for half its value, to the Heritage IRA." He smiled. "When those three letters enter a conversation the temperature usually rises, and this case was no exception. Understandably, the IRA quickly became favourites for the murders..."

"Hang on a tick," I intercepted. "Have I missed something? What murders?"

"Sorry, sorry. The two trawlermen, up near the family farm. Couple of bullets, very amateurish, very messy, but still rendering the victims very dead."

25

He'd hooked me in classic style by holding back a crucial piece of information, the two killings, then dropping it into a lull. In the space of twenty words he'd shifted the emphasis of his story: a family smuggling business had evolved into a major drugs trafficker with links to the Heritage IRA who in turn murdered anyone who got in their way. He reached out for his glass and knocked back what was left in a single gulp. I must have looked surprised and offered him another, but he declined. So did I when I offered myself a top-up.

"The wives had reported their husbands and Kinsella missing, but since they weren't twelve-year-old kids, a file was opened and left dangling. Until the body of one of the trawlermen was found a couple of weeks later in a ditch. Ten days after that his brother-in-law rose to the surface of a slurry pit. Kinsella's body still to be found. When questioned the wives didn't know a thing about heroin, Latvia or the Heritage IRA. They gave up the name Aaron Flaxman willingly, saying he was a top dog sort of bloke, alpha male, gave the orders and woe betide anyone who didn't follow them. But as for him being a murderer, well..." He smiled. "You know how the rest of it goes: unthinkable, can't believe he would do that, he's just an ordinary bloke. Be that as it may, the trawlermen's blood and brain matter were found in the back of a pickup belonging to Flaxman and he was charged with their murders. He's on remand in Stamford.

"Then one night, middle of April, the local police got a call to Speaker's Farm. Aaron Flaxman's father had shot an intruder, winged him. The intruder turned out to be Liam

Kinsella and this was the fourth time the old man had caught him poking around the farm."

"Looking for the overweight copper?" I asked.

Blackwell nodded. Kinsella had maintained he was just hiding out, had been for weeks, and when asked about the heroin he was deeply offended. He hadn't signed up to bring in stuff like that, nor had the dead trawlermen. When they'd objected Aaron Flaxman had shot them. How did Kinsella know this? He'd seen him do it!

Blackwell thought he'd better boil all that down so that I could digest it more easily. "In other words, this scruff-bag Kinsella was manna from heaven, the best break the local crime squad had had. He'd been standing thirty feet away when Flaxman pulled the trigger. And for a case that didn't have much going for it, bar some blood and brains in a Chevy pickup, Kinsella's willingness to talk was a godsend."

I'd retained most of what he'd said, aware that none of it was as important as the detail he'd left out. I stood up and went over to the sink, filled a jug and poured water into the coffee maker.

"So where do I fit in?" I asked.

He looked at me, scrunched up eyebrows. "Who said you did?"

"You mean you've come all the way from ... where is it you live?"

"Guildford, Guildford."

"You've come all the way from Guildford-Guildford to tell me about two trawlermen who've been shot dead? You've taken me all round the bloody houses to find out if

27

I'm living here alone and, if so, who visits." He looked away, and I shifted to get back in his eyeline. "The first thing you mentioned at the gate was through traffic. You went on to Laura, the kids, my lady who does! Why?"

The only thing either of us could hear, once I'd stopped making the point, was the water pumping through the coffee maker, slowly, arthritically. I'd been meaning to descale the thing for weeks, never got round to it. Blackwell was chewing his bottom lip, wondering how to deal with the fact that I'd rumbled his technique if not his purpose.

Eventually he said, "Pupil goes back to teacher. I guess I came for advice."

"Advice, my fanny!"

For a moment the man behind the long, drawn-out crawl towards me reared up on his hind legs. "For Christ's sake, Nathan, you never could take anything at face value, never mind a compliment! Why else would I be here? The pleasure of your company?"

After some deep breaths he returned to his main purpose. Aaron Flaxman, he said, was coming up for trial. It had been fast-tracked and was due to begin end of September.

"Trial where?"

"The Bailey. That aside, with Kinsella's evidence it's gone from being a possibility that he goes down to an almost dead cert."

Was I familiar with the 2005 Serious Organised Crime and Police Act? I wasn't and had no intention of becoming so. It was an overloaded ark of bureaucratic fence-sitting and back-watching, Blackwell said. It was designed by twelve-year-old lawyers to make the job of catching scumbags like Flaxman harder than necessary, but in so far as it applied to this case everything had been done; the evidence had been properly assessed and an Immunity from Prosecution agreement for Kinsella was in the pipe-line. Right now he was safely tucked away waiting for the trial to start. As for Aaron Flaxman, he was on remand in Stamford, an old prison near Grimsby.

Blackwell looked at me as if I knew what was coming next. I hadn't the faintest.

"My advice?" I prompted.

He fumbled for words as I took down two mugs from the dresser, both of us aware of the irony that, having insulted him, I was now going to serve him coffee. I went to the fridge for the milk and once my back was turned to him, he blurted it out.

"I'd like to use this place as a safe house for the main witness, Liam Kinsella."

I turned back to him, milk bottle in hand, and he waited, some time I imagine, for my mouth to close.

"You'd be paid, of course. Believe it or not, there's a contingency fund..."

"You want me to put up a murder witness in my house?"

He said yes, that was the gist of it, but like all bare facts it could gave the wrong impression and the truth in this matter was only half the story. I suggested that was a contradiction in terms and asked for the other half. He searched for words that wouldn't upset me, couldn't find any.

"We think there a chance someone'll come after Kinsella before he can testify."

"Fantastic! When the Heritage IRA turn up, we'll break open a few cans of Guinness, have a ceili. Who the hell are they, anyway?"

He explained that after the Good Friday agreement in Ireland, when everybody was meant to love each other, it didn't quite work out that way and split the IRA into factions: Continuity, Real and Heritage. Flaxman's family had tenuous connections to Heritage. He could see, from the look on my face, that none of that had put me in a better frame of mind. He held up both hands to fend off the immediate future.

"Nathan, if you don't want it to happen, that's an end..."

"Why weren't you straight with me, right from the start?!"

He had an answer for that as well but I didn't like it. There was a chance the current list of safe houses had been compromised. The situation here in Winchendon, quiet village, no through road, few callers, was perfect, but if at any point I'd said one of the kids was living here, or I was in a permanent relationship, he'd have called it off and I'd have been none the wiser. I translated that for him. He hadn't wanted me to know that he was reeling me in.

I screwed the top back on the whisky, took the glasses to the drainer, then moved the odd item of furniture out of harm's way. He must have recognised the signs from the old days. Any second now I would reach for someone's head and slam it down on a hard surface, and since he was the only person in the room...

"I'd better go," he said. He took his anorak from the back of the chair and stroked out non-existent creases.

"Before you do, Tom, hear this. Your family might not give a toss if a bunch of Paddies break in and blow your brains out. Mine would. They'd be..." I pretended to search for the word. "...upset."

"It wouldn't happen, Nathan. You'd have a top flight team here, armed, experienced..."

"Christ Almighty, now it's a house party! Listen, you may not figure much in your kids' lives. Each to his own." He was shaking his head now, avoiding my gaze. "I mean all you've said is that Georgina got married, and you didn't seem too chuffed about that! What about the boy?"

"Graham?"

"Not a mention. I never knew a man who didn't boast about his son, no matter how well or badly they got on..."

"We lost him."

Even though I'd understood him completely I still asked, "What do you mean, you lost him?"

"He was killed, just before Christmas. Big pile-up on the A34. Three cars. I just hope he died before they burst into flames. Strange thing to say, I know..."

I didn't want him to stop talking because it meant the next words would have to be mine. He spared me.

"It's difficult telling people. They're sympathetic, of course, but most of them don't know when to stop. For Karen it just relives the whole business. For me, I have to go right back to the first days, seeing her through it while grieving myself..."

"Fucking hell, Tom," I said.

He smiled, faintly. "I knew you'd have the right words, Nathan."

I slumped into the chair at my end and watched as he put the anorak back on and zipped it up. He gestured for me to stay seated as he stretched out a hand.

"Good to see you. You haven't changed."

He went over to the door and as he reached it, grabbed the handle, a hundred voices in my head were begging me not to say what came out of my mouth next.

"Hang on a second."

The handle snapped back and he turned to me.

"This case is important to you, personally? Have you got drugs in the family?"

"Not that I know of. You?"

"Connor. He got a grip on it but it wasn't easy. Sit down again." He protested with a painful grimace. "Take your coat off, switch that bloody coffee maker off, pour us both some."

He did as I'd asked and came slowly back to the table with two mugs. "This may sound trite, but losing a child does so many things. Graham's death made me consider the morality of what we do in our job sometimes. I think we fall short too often..."

He broke off as if he'd said too much or maybe not enough. Either way, I could hardly challenge him.

"How long would this Liam Kinsella be here?" I asked.

"Four, five weeks at the most."

"How many people apart from him?"

"Just two from Special Ops. Fewer the better, or at least that's what I tell myself. Truth is, I haven't got the resources."

I nodded. "No spare box of coppers lying around."

I asked him to give me twenty-four hours to think it over, which would involve putting the matter to Laura Peterson. He understood my wish to do so completely. She came to my house far too often to be left out of the loop. Besides, he added with a smile, it would give him a day to check on her, the gardener and Jean Langan, my lady who does.

As we drank our coffee he spoke wistfully about his dead son, the things he hadn't done for him and with him. It wasn't self-pity, but in the space of twenty minutes he beat himself up so badly that a decent referee would've stopped the fight after the first round. When he was done he gave me a couple of chances to backtrack, to say no to the whole dumb safe-house project. I didn't take them. I had an uncomfortable feeling he'd known all along that I wouldn't.

- 2 -

I took Laura to The Thatch in Thame that evening and we sat in a corner of the old restaurant, all low beams to crack your head on and sudden mirrors to record the passage of time. It was both the right and the wrong place to have chosen: good because the noise from other customers muffled what I had to say, bad because their conversation tested my legendary tolerance.

The clientele was largely mid-thirties, middle-incomers, and a dozen or so were celebrating a birthday at the next table. One of the women caught my attention immediately with her harsh, painful face, blonde hair framing it on three sides. She wore a black, silky dress that had seen younger, slimmer days, but her defining feature was the rapid gunfire laughter, ten degrees louder than anyone else's, and the more she drank, the more easily it was triggered. I looked at her critically once or twice until I realised that her friends also found her annoying; indeed they were doing their best to sideline her, a fact which gradually made me change sides in this undeclared battle of wills. At eight o'clock, shortly after we arrived, I could have killed her; by nine I would have laid down my life for her. I digress...

Laura was intrigued to know why there'd been a departure from our normal routine on busy days of a quick supper at the pub in Winchendon. I told her that, much as I loved Annie McKinnon's home cooking, a private conversation in The Crown always became public knowledge within twenty-four hours. Nobody knew how it happened; it was something to do with English village life being made that way.

She'd had a long, hard day at the surgery and was still concerned about one of her younger colleagues who'd had a lump removed from her breast a month ago. Laura was keen to support this newcomer to the practice and, rather than bring in a locum, she was sharing Doctor Sheila Bright's workload with another partner. I'd voiced my opinion, in spite of it not being asked for, that the seventy-, eighty-hour weeks couldn't go on for much longer. Laura said they could and would until Sheila's health was restored.

Though tired she was looking pretty good, better than some of the birthday crowd close by. She's one of the few middle-aged women I know who look decent in jeans anyway, and that's mainly to do with the long legs. Above the waist she was wearing a black velvet jacket and a mass of her favourite silver jewellery.

Over one of the house specialities, devilled kidneys on toast, I told her about the murder of the two trawlermen, then explained what Tom Blackwell had asked for and I'd virtually agreed to. She blinked at me, troubled by some new contact lenses.

"You mean his star witness is coming to stay at Beech Tree along with two police officers for a whole month?"

I couldn't work out if she was troubled or thrilled by the prospect but opted to assume the latter.

"What sort of chap is this Tom Blackwell? If he's an old friend, presumably you can trust him?"

I corrected her quickly. Blackwell wasn't a friend, he was an acquaintance, a man trying to do the right thing.

"So, you believe he's a ... moral man. Isn't it odd that we, the general we, find that word so difficult to use these days?"

She sat back in her chair, taking her wine with her. A few moments later she came forward again with another question.

"Why did he come to you, you in particular? There must be dozens of acquaintances he could have called upon."

"I haven't given it much thought."

"Well, is there anything in your joint past that might explain it? A case you worked on, people you knew?"

"He was on an inquiry I led, for less than a year."

A waitress brought a cake to the next table, four candles on it, one for each decade rather than a burning forest to emphasise the advancing years. The celebrant blew them out and his friends began to sing 'Happy Birthday' with such gusto that we fell silent. When it was over and the clapping had died down I sat up straight, hands behind my head, and tried to stretch Tom Blackwell out of my mind. He wouldn't go. And then Laura jabbed me with a shot of feminine perception.

"Why the uncertainty, Nathan? I mean it's not just about the possible danger involved, is it? You invite that at the best of times."

I must have smiled, or something equally impetuous. She repeated her question. I explained as wearily as I could that I hadn't wanted Liam Kinsella shacking up with me, especially after Blackwell had hinted at a possible IRA connection. Like he'd said, mention of those three capital letters has an effect, one where the listener imagines either a spent force or a re-emergent threat. Laura simply said that Kinsella was a hauntingly beautiful name and asked, for the third time, why I had misgivings. I told her about Graham Blackwell's death and she was horrified by it, the more so probably because her own brother had died in a road accident at a similar age. She reached across the table and took my hand as if somehow that might convey her empathy to Tom and Karen Blackwell. I then came out with what I'd been reluctant to believe.

"I think he used his son's death to persuade me, to make me change my mind. He worked it into the conversation in order to get the result he wanted. What sort of man would do that?"

She withdrew her hand and thought about it, then said, "That could just be you, thinking the worst of everyone as usual. And it doesn't alter the fact that his son is dead."

On the way home to Beech Tree, Laura gave a more considered diagnosis. She was driving, being less over the limit than I was, and began her summary with the ominous words, "I've been thinking..."

I turned and looked at her profile as she kept her eye firmly on the road ahead. I always homed in on her nose. A proper nose, my son Jaikie called it. Lips slightly forward, kissable, though not from that angle. Chin jutting. Above it all, the sizeable forehead shielding all those brains. If I'd been voicing those thoughts when we left The Thatch, no wonder she'd offered to drive.

"Blackwell said he came to you for advice."

"Advice, my fanny!"

She turned to me momentarily.

"That's what I said back to him," I said.

"Pupil goes back to teacher," she quoted. "We always think our teachers know more than we do, and it's usually true."

There was something definitely off about this case, she went on, and if she'd sensed it then Blackwell probably had and I most *certainly* had. Okay, we couldn't put a name to it, but what did we have so far? One, the trial was being rushed; two, it was laughable that he'd run out of safe houses, and as for three, there being only two police officers available...

"And one of them is evidently a girl," I said, unwisely.

She let it ride. Aware that something was skewiff, she continued, Blackwell wanted to bring his star witness into my presence to see if I could put my finger on it. More than that, however, he believed that when I discovered what was wrong I would do something about it, poke my nose in as per usual. I would cross lines, cut corners, break rules that he as a serving officer couldn't afford to. She slapped the steering wheel and waited for my reaction. I told her that what she'd said made sense but I didn't believe it. We fell silent, consideration on my part, a slight sulk on hers.

"I know one thing he's got wrong," I said, eventually. "The murders were very amateurish and very messy, according to him. That doesn't sound like the IRA to me."

- 3 -

Later that evening I went up to my cabin to talk to my kids. I don't actually *talk* to Fee, Con, Jaikie or Ellie, of course. We've developed this e-mail forum: one of us starts a thread, the others follow up, and if ever proof were needed of how powerful a misplaced word can be then our brief exchanges provide it. Two years ago, from their faraway laptops or mobile phones, they would ramble on about each other, themselves or maybe nothing in particular, assuring me that some invisible chain held us together as a family. Now, along with an entire generation, they've shortened their missives, shortened the very words they use, and left me fearing that the result will be estrangement.

This particular exchange was going to be tricky and the smart thing would've been to say nothing. In a month it would all be over, Flaxman would've been sentenced and Kinsella would've changed his name. But I tried to persuade myself that something primal was at work as I sat down at my computer on that late August evening. Beech Tree was my kids' home as much as mine and I was about to place it in jeopardy by letting a murder witness stay there. I hadn't signed an agreement in blood with Tom Blackwell to keep quiet, so why shouldn't Fee, Con, Jaikie and Ellie give their opinion? I made a pig's ear of it by obscuring the real question with a trivial one which took on a life of its own.

The clocks on the wall told me what time it was in their parts of the world. It was two in the morning in downtown Katmandu where my daughter Ellie worked in an orphanage alongside her American boyfriend, Terrific Rick.

"Hi Ellie," I began. "Just wanted to run something past you, you being the dog whisperer in the family. I've been offered another one. German Shepherd cross with a Labrador, young, male, biddable and good looking. You saw Dogge at Xmas. Can she cope? Dad x."

Even as I pressed the key to send it I was staggered by its cack-handedness. Nevertheless, over the next few hours I received a series of replies starting with Ellie's.

"Hi D! Sounds like my ideal man! It's yr house. Hve as many dogs as you wnt. Crse Dogge can! E x."

As I'd expected Fee wasn't far behind, having heard the news from her sister. No messing with Fee, she went straight for it.

"Dad, what's wrong? What do you want another dog for? Is Laura okay? What's happened? Fee x."

With Fee I knew it was a fine balance: respond too soon and she'd suspect, leave it too late and she'd worry.

"Absolutely nothing wrong," I replied half an hour later. "It was a genuine question. I mean is it fair that I get a young, boisterous dog in when Dogge's in her declining years? Will she feel pushed out?"

Jaikie was next. "Dad, mate, Fee's been on, yap, yap, yap. If you've got something wrong with you, get it checked out."

This was going badly. It had jumped tracks from being about a fictional new dog to me having a terminal illness.

He went on to say that I should mosey on down to Chiswick next week for lunch, only not Monday, he was seeing the guys at Working Title (*Four Weddings*, *Bridget Jones*). Him and Keira Knightley in something together? Not Tuesday either, he was doing a voice over. Wednesday he was having lunch with the CEO of Cloud Eight (*Slumdog Millionaire*). Thursday was out as well, but it was reassuring to know that he was his usual self-obsessed self. He did have the grace to end with a PS. "Repeat, get it checked out immediately, okay?!"

Ellie must have picked up on his concern along the way and it resulted in, "Dad, tweet from J earlier. This illness, what does L say?"

I responded with attitude. J and L are the human beings known to me as Jaikie and Laura, are they, my love? Laura says the usual. Less booze, less coffee, more exercise. Maybe I did need another dog.

There was one voice missing. It belonged to Connor, who'd become increasingly difficult to reach. To account for his silence, this departure from the family norm, his siblings had turned as one on his current girlfriend, a French Creole beauty from New Orleans called Marcie. None of us knew her, none of us had even met her, but we all disliked her. I put Con on a nearby shelf, to worry about in spare moments.

- 4 -

Blackwell and I didn't meet again until his two Special Operations Unit officers moved in to Beech Tree four days later. We'd spoken on the phone a few times, though he'd have preferred an e-mail exchange. Fair enough, but with people who manipulate the truth for a living, such as policemen, e-mails allow the writer to disappear behind their style and the substance is always the loser, so I insisted that we iron out wrinkles ear to ear. We dealt with stuff like who was going to sleep where, the location of the temporary armoury and, most importantly, what the cover story would be.

Basically, the male SOU officer would be a distant cousin of mine, staying with me for a few weeks along with his wife, the female officer. Kinsella would be her step-brother – the 'step' part would cover the lack of family resemblance. A gathering of the clan, then, should anyone ask, and on the occasions Kinsella was due in court they would all have gone out for the day to visit the likes of Blenheim Palace, Waddesdon Manor, Windsor Castle.

When the two SOU officers arrived I was standing at the kitchen window, six thirty in the morning, waiting for the coffee maker to squeeze out a pot of wakefulness. I still hadn't descaled it; I'd simply stopped listening to its agony.

A Ford Focus drove down Morton Lane and paused outside Beech Tree. Detective Constable Petra Fairchild got out from the passenger side, opened the five-bar gate, the car drove in and she closed the gate behind it. Sergeant Bill Grogan emerged, slab by slab, from the driver's side, looked up at the place and mouthed the words, "Fuck me!"

I ground some more coffee.

Grogan wasn't just a large man; he was a cumbersome one as well. Throughout his stay I was to hear regular collisions between him and a low beam, an impact followed by reverberation and strangled expletives. That just about sums him up. He was someone who made his presence felt more than heard, a man of few words, at least in the beginning, and it's a breed I'm not familiar with. He dumped a holdall on the kitchen table, nodded at me, then asked if I minded him looking over the house without me as a tour guide. I did mind, but it seemed unhelpful to begin our relationship with disagreement. That would follow soon enough. Off he went.

I would've said the only thing he and his colleague had in common was that neither of them wanted to be there. Fair enough, I'd found myself in that situation many times and who was to say I hadn't landed there again, but it was a month out of all our lives, no more. A job that needed doing. So why did Grogan and Fairchild worry me? Habit, pleasure or something real?

For a start, I couldn't see them as a married couple, certainly not in the same bed together. Beyond the fact that he was pug ugly, jowly before his time, and she was seriously attractive, age was the main stumbling block: he was late forties to her thirty at the most. His clothes were plain dull, hers quiet but expensive: a leather bomber jacket, burgundy in colour, jeans and what my mother would have called 'plimsoles, probably from Woolworth's'. My mother would also have gone to town on the spiky auburn hair which even I could see had been cut by someone who knew what they were doing.

Fairchild placed her own sporty-looking shoulder bag on the table and felt the need to apologise for her partner.

"Sorry, he's not happy with the arrangements."

"D'you know why?"

"Same reason I'm not. The place is miles from any backup and there's just the two of us if anything goes wrong. It feels like a plan thrown together by someone who's never done a day's police work in their life."

I think she expected me to rear up in defence of Tom Blackwell at the criticism. The trouble was I agreed with it. I asked how she took her coffee. Black, no sugar.

Grogan returned from his tour of the house, ducked into the kitchen from the hall and rocked his hand at Fairchild before turning to me.

"Thought you had a dog," he said.

Picking up his style I replied, "Have. Neighbour."

Fairchild gave an inward hiss. "That may not have been such a good idea. It might be helpful to discuss any changes before you make them."

I rocked my hand in mid-air as Grogan had done.

"Does this mean the house isn't as bad as you feared?" I asked him.

"Did I say that?"

"No, and that isn't what I asked you."

"Not much wrong with the house," he said. "It's the job itself: cobbled together, last-minute stuff." It was a clipped voice with a Sarf London accent. "Who the hell is this Liam Kinsella, anyway? Who's Aaron Flaxman, come to that?"

"Well, if you don't know that..."

I stopped when I realised he wasn't kidding. He really didn't know either of the names, only that he and Fairchild were charged with keeping one of them safe until the murder trial of the other was over.

"Maybe that's Blackwell's idea of security," I said. "The less you know..."

Grogan stared at me, no doubt wondering how he'd survive a month in the present company, plus Liam Kinsella. By way of a gesture, and to raise the falling temperature, I said there were beers in the utility room, ice in the freezer, spirits in the dresser, they should help themselves. That didn't go down well either. Grogan said he didn't drink.

"I'm going to get the rest of the gear from the car," Fairchild said. "Where's the bread oven?"

She hadn't had a sudden urge to knock up a batch of granaries; she wanted the bread oven by the inglenook, which Blackwell had told her about, for storing four Glocks, a couple of Taser pistols and a Taser rifle. God knows how two SOU officers, with such a skinny assortment of weapons, were meant to tackle the Heritage IRA if they came calling, but that's budget cuts for you.

The call came at six o'clock that evening and was a hit-and-miss affair. Tom Blackwell spoke to Fairchild, who moved around the ground floor of the house asking the eternal question: why was it so difficult to get a signal here? I gave her the eternal answer: the walls are too thick. Whether it makes technical sense or not, I've no idea, but it usually sends people out into the garden.

Fairchild returned thirty seconds later, saying that Blackwell wanted to speak to me, and after our own round of 'can you still hear me?' he asked if I would go with Fairchild and Grogan to pick up Kinsella. He'd be supervising the handover and had one or two things to say to me, face to face. The call finished of its own accord.

"You're meeting at Chestnut Farm," I said. "The farmer's a friend of mine, Martin Falconer."

Grogan nodded slowly as if the remark had been highly charged. "Blackwell didn't say."

"Seven thirty, Bryant's Lane."

For all its lack of planning, it seemed an over-elaborate handover to me. Why not bring Kinsella straight here to Beech Tree? It was hardly the middle of Trafalgar Square.

"Last-minute decision stuff," said Grogan, with the umbrage of an old-school copper being asked to keep pace with the times.

He turned away, leaving any polite chat to Fairchild. She was trying to make light of a broken fingernail when in truth it was annoying the hell out of her.

"Presumably Blackwell told you he wants me along for the ride?" I said.

"Yes," she said, beginning to root around in her shoulder bag.

"There's one in the dresser, the apothecary drawer."

"One what?"

"Emery board."

She thanked me and five minutes later the job was done. It was shorter than the others but just as round.

We arrived at the bottom of Bryant's Lane half an hour before we needed to, a habit I'm still trying to break, and Fairchild parked at a metal gate, chained and padlocked. The sheep beyond it seemed to log away our every move from that moment on and managed to upset Grogan almost immediately. After staring back at them for a while, he muttered, "Stupid fuckers."

It broke the ice, perhaps because it was the first thing all three of us agreed on, and for the next twenty minutes we small-talked our way round each other, trying to keep hackles down. We slipped just once when after some colourless chat about police pay and pensions, obligatory wherever two or three coppers are gathered together, Grogan asked if I knew why Blackwell had chosen my place as a safe house.

"I don't," I said. "Do you?"

"No, and I couldn't care less."

"Why ask, then?"

He hardened a little. "I'm being friendly."

Fairchild chipped in. "My guess is he knows he can rely on you."

That didn't help any. "Rely on me for what?"

She looked at Grogan for support but he was too busy examining the middle distance.

"Well, in general," she said. "He knows you from way back, so he's thought..."

Her explanation tailed off and we eased away from each other.

I don't think I'd ever been down Bryant's Lane – it doesn't lead anywhere – and unlike most of Martin Falconer's land, this patch was dank and still, spooned out as if someone had once tried to create a lake there. Maybe they had and Martin had drained it for grazing. He was known to our resentful Parish Council for his earthworks.

I became aware of a fluttering sound in the far-off stillness. It grew quickly into a recognisable clatter and yet still I asked, "What the hell is that?"

Grogan nodded in a north-easterly direction and said sourly, "Chopper, by the sound of it."

We'd expected a car, but within two minutes a Eurocopter EC135 descended to Bryant's Field with blades glinting in the sunset as if wielded by some demented samurai. The sheep rose and ran for cover, still chewing leftovers. Once the pilot had settled the aircraft the door opened and a skeletal set of steps unfolded to the ground.

Blackwell was first down them, clocked us by the gate, then beckoned his travelling companions to join him.

Grogan's reaction to his first sight of Liam Kinsella was much as I'd expected: indifference to the man himself and contempt for those who'd made the arrangements. Kinsella was dressed head to toe in battered denim – jeans, shirt, jacket, stained and oily, as if he'd just been rolled out from under a lorry engine. He had shoulder-length black hair, greasy and matted like his beard, both adding ten years to the thirty-two he supposedly was. He was protesting, answering back to those around him, mainly out of fear, but with good reason given that he was meant to be Tom Blackwell's star witness, not his prisoner. Surely a certain amount of trust should have developed between them by now and yet he was handcuffed to an Organised Crime Command poster boy, nattily dressed with not a mark on him, who, while holding his charge close, was also at pains to keep him at a distance. Kinsella was the shorter, slighter of the two and gave the impression of being dragged along like a manky child.

Blackwell reached the gate, climbed over and shook my hand. "Good of you to come, Nathan."

He turned as Poster Boy unlocked the handcuffs and side-vaulted the five-bar gate. He reached back, grabbed Kinsella by the denim and lifted him over. Above the protestations Blackwell introduced Fairchild and Grogan to him.

"And who are you?" Kinsella asked me.

"Hawk. I thought you'd be ... cleaner."

Poster Boy handed Grogan the cuffs and key and began stroking non-existent detritus from his jacket. In grim disbelief at what was being asked of him, Grogan snapped the loop to his own left arm.

"Jesus, at least when I got here I thought..." Kinsella tried.

"Car," said Grogan.

He opened the back door and pushed his other half in ahead of him. Blackwell gestured to Fairchild, her cue to get back in the car and start the engine, then he reached out to shake my hand again.

"You said you wanted to speak to me," I reminded him.

"Oh, yes. I wanted to check we're all on the same page. We are, aren't we?"

If there was any doubt about that, he said, there was still just enough time for me to pull out, for Kinsella to be taken back to wherever they'd brought him from. He took my silence as approval of the plans as they were unfolding.

As I watched him return to the Eurocopter, watched the aircraft rise, turn in the air and head north-east, I wondered why I'd let him off the hook so easily. I should have made him account for calling me out when I suspected that he'd done so just to remind me who was running the show. I should have gone on from there, voiced Laura's reasoning that he wanted my expertise during the lead-up to Flaxman's trial, to say nothing of Fairchild's unwarranted belief that he could rely on me. What stopped me, I'm ashamed to admit, was vanity: I was flattered to have been chosen for a job that he feared his own people might not be able to handle.

- 5 -

I've never watched those reality television programmes where disparate groups of people are thrown together in the same house and left to get on with it. It's tough enough being shacked up with people you know and love. My own way of handling the in-house battles of family life had always been to position myself right at the front line, having the first and last word. Or at least that's the delusion I cherish.

One aspect of life with these passers-through had to be dealt with immediately. Kinsella hadn't had a bath for months, he boasted, and the stench of ever-ripening sweat which clung to him was enough to choke on. I was surprised they hadn't made him shower at wherever he'd been held previously, but, as we soon discovered, Kinsella was a great one for quoting his human rights. He'd probably used it as a means to keep himself filthy. He could have his tattered clothes back, I said, once they'd been through the wash. He could keep his tangled hair and stupid beard. He could even go without cleaning his teeth, so long as he breathed away from me. But he was going to have a bath.

He objected immediately and I outlined his options. He could do it himself, with me and Grogan standing over him, or failing that Grogan would hold him down and I would scrub him clean with the head of a yard broom.

"Guantanamo," he muttered. "It's Guantanamo Bay. Water torture."

"You'll thank us in the end," I said.

While Fairchild ran his clothes through a delicate wash cycle, in case they fell further to bits, he play-acted his way through a supervised bath, demanding bubbles and ducks, and as he towelled himself down I handed him deodorant and talcum powder and informed him that this would be a regular event. Friday night would be bath night.

With him smelling bearable, a routine was soon established during which Grogan was never more than six feet away from his charge. Two areas were difficult, as you might imagine: lavatory and sleeping. Suffice to say that Kinsella was never allowed to close the door when he used the toilet and I often heard him complain about having to watch Grogan take a shower, but it was done in semi-jocular fashion so I thought nothing of it. Grogan also slept beside him on an old futon I'd dug out. He warned Kinsella at the outset that he slept like a cat, so God help him if he tried making a run for it. They turned in every night at eleven, slept right through and were both four square at the breakfast table by seven o'clock the next morning. Their conversational style was such that Kinsella, as he gained confidence, took the piss gently and Grogan responded with two-word threats or put-downs. Fairchild clearly found Kinsella's remarks amusing, which often they were, but she tried not to let it show.

Fairchild had taken Ellie's old room with its feminine ambience, its sweet smell of something I've never identified, its legion of soft toys in family groups. They were a direct link to her mother, Ellie said, and when she'd gone off to Nepal with Terrific Rick she could only take a few of them with her, insisting that I leave the rest exactly as they were. When she had come home the previous Christmas they'd been the first things she had checked on.

The visitors had been living with me for nearly a week when a plaintive text from Laura Peterson reminded me that she still hadn't met my house guests. I apologised and we arranged that she would come round early the following morning and join us for breakfast. That fitted in with her plans perfectly, she told me, but, conscious that it wasn't going to be the social event she'd hoped for, I explained that Grogan was pretty bloody in the morning, Fairchild was no ray of sunshine either and Kinsella was in need of another bath. It didn't put Laura off and she duly arrived at about 7.00 am and stood just this side of the back door with an oddly shaped smile on her face.

I could pick up the next half hour of my life, put it down in another time and place, and it would fit perfectly. It was made up of the challenges and surprises which in kind, if not exact detail, have typified my existence. It began with a classic blunder on my part.

"Hi! Surgery?" I asked.

"Don't be silly."

"Sorry."

I went over and kissed her on the cheek, at which point she seemed to deflate a little.

"I'm missing something, aren't I?" I said.

"Yes." Seeing no hope of getting me up to speed she moved on. "I'm having a day off today. I'm going into Oxford with Sheila Bright. She's got an appointment at the John Radcliffe for chemo, after which we're going to Brown's for lunch, if she can manage it. Then shopping."

"Ah, if you're going to the covered market, get me a crab from..."

"Nathan, does this look like mutton dressed as fish?" she blurted out.

She stood there, hands splayed, demanding a response. She was referring to the clothes she was wearing: soft lace-up boots, fashionable leggings and a sparkly smock top. She'd hoped I would say, straight off, how fabulous she looked. I dug deep.

"Laura, the reason I didn't notice was that everything you wear looks absolutely..." I was floundering. "...terrific. I've never seen you looking anything but..."

"Nathan, please." She looked away, over my shoulder and out through the window by the sink. "Just tell me why Ben Gunn is sliding down the roof over the living room?"

From her allusion to the castaway in *Treasure Island* I knew exactly who she was referring to and turned to see, through the window, Liam Kinsella making his way down the thatch over the extension, using the chicken wire which held it in place to aid his descent. He must have come out through the attic room window above, dropped down onto the roof and was now heading for the wide blue yonder.

I've never been sure what kicks in at moments of crisis, just grateful that it usually does. Clearly, if a loved one is in danger a whole raft of instincts combine to help in the ... interception process. Kinsella certainly wasn't a loved one, nor was he my responsibility, but within seconds I'd seen myself turn to the back door, yank it open and leap out onto the gravel just as he dropped the nine or ten feet from the edge of the thatch. He crouched into a classic squat to break his fall, sprang up again and ran. I could already hear Grogan, inside the house, crashing down the stairs, curse by curse.

I caught up with Kinsella at the big beech tree and kicked out at the back of his knee. He went down in a flurry of anger, the gist of which was, "Bastard coppers, you never bloody change, never lose the will to make other people's lives a misery..."

He was trying to get to his feet and when he reached all fours I kicked his arms out from beneath his shoulders and turned to see Grogan, loose vest, boxers, nothing on his feet, prancing over beech husks towards us. I stepped back and when he reached Kinsella he stood over him and punched him in the neck. Kinsella dropped again. Grogan showered him with expletives.

"You fucking sod, give you an inch you take a fucking yard! No more of that, you little shit!"

It was the first time any of us had seen Grogan's temper. We knew it was there, we knew that unleashed it would be dangerous. Kinsella groaned. Grogan stooped down and punched him again, then again and then again. It wasn't me who stopped him, it was Laura.

"Hey! Just a second!" she called from the kitchen door and headed towards us.

Grogan froze, fist clenched, conscious of a stranger looking on. He must have missed her on his way across the kitchen, leggings and sparkly top notwithstanding. He looked at me.

"This is Doctor Laura Peterson," I said. "Laura, Sergeant Bill Grogan. On the ground, Liam Kinsella. At the back door, Detective Constable Petra Fairchild."

They turned to see Fairchild, who was looking pretty good, considering. A shiny pink dressing gown was tied firmly at the waist and she was spiking up her hair.

"What's happened?" she asked, approaching.

"Your star witness just made a bid for freedom, though why he should need to's a mystery. I've made coffee, by the way."

I led them back into the house. Grogan, who had dragged Kinsella in behind me, threw him into a chair with such force that it tipped backwards. Arms and legs akimbo, Kinsella struggled to keep upright and just about managed it.

"Five minutes," Grogan said to me. "Keep an eye."

He meant that he needed five minutes to go and get dressed and would I mind making sure that his charge – his prisoner, it seemed – didn't make another break for it. He nodded at Laura, a mixture of gratitude that she'd stopped him from doing serious damage to Kinsella and apology for having been caught in a state of undress. As he passed her I saw her eyes stray to the tattoos on his bare flesh, the neck and upper arms. They were violent and tribal and at some stage he'd tried to have them removed with minimal

57

success. He left the kitchen and we heard him go up the stairs two at a time.

Laura clapped her hands, just once, to alter the mood.

"Right, what does everyone have for breakfast?" She went on to stress the importance of the first meal of the day.

"Would you like some help?" Fairchild asked.

"Thank you, dear, get some bowls out..."

"So you're the lady of the house," said Kinsella.

"I most certainly am not."

"All the same I apologise for what you've just witnessed. My part in it, at least. As for the others involved..."

"Kinsella, zip it," said Fairchild, pointing above her head. "You're in a heap of trouble as it is."

Laura took a packet of Quaker Oats from the cupboard and measured a couple of mugfuls into a china bowl. She added milk, a rough amount, stirred the result and placed it in the microwave. It might have been breakfast in a million households across the country. I was pouring coffee. That was becoming routine. In the morning I poured coffee, in the evening I poured wine or whisky.

I set a mug of black down in front of Kinsella, pointed at the sugar. He muttered his thanks and drew up to the table.

"Mr Kinsella, where have you been living?" asked Laura.

It seemed an almost surreal question to ask, given the circumstances.

"You mean where was I brought up? North Wales."

"Yes, but where have you been more recently?"

He smiled. It wasn't just the facial hair that was discoloured and matted; the teeth were glued together with yesterday's food, if not the day before's. The breath, if you were unlucky enough to catch it, was lethal.

"Living rough," he said. "Then even rougher, behind bars."

"Protective custody," Fairchild modified.

"That would explain it," Laura said. "You have head lice and, of course, the nits that go with it."

There was an immediate silence. I was the only one in the room with chalk-face experience of what Laura's words meant. Con had arrived home from a new school one day with head lice. No matter how much the school nurse tried to persuade us there was no shame attached, it didn't really work until we realised that everyone in the school, teachers included, had fallen prey.

"It's nothing to worry about," said Laura.

"I had a bath last week," he protested.

"Makes no difference. You will need treatment. All of you."

The microwave pinged just as Grogan re-entered the kitchen, fully dressed. He went over to Kinsella, grabbed him and the chair as if they were one, and dragged them to the far radiator. He took a pair of handcuffs from his pocket, snapped one loop round Kinsella's left wrist and the other round the inflow pipe which ran up the wall. Common sense would say it was a temporary measure, mild retribution on Grogan's part, to be reversed when he'd regained his composure.

"He's got head lice, Bill," said Fairchild.

"What?"

"Head lice, Sergeant," said Laura, believing that a medical voice would soften the impact.

Grogan's eyes focussed serially on various parts of the room and Fairchild stepped in between the two men. Laura went to the rescue.

"And if you'd allow me, Mr Kinsella, I'd like a quick look at those lesions around your mouth."

Grogan moved away to give her access.

"Now would you turn your head and part the hair at the back of your neck for me?"

He did so. The hands were filthy, the nails black and broken. The neck was ground-in grey. We'd missed it at bath time. As for the sores on it, some were scabby and peeling, others were fiery red and suppurating.

"How long have I got, Doc?" he asked.

"The two often go together, though it's some time since I've seen it in an adult. It's a result of scratching, which itself is a result of the lice. Impetigo."

"You filthy bastard," Grogan muttered.

"Not at all, Sergeant. The cleanest of people can..."

Realising that any defence of Kinsella along those lines was futile, she broke off.

"Treatment?" said Fairchild, plaintively.

"Yes, I'll deal with it this evening. Porridge, everyone?"

She and Kinsella were the only ones who ate the porridge with any indifference to the creatures roaming his head, the eggs they had laid and the weeping sores on his face and neck. I looked across at the radiator where he sat, hunched up and spooning from the bowl on his lap. His left hand was still clipped to the down pipe. The punches he'd taken from Grogan were swelling up. The whole effect was positively Dickensian, made all the more so by the yellow smile he gave me.

And then the front doorbell rang. It was seven fifteen, so God alone knew who it was.

"I'll see to it," said Grogan.

He felt for his Glock. It wasn't there. He'd left it upstairs in the rush to get dressed. Fairchild rose. She wasn't wearing hers either, not under the pink dressing gown. Again they exchanged a glance.

"Bodes well for when the Heritage IRA get here," I said, then called out, "Who is it?"

"Dad, it's me," came the reply.

"Come round the back, love."

It was my oldest daughter Fiona, or Fee as she's more affectionately known. I'm usually so pleased to see any one of my kids. Usually. She entered, closed the door behind her and, never one to admit she didn't know what to make of a situation, she smiled round, hoping it would become clear without her needing to ask.

"Fee, you're just in time for breakfast," said Laura, brightly. "There's plenty left."

"Thanks, yes. Where's Dogge, Dad?"

"Jean Langan's."

- 6 -

I didn't get time alone with Fee until ten o'clock, by which time everyone in the house was fully dressed and Laura had gone off to Oxford with Sheila Bright. Grogan and Fairchild hadn't the nerve to question Fee's presence here, or ask how long she intended to stay. Shame, really, because I wouldn't have minded knowing myself.

We'd gone to sit on the bench under the big beech tree and for some peculiar reason, certainly to do with my house guests, we spoke in a whisper. She said I was wrong to think she'd been worried about me, based on the 'new dog' ruse. She'd been in touch with Laura immediately afterwards and discovered I was as fit as a flea. A favourite description of her mother's, she reminded me, applied to just about anyone who wasn't dying.

So why had she come home? She was taking stock of her life, she said, and the terrifying fact that she hadn't done much with it. She intended to give herself time to rethink, to reappraise, to reinvent...

"In other words you've dumped him," I said. "Why, if you don't mind me asking?"

"Is it mean to say that he's too short?"

I turned to her and smiled. "Well, he is Japanese."

As a girl she'd had masses of dark brown hair which she had cut short at sixteen, and there it had stayed. People could see her face better that way, she maintained. She was enviably tall, though never as tall in the flesh as she was in her e-mails. Whenever she wrote to me she projected the height that goes with a terse verbal style, the extrovert efficiency that marks out a violet who never shrinks.

"His height can't be the only reason," I suggested.

She said there were cultural differences which hadn't been apparent when they'd first met in Tokyo's Electric City, just after the earthquakes, when Yukito was trying to establish his electronic gadgets business. She'd set up the marketing side of the company, selling stuff to Australia, New Zealand, America, Britain. However, she'd come to believe that flogging torches which shone brighter or duller at the verbal request of the person holding them wasn't really her life's ambition.

"I mean how many murderers had you caught by the time you were my age, Dad?"

"Four, though I'd had help. Correction, at your age I *was* the help."

She smiled and looked over at the house. "Now you're the fount of all wisdom, the one they come to when they've got a problem?"

"Who told you that?"

"Laura. Anyway, isn't it what you do these days? Sort people out? Even unwashed cavemen?"

"Apparently."

"Don't go all coy, Dad. Doesn't suit."

Rather than defend myself against the coyness charge I explained that I'd had the situation dropped on me by an old acquaintance, Tom Blackwell.

"I remember him," she said, and she proceeded to give me a younger, over-flattering description of the man.

I told her about the pending murder trial and how Kinsella was the star witness who had turned against his associates.

"Why was he chained to a radiator?"

"He tried to make a run for it this morning."

She wanted chapter and verse on that as well and wouldn't rest until I'd given it, then stood up and went close to the spot where I'd brought Kinsella down. She stooped and examined it, like a girl guide.

"Here's where you caught up with him?"

I nodded and she looked over at the house again, specifically at the extension roof.

"Where were you when he jumped?"

"By then I was out of the door, hot pursuit..."

I thought she was going to ask how a man more than twenty years my junior hadn't managed to outrun me. She must have read my mind.

"That makes sense. You're a fit guy; why wouldn't you catch him? And he is out of condition."

"Faint praise," I muttered.

She cautioned me to be serious.

"Where was he going, Dad? To a rendezvous, a car, a push-bike? What were his plans?"

I stared at her for a moment, then turned and hurried back to the house.

All three of my unwanted guests were in the kitchen and something about my demeanour when I entered must've put them *en garde*. Kinsella was handcuffed into Maggie's dad's rocker, reading a magazine. The greasy hair didn't move as he looked up at me; only the beard parted as he smiled at Fee. The teeth still hadn't been cleaned. Fairchild was seated at the table, working on her laptop. She closed it. Grogan was descaling the coffee maker. It felt like a fair exchange, given that I was taking over his job. I stood in front of Kinsella at a reasonable distance from the smell.

"Uncuff him," I said to Grogan.

"Hang on a second..."

"Do it!"

He went over to the rocker and unlocked the handcuffs.

"Empty your pockets," I said to Kinsella. "Whatever's in them, place on the table."

Kinsella smiled again. "You mean loose change, hanky, the good luck charm..."

"I mean the keys to their car."

He stopped trying to be smart, smiled at Fairchild and then reached into his back pocket for the keys to the Ford Focus. He tossed them onto the table and raised his arms in a bang-to-rights gesture. I glanced at Grogan. His eyes were roaming the room, trying not to settle on anything he might grab and break, but eventually he gave way to anger and swooped on Kinsella, who backed away. I stepped between the two of them and pointed at Grogan, who all but took his clenched fist in his free hand and moved it to a place of safety. I turned back to Kinsella.

"Take your shoes off."

He gave me the smile. "Denying me footwear? That's surely a human rights issue..."

"Take them off," said Fairchild.

Delighted to be the centre of attention, he pulled off the tattered trainers and handed them to Fairchild, who held them at a distance.

"Bin 'em," I said.

Fee toed the pedal bin, the lid yawned open and Fairchild dropped them in.

"Socks?" Kinsella asked.

"I'll ram them down your fucking throat..." Grogan began.

"Shut up, the pair of you! Kinsella, you were described to me as a 'terrified down-and-out who'd had a crisis of conscience'. Maybe that's the game you play on Saturdays. Sunday you're a pushy little piss-taker. Monday? Tuesday? What are you then?"

I asked Grogan if he'd be informing his boss of Kinsella's bid for freedom. He didn't see any need to bother Blackwell, since the matter was being dealt with. He hoped I agreed.

I said to Kinsella, "So you're their star witness?"

He smiled, gelatinous teeth. "Well, I..."

"Only, if you're having second thoughts, there's a way out. I'll suggest to Commander Blackwell that he cuts you loose, then tells Flaxman all about it. Without your testimony he'll get off and you'll be the first person he goes looking for. The man murdered two trawlermen, cold blood. Police reckon he was after you too. You'll be dead by Christmas."

About an hour later Fee knocked on my cabin door and entered. She gazed round, her eyes coming to rest on the four clocks.

"Tokyo, seven in the evening. He'll be going off to Elio's. Italian restaurant. You'd love it." She took a deep breath and changed the subject. "So ... this is your hidey-hole. I don't think I've ever been in it."

"It was here when I bought the place."

She smiled. "You don't have to apologise for having it, Dad."

She went over to a photo on the wall, all six of us a century ago, and straightened it. It hadn't needed it; she'd just wanted to put her hands on it.

"What's going on in the house?" I asked.

"Breast beating. Grogan accusing Fairchild, Fairchild just about holding her own..."

"Accusing her of what?"

"The car keys. Her responsibility, he says."

"He's the one at fault!" I said, too loudly. "Senior officer."

"Kinsella's loving it."

She came to the desk and started to tidy it, straightening the piles of bills in their clips. It's genetic: her mother used to fiddle with paperwork, unfold it, straighten it, put it in a different order to mine.

"Loving it how, why?" I asked.

She shrugged. "They disagree, he plays on it, they argue even more. You know what their trouble is?"

"Cabin fever."

She shook her head. "Future tripping. Know what that is?"

I answered as best I could. "A journey one will take sometime in the, well ... future?"

"It's the habit of trying to deal with a problem long before it happens. You do quite a bit of it."

"I call it forward planning," I argued.

"That's different. Forward planning's a straight line to an objective. With future tripping you come at something from all angles and never reach a conclusion. Fairchild's an expert at it."

Fairchild's latest future trip, Fee told me, involved the visit by the Crown Prosecution's legal team, due sometime next week to interview Kinsella. Did he understand what was being asked of him? Would he keep his word and give evidence at the trial? Should she and Grogan be present for the questioning?

"What does Grogan say?"

She smiled. "Basically, fuck everyone."

There aren't many things which bring all human beings down to the same level, unless you count war, plague or famine, but being treated for head lice is one of them. I won't dwell on it, but Laura lined us up just before lights out and made us douse our heads with an oil that boasted a double-barrelled name. We had to wear it all night. By morning the lice would be dead. Then, she said, we would need to shampoo our hair, even those of us who didn't have much, and wet comb each other like gorillas to remove any remaining nits, the eggs which had the power to cling to their hosts no matter what. She'd bought a selection of nit combs for us to choose from and tried to make the process sound like fun. And I said a moment ago that I wouldn't dwell on it...

- 7 -

Over the next couple of days the nit combing ran its course and the ointment Laura had prescribed for the sores on Kinsella's face and neck started to work. As she examined them just before supper one evening, Kinsella said, "Mr Hawk, that Lewis chess set in your living room, is it just for show? Are you a player?"

"I'm not."

Laura glanced in my direction, then went back to the sores.

"I saw that, Doc. He does play, he's just scared I'll beat him."

"Well, I'm not," said Laura. "I used to captain my school team. I'll have a game with you sometime."

"This evening?"

"Very well."

"Fantastic! I bet you're good. Are you good?"

She smiled, went over to the sink and began washing her hands more thoroughly than most people ever contemplate, forbearing to lecture us on the subject even though it had become her latest hobby-horse. Kinsella followed her there for an answer.

"How good?"

"We'll see, won't we?"

Grogan ducked into the kitchen from the hall with a visible aura of panic clinging to him, the one reserved for lost dogs or misplaced children. His eyes came to rest on Kinsella, who'd been out of his sight for five minutes, and he relaxed. It was a game they'd started to play and in the scoring so far Kinsella was way ahead.

The conversation over supper was too girly for my liking, and I'm sure Bill Grogan felt the same, given that it centred on men's fashions, childbirth and calorific values. Kinsella tried to hijack it. He'd been overweight as a kid until he'd started playing football. With practice twice a week and a match on the weekend he soon slimmed down. Laura praised his parents for getting him out in the fresh air instead of letting him solidify in front of a television. At that point Kinsella made a bid for our sympathy. Far from being model parents, his mother was completely under his father's thumb, afraid to challenge him on any of his shortcomings, and she ended her life as a haggard, neurotic parody of the woman she might have been. The girls made a few sympathetic noises, then went back to their conversation, this time about skin-care products, Charles Dickens and breast cancer.

"On the subject of staying healthy," said Fee in her patrol leader's voice, "I think we should all go jogging, starting tomorrow morning."

There was one hell of a silence. Only Kinsella thought it was a good idea. He'd done quite a bit of jogging in his time, a couple of half-marathons, though never in bare feet. He tried to whip up our enthusiasm and failed.

"Oh, come on!" said Fee, gesturing at what remained of supper. "We can't just sit here, packing away more and more calories, never burning any off."

"I agree," said Fairchild, hands straying to her hips.

"Settled, then!" said Fee. "Seven thirty, tomorrow morning?"

Grogan wasn't so much lost for words as disinclined to use any.

We cleared the table, a team effort, after which Kinsella asked Laura if she was still up for a game of chess. She said she was looking forward to it and suggested that he go and set up the board in the living room. Once he'd left the room Grogan muttered a two-word instruction to her.

"Thrash him."

"Are the rest of you going to sit and watch while I do?" she asked. "Or have you other plans?"

"Fee and I'll mosey up to The Crown, I reckon. Care to join us, Fairchild?"

She was about to say yes, but a slit-eyed look from Grogan changed her mind.

The Crown was pretty busy for a weekday and, since Fee hadn't been there since Christmas, she received quite a welcome, people asking how she was, how life in Japan was treating her but, more importantly, had it started raining outside yet? Fine, fine and not yet, she was able to tell them. Most people thought she looked radiant, of course, but one or two inquisitors wanted to know the real reason for her trip home. Was it just to check on the old man, make sure he was behaving himself? She'd made a pact with herself, she told them, to return at least twice a year, and if she hadn't got the summer visit in sharpish it would soon be Christmas again. That gave everyone a chance to bemoan the passage of time.

We settled at the bar and when Fee asked Annie McKinnon how Roberta, her two-year-old daughter, was, I thought I sensed envy in her voice. Annie must have caught it too and, without ceremony, asked after Yukito almost as if she were inquiring about his sperm count. Just as bluntly Fee told her that she and Yukito were history and, to Annie's delight, launched into a detailed account of the break-up. I was glad to see that an old friend, Jaikie's Latin and Greek teacher, was in the snug and apparently on his own, finishing off a crossword someone else had started. I took a drink through to him.

John Demise rose to greet me and we broke into the usual square dance of embraces before settling down to chat about cabbages and kings. Over my shoulder he caught Fee's eye, through in the main bar. He waved, she waved back and he seemed to drift off for a moment; he'd once told me how Fee reminded him of his late wife, Susie. When he returned, he said, "I didn't know you had an extended family, Nathan."

"I don't. That's Fee, my daughter."

"Yes, I know that's Fee," he said, with a teacher's irritability. "I'm talking about your cousin, Bill."

He was referring to Grogan who, for cover purposes, was my mother's nephew. The trouble with people like John

Demise is that you tell them some trifling detail and they remember it forever.

"So he'll be Auria's son, will he?"

"Yes, yes," I said, trusting that at some stage I'd tested the logic of that. "You met him?"

"No, not him, his wife, Petra. If I ever decide to get married again I'll advertise for someone just like her. Poor Susie, eh?" he added. "The moment her back's turned."

I smiled. "Give it to me in Latin, may not sound so bad."

He gazed into the middle distance for the translation. *"Quando tergum suum convertum, ceterae feminae converto."*

"Sounds worse. Where did you meet her?"

"Durham University, 1965."

"Not Susie, my cousin's wife, Petra."

"Oh, in the post office queue at Stone, couple of days ago."

I hadn't made it my business to check on every move Fairchild or Grogan had made since they'd been with me, but something about the words 'post' and 'office' retains the power to disconcert coppers of a certain generation. It has something to do with them being robbed every five minutes.

"What was she doing in Stone Post Office?" I asked.

"Posting something." I acknowledged his gentle dig. "A parcel. Somebody's birthday, given that the wrapping had 'Happy Birthday' written all over it."

"Dead giveaway. No one in the family, so I guess it must be, well..."

Leave something like that dangling and, if the other party has the knowledge, they'll usually share it. Besides, it's in a teacher's blood to pass on information.

"Someone in Grimsby," he said. "I know you're supposed to stand well back when those in front of you are at the counter, but there's something about the name Grimsby that cuts right through the air."

I'd suspected there might be something fishy about this case ever since the name Grimsby first came up, way back when Blackwell asked if he could billet Kinsella on me. So far there'd been nothing much to go on, apart from my natural feelings of mistrust, but this was promising. An SOU officer, charged with protecting the main prosecution witness, had sent a parcel to someone in the town where Aaron Flaxman murdered two trawlermen. Who and why? Who was it addressed to, why had she sent it? It smelled decidedly off.

Walking home from The Crown, arm in arm with Fee, I might have been any middle-aged man strolling late at night with his daughter, each of us happy to place our private worries on the back burner as we chatted. Had they been brought to the boil, Fee's would've concerned a man called Yukito whom she'd spent two hours being disloyal about to Annie McKinnon, something she doubtless now regretted. Mine would've homed in on Grimsby and birthday presents being sent there. And, beyond that, why I'd let Tom Blackwell lumber me with his star witness. Hadn't experience taught me that such unguarded generosity would land me in trouble?

Under the glare of a security light we'd triggered, Fee suddenly said, "Dad, what about the shoes?"

"You mean Kinsella?"

"I mean his feet. I bet it's true, you know, it's an abuse of human rights to deny a man footwear."

"Nonsense! There are whole races of people who've never worn shoes in their lives."

"Not in the North of England, or wherever he comes from."

"North Wales."

"That might be a special case, but I still want an answer."

She'd always been a persistent girl, argumentative and fearless, all qualities I admire so long as they're not directed at me. I'd also disregarded her Grand Plan to save the world one creature at a time, a mission she'd inherited from her mother.

"It's out of my hands," I said, as we turned into Morton Lane.

She stopped dead and the arm lock she had on me forced me to do the same.

"You know that's rubbish, Dad. Bill Grogan would do anything you told him to. He'd whinge, he'd pull his face, but given enough time to sulk he'd fall into line."

"And Fairchild?"

She took her time answering that. "I'll let you know when I've sussed her out. Meantime, she's so happy to have a job with the boys it's embarrassing..."

I smiled at her. "Since when did you become such an expert judge of character?"

She let go of my arm and stood facing me, ready to do battle, just as ready to fall back in defence. "Since needs must."

She meant when she'd stepped into Maggie's shoes, nine years ago at the age of twenty-one, and started organising the lives of four other people: Con, Jaikie, Ellie and me, everything from laundry to the weekly shop via vetting her brothers' and her sister's friendships. She'd done it from choice, she once told me, not because I'd asked her to, and The Others had responded well enough. The only problem was she had yet to fully release her grip and, in an odd disfigurement of family power, all three of her siblings knew they would always answer to their big sister.

As we approached the house I could see the lights were still on, silhouettes were moving behind curtains, people were still up. Why that should have bothered me I'm not sure. I'd have been equally concerned had the place been in total darkness. It was all to do with not being in charge, Fee said when I put it to her, a long-held belief that other people were incapable of doing their jobs, especially without my leadership.

Fairchild was in the kitchen making camomile tea for bed, and clearly she wished she'd come to the pub with us since watching a chess match has never been much of a way to pass an evening. I was glad she'd stayed at home and spared me the embarrassment of John Demise drooling over her. I decided to save my questions about the parcel she'd sent till the following morning. The jog.

Through in the living room Kinsella was giving an elaborate display of defeat, gracious enough in tone, but still very much a performance. He was on his feet, circling the chess board, occasionally clutching his head with both hands as if he would tear it from his shoulders and bowl it across the room.

"This is one hell of a clever lady, Mr Hawk!" he said as I entered. "Three games we've had, three times she's wiped the floor with me!"

The lady herself was far too modest to crow about her success and was busy packing away the pieces as he spoke, but at least Bill Grogan shared the delight that was duly hers. He was smiling, not something he did easily, covering more vocal delight with a round of stretches and yawns, indicating his readiness to turn in. He may not have found the three matches as lively as their equivalent in rugby league terms, but the results were far more rewarding.

Once he and Kinsella had gone upstairs I found myself refereeing a different kind of match, an undeclared stand-off between Fee and Laura. I can't say I hadn't been aware of it up until then, but in the time I'd known Laura the need to confront it had never arisen. The previous Christmas, for example, she'd spent every night at her own house due to weight of numbers in mine; the summer before in Los Angeles, we'd all stayed in the Beverly Wilshire, and hotels are different with a social structure all of their own. However, from Fee's point of view, when the woman who has taken your mother's place moves into your father's bedroom something Freudian happens between the three of you and can't be ignored. So, as Laura began to gather up the debris of her visit prior to going back to Plum Tree Cottage, I said, "Laura, we've both got a heavy day tomorrow; why don't you go on upstairs? Fee and I'll finish the kitchen."

She glanced at Fee. "Well, if you're sure you don't..."

"I'll be five minutes."

Laura swept her stuff into a sort of carpet bag she'd grown fond of, pecked Fee on the cheek and headed upstairs.

"Did you have to make her feel so uncomfortable?" Fee hissed.

"Pardon?"

She stepped in close, the better to get in my face while keeping her voice low. "We all know what's going on here, Dad. You're having an affair with a middle-aged woman..."

"It is not an affair, it's a relationship."

She found the correction pedantic and trifling. "Alright, you're having a relationship with a very smart lady and all of a sudden your oldest daughter pops up. Well, I'm sorry, it can't be easy for her."

"Please don't apologise..."

"And it certainly isn't easy for me!"

It was difficult to know how to put the brakes on this one and I had a nasty feeling it was about to veer out of control. The best course was to keep listening.

"Thing is, Dad, when Mum died I went into action, but once things settled down I realised that my best friend and confidante had just ... upped and left me to cope with you lot. In a way I blamed her but you're right, I had no one I could count on for unconditional love. I mean you, yes, but..."

Oh, good, I thought. Fee spotted my self-pity immediately.

"Don't hang your head, Dad! Of course I could come to you. I mean I hope you'll always be – well, I'm sure you will..."

I don't think either of us knew what she intended to say next.

"I wasn't hanging it," I said. "But there is something I've neglected; kept trying to find the right moment for nine years. I never thanked you for taking over. So ... thank you."

She looked at me until I wondered if again I'd said something pedantic and trifling. And then, without the slightest warning, her eyes filled up and she broke down in silent floods of tears.

It took half an hour or so to get Fee back on course again and she made most of the running herself, not because I'm useless when it comes to tears, but because she can't stand being seen as vulnerable.

We'd adjourned to the kitchen and sat at the corner of the table, pushing whatever needed clearing away to one side. She spent the next twenty minutes saying she didn't know what had come over her, blaming jet lag, the wine she'd drunk at The Crown, advancing years, all thirty of them come June. I spent most of the time not saying that she'd just broken up with a man she loved, which, even if voiced, wouldn't have been the whole story. With a deep breath and a slap of the table, she finally became her old self again and told me not to fuss, and certainly not to tell Laura. It would only make her feel worse and I'd caused her enough embarrassment that evening already.

When I eased open the bedroom door I'd expected the room to be in darkness and Laura to be sound asleep in her side of the bed. Instead she was wide awake, leaning back on upended pillows, reading from her tablet. She smiled, cautiously. "Is Fee okay?"

"You heard?"

"No, but I have a good imagination. Yukito?"

I sat down on the edge of the bed and reached out to her. "Yukito and other things. She misses her mother. We never gave her the chance to grieve properly, The Others and me, we just set her to work taking Maggie's place."

"That can be dealt with," she said.

I nodded. "But at least you made Bill Grogan's day."

She folded over the cover of her tablet and switched off the power, then considered what she was about to say. It was a developing habit, taking her listener to the brink of new information, then pausing to ensure their full attention.

"I didn't win," she said, eventually. "He allowed me to win."

"He was scared of what Grogan might do to him otherwise?"

"Either that, or he was being gallant."

"Gallant? It was only chess, Laura. It wasn't a sinking ship or even a door that needed opening. It was a game."

"Yes, but one that requires considerable mental abilities."

She thought for a moment, deciding if what she was about to say next would irritate or pacify me.

"He wanted to do medicine, you know. Science A-levels at school, four grade As, but his parents couldn't afford to send him to medical school."

"Which one?"

"I didn't ask."

No names, no pack drill: he was a dab hand at not giving much away. Gallant he might be, but he was still filthy, ragged, smelly and proud of it. When she saw the sceptical look on my face, Laura came gently to Kinsella's defence.

"It does happen, you know. People fall by the wayside. And that is shameful."

She launched into the case against an education system that still denies the best brains an opportunity to contribute. His home life had been truly dreadful, by the sound of it, with him needing to work even when he was at school.

"If he was working, how come he got good A-levels?"

"That's what's so remarkable, but is it any wonder that he fell into bad company?"

I smiled as best I could. "What's remarkable to me, Laura, is that you believe his bullshit."

She folded her reading glasses with unnecessary care and laid them on the bedside table. "I'm sure you meant to include the phrase 'with all due respect' somewhere in that sentence," she said quietly.

"With all due respect, I'm afraid I didn't."

- 8 -

We'd been asked to assemble under the big beech tree at 7.30 next morning, all of us except Laura, who cycled off to the surgery on the pretext of getting some paperwork done. We'd had a sort of breakfast an hour earlier, bran flakes and coffee, just after Fee woke the entire household with a ship's bell application she'd downloaded to her phone.

Jaikie's old trainers and tracksuit fitted Kinsella like gloves, and as I went out to join the others he was already jogging on the spot and stretching out as if murder trials were something that happened in other worlds, nothing to do with him, the main witness on whom the case depended. Fairchild offered him an elasticated tie for his hair and when he accepted it she took courage in both hands and put it on for him. She was looking pretty good. Pink, head to toe: zipper top, leggings, running shoes, sweatband round her forehead, all of it very budget, but showing off the face and figure which had so appealed to John Demise in the queue at Stone Post Office. Bill Grogan looked as grim as the reaper himself but at least he was wearing a side-arm under the grotty old tracksuit top. He engaged me in one of the longest conversations we'd ever had.

"Guvnor, d'you have a length of rope I can use?"

"You gonna hang yourself, Bill?"

"I'm not what you call a natural runner. I've a feeling this bastard is. Leastways, he's got a few years over me. I'm going to tie him to me."

"Have me pull you along?" said Kinsella, feigning outrage.

Grogan turned to him, opened his tracksuit top to reveal the Glock. "Make a break for it, son, this time I will fucking shoot you."

Fee waded in immediately. Wasn't it time we started trusting each other? Firearms notwithstanding, how on earth could Grogan or Kinsella run if shackled to each other? And suppose we passed anyone we knew, someone in the village: what would they make of it? Grogan just looked at her and held his tongue. I went off to the shed and found a length of rope.

We set off soon afterwards, on a five-mile loop of the Aylesbury Ring which for the first mile took us down across Martin Falconer's land, well away from the prying eyes of neighbours, and it was indeed a beautiful morning to be out and about. By the time we reached the bridge over the Thame at Lower Winchendon, with the prospect of a steep incline ahead of us, the runners had been sorted from the plodders. The fact that Grogan was lagging behind came as no surprise, any more than Kinsella's false bonhomie did as he ran beside him with absolute ease, making play of the umbilical cord between them. Fairchild had struck out, long legs and youth on her side, and soon gained a distance of half a mile or so. Fee ran back and forth between the two camps, like the proverbial PE teacher giving praise to front runners, spurring on those bringing up the rear.

I put on a spurt and caught up with Fairchild, unable to speak fluently for a minute but eventually finding a style that suited the pace she was setting.

"Friend of mine ... took a real fancy to you ... the other day."

She turned and smiled. It was the nicest thing I'd said to her since we'd met.

"Guy you met in Stone Post Office ... posting a parcel ... to Grimsby."

She'd had a feeling the niceness wouldn't last and tried to handle its passing with silence. I was getting some of my breath back.

"Who lives in Grimsby, Petra?"

"I think that's my business," she said, softly.

"I disagree. Too much of a coincidence to actually be one. These trawlermen were murdered there, now you send a birthday present to the same town? You can tell me or you can tell Grogan."

Her face hardened. "Who the hell do you think you are?"

We'd reached the ridge and normally the view ahead, down into the valley overlooking the Pollicots and Chilton, would make anyone pause and relish it, to say nothing of getting their breath back, but Fairchild used the descent to try and outrun me. I called after her, turning so that Grogan, even though he was way behind, might hear as well.

"Who lives in Grimsby that you don't want us to know about?"

She stopped dead and I waited for her to re-join me, which she did at walking pace.

"I was posting a parcel for Liam Kinsella."

"You bloody what?"

She stood facing me, arms folded. "Where does it say in any briefing I've had that I can't do the guy a common or garden favour?"

No wonder Fee hadn't sussed her out yet. She was too full of surprises.

"Nowhere. It shouldn't need to."

"Then please enlighten me as to why posting a parcel for him has got your knickers in a twist? Or was that the uphill jog?"

Grogan, Kinsella and Fee were still far enough away not to overhear our discussion.

"This man is testing you, me, Bill Grogan, my daughter, Doctor Peterson, to see how far he can push us."

"And why's he doing that?" she asked with a roll of her head.

"Drop the attitude, Fairchild, you might learn something. I don't know what he's up to, but if you start doing odd jobs for him, God knows where it'll..."

"You sound just like Bill Grogan and a hundred other old coppers I've met. No logic to any of your prejudice, just fixed ideas about some poor kid caught up in the justice system..."

"Forget the hundred others," I hissed. "Just listen to me, you stupid..."

For some reason I broke off. I like to think that her being a woman had something to do with that.

"Please, don't hold back," she taunted. "Forget the pink, see blue."

I took her up on that but stepped back a pace to emphasise the danger she might otherwise have been in.

"If you were a member of my squad I'd probably have grabbed your head by now and slammed it down on the nearest hard surface..."

"Charming."

"I'd have said, 'You stupid bastard, are you blind or just thick?' Kinsella is a man with a plan. Don't ask me what it is yet..."

She shrugged, as if I'd proved her point about fixed ideas.

"...but don't kid yourself he's had a moral awakening, all to do with heroin. He tried to escape the other day and as the trial gets nearer he'll try again. Just make sure you're not standing in his way when it happens. What was in the parcel?"

"A silk scarf."

"You bought that for him?"

"Yes! From a shop in Thame. Ten quid."

"Wrapping paper? Card?"

"From the newsagent next door."

"Then you brought it all home, snuck it in past Grogan, got Kinsella to sign it, went out again and posted it? I'd say this was more than a favour; I'd say this was busy."

She sighed irritably and looked away, hopefully in the first stages of realising that maybe I had a point.

"Who was it to?"

"A woman called Emma Jago. An old friend."

"Miss? Mrs? Doctor? Baroness?"

"Just Emma."

Fee was calling from a hundred yards behind and below us. "You two alright?"

"Address?"

"The Amethyst, Grimsby. I even remember the sodding postcode. In fact I doubt I'll ever forget it now! DN31 7SY."

"What did the card say?"

"Oh, for Christ's sake!" She squared up to me again. "It said 'Happy Birthday, Emma'. What are you going to read into that?"

"The fact that he's got you jumping like a Mexican bean. And why the hell I'm covering for you, God knows, but do anything like this again, I tell Grogan, I tell Blackwell."

She nodded and I called back to Fee. "We're okay, just wondering whether to go back or go on."

I received the expected reply. "Onward, onward!"

- 9 -

A few days later, the Crown Prosecution duet of solicitors paid us a visit and whereas I'd expected Kinsella to be nervous he was the complete opposite: urbane, gracious and polite. So this was the way he behaved on Wednesdays, I remember thinking, but given his appearance and the pungent smell coming off him, his apparent confidence still seemed a curious paradox. Certainly the young woman solicitor was taken aback when he helped her off with her coat, then hung it in the hall on a stand I'd virtually forgotten was there. He chatted with her and her boss about the weather, their journey here, the peace and quiet of the village, and then showed them into the living room. Grogan, not good in social situations at the best of times, and Fairchild, unwilling to usurp his seniority, both hung back.

The male solicitor introduced himself to the company as Henry Sillitoe whose job today was to examine the evidence against Aaron Flaxman and make sure that it was presented as Kinsella intended. He was mid-fifties and fancied himself, full head of hair, going grey at the temples, and a face like chopped wood, grainy and knotty, liable to give off splinters. The eyes were blue and he was well over six feet tall. I remember that because Kinsella kept warning him to mind his head on the beams. As far as I was concerned, having taken an immediate dislike to him, he could bang it on them as often as he liked.

His female lieutenant was called Marion Bewley, late twenties and pretty in a pinched sort of way, with auburn hair that tried to meet under her chin and nearly made it. She had teeth on which a small fortune had been spent, but what I liked most about her was her keenness, her excitement at being here: she was nervous, yes, but looking forward to the task ahead with no hint of the jaded attitude she would almost certainly develop as the years went by. Against her was the fact that, in spite of his appearance, teeth, grease, flaking sores and all, she was clearly impressed by Kinsella, but then the legal profession doesn't boast many comparisons for her to have based her judgement on.

They sat on the leather sofa with a low table pulled towards them on which they spread their various notes and photos. Sillitoe asked if Kinsella would mind Miss Bewley recording the conversation, as much for her own career development as anything. And for him to cover his arse, I thought, but didn't say so. Kinsella was more than happy to go on record.

Fee brought in a tray of coffee and Kinsella rose to thank her, then asked our guests if they wanted biscuits with it. Neither of them did. He asked if they took sugar. Marion Bewley asked for a smidgeon, thus betraying her Northern origins.

"White or brown?" he asked.

"Brown, if you've got it."

"The healthy option."

I wanted to smack him right there and then but with lawyers in the room it would've been unwise. He passed her the pot containing the demerara.

"Shall we get on?" Sillitoe asked.

He took a deep breath and informed us that Sir James Garrod QC would be presenting the case against Flaxman, which augured well for the Crown's prospects...

"Why isn't he here today?" I asked.

Though I say it myself, I rarely enter a room where those already there don't acknowledge my presence, so imagine my distress at this jumped-up solicitor's apparent resentment at me being in my own house.

"He's in court," said Sillitoe, glancing at his watch. "And this is very much a preliminary stroll through the evidence..."

"The trial begins in three weeks," I reminded him.

"I'm well aware of that. Even if he'd been available, I doubt he would have joined us. Being of the old school, he's sensitive about the practice of coaching, or anything which might be misconstrued as such..."

"Does any of this make any difference?" Kinsella asked me. "I mean as long..."

"Sit down, Kinsella, button your lip."

The room fell silent, except for the rattling of a teaspoon as Bewley stirred her smidgeon into her coffee. Even that ceased as she thrilled to the tension in the air. Sillitoe gave me that smile which solicitors of a certain age have perfected, thin, cruel and expensive.

"Forgive me, I understand that you own this charming house, but unfortunately that doesn't mean..."

A voice on the edge of the room overtook his. It belonged to Fee and because I liked what she was saying I didn't stop her saying it.

"I don't think you know who you're dealing with here, Mr Silly Toe. This man is my father; he is ex-Detective Chief Inspector Nathan Hawk, late of the Hamford Crime Squad where he solved thirty-five murders. Since leaving the force he's found four more killers, just by way of a hobby, so imagine what he could do if he really put his mind to it."

It was the last sentence that wrong-footed everyone, especially me, but it did the trick. Sillitoe had actually heard of me on the legal grapevine.

"You're the man who found John Stillman's daughter? Brought her killer to justice?" I nodded and he glanced wearily at his sidekick. "I wish I'd known that beforehand. To business..."

He shuffled a few A4 documents and in a fresh voice said that he would take Kinsella through the case, examine the evidence as he believed Flaxman's defence would see it. As he leaned forward to speak I held up a hand to stop him.

"Before any of that, I'd like to see a copy of the Immunity from Prosecution agreement Mr Kinsella was given."

"Yes, indeed, I was hoping Mr Kinsella would sign it this morning..." He glanced at my outstretched hand. "May I ask why you'd like to see it?"

"Because I don't think you guys can be trusted, but maybe that's the old copper bouncing up and down inside me."

He smiled again. Bewley passed me a copy of the letter. I took my time reading it, then looked at Kinsella. "Have you seen this?"

"Well, yes..."

"Is that your way of saying no? Tell me what it means."

He moved aside a bothersome hank of greasy hair, skim-read the letter and shrugged his understanding of its contents. "I give evidence against Flaxman, I don't get charged in connection with the murders."

He handed the letter back to Bewley with a smile which she returned quickly.

I jabbed Kinsella to regain his attention. "Like I've said before, you'll be dead by Christmas. D'you know what a 'scoping' interview is?"

"Yes. No."

"Forgive me, I thought I was the one..." Sillitoe began.

I raised a hand to stave off the interruption. "You've had a scoping interview with the Humberside Crime Squad and then received this, a proffer letter, outlining details of the witness protection programme you'd come under."

"New identity, yes..."

"In your dreams. You're not some double agent, the victim of a terror squad or the one who got away from a gangland boss. You're a cheap jack smuggler. This letter offers you immunity from prosecution in the case against Flaxman. They can still do you for the contraband – the fags, the booze, the perfume, electronics, to say nothing of the heroin."

I turned my fatherly gaze on Bewley, who thought she'd better contribute and did so by promising to make a note of everything I'd said and ensure that Mr Kinsella was fully immune before the trial date. He smiled at her again, poor girl.

In truth I should've counselled Kinsella to call a halt to proceedings, at least until he was safely behind the skirts of the witness protection scheme, total immunity, on paper, signed, sealed, delivered. More disturbingly, I wasn't sure why I'd leapt to his defence. Was it because I saw 'some poor kid caught up in the justice system', as Fairchild had put it? Or had I relished the chance to pick a fight with the lawyers in the room?

In yet another fresh voice, Sillitoe began again. "So, on the understanding that the conditions Mr Hawk has outlined will be met, I propose to take you through..."

"I've got another question. Why's the case being tried at the Old Bailey? Why not on home turf?"

"Couple of reasons," he said, wishing he'd handled the day differently. "Flaxman's defence didn't think he'd get a fair hearing there. The judge agreed. Flaxman's a local ne'er-do-well with a reputation, known to police, social services, media. And then there's the Heritage IRA connection, calling for maximum security."

I put on my sarcastic face. "1973, security was pretty tight, but it didn't stop an IRA car bomb right outside the Bailey."

"Things have ... improved."

He waited, eyebrows raised, to see if I had further questions. I gestured for him to carry on with the morning's business. He turned to Kinsella.

"I propose to take you through the events leading up to the murders of the two trawlermen. Will you please answer my questions briefly, clearly and, of course, truthfully? On Saturday April 12th last year did Mr Aaron Flaxman call on you at the house you were renting in Montgomery Terrace, North Cotes, Grimsby?"

"You know he did."

Sillitoe closed his eyes in an elongated display of patience. "Mr Kinsella, we will go through the evidence as if it were a play, for example, one which no else in the room has seen."

"Then yes, he dropped round for a chat."

"What did the two of you talk about?"

"Aaron wanted me, him, Vic Wesley and Freddie Trent to meet that afternoon."

Sillitoe gestured round the room. "Before Victor Wesley and Frederick Trent were murdered, how were the four of you involved?"

Kinsella turned to us, a right bloody performer, and explained they were the two trawlermen who'd imported contraband from Europe, instead of fish.

"Did Mr Flaxman tell you what the meeting was to be about?"

"Yes. Freddie and Vic said they hadn't agreed to bring in heroin. Aaron wanted my help to change their minds."

"Where was the meeting to take place?"

"At Speaker's Farm, his dad's place."

"What time?"

"Five o'clock."

"So, you went to the meeting...?"

"Right, only I was late. It was nearly five thirty when I reached the gate, the cattle grid..."

"In your car? On foot?"

"Car." He smiled. "I see where you're going. You want to know how I saw what I saw..."

"Mr Kinsella, refrain from commenting on the questions put to you, especially when we're in court. Did you drive up the main track, from the gate to the farm?"

"No."

"Tell the court why not."

"It was a new car. The track was rutted with mud, a foot deep in some places, so I parked at the gate, put on the wellies and walked."

"Down the main track?"

"No, across at an angle, through Speaker's Wood."

Sillitoe dropped his courtroom pose and explained that at this point Sir James would show large-screen aerial photos of Speaker's Wood, an area of 119 acres, mature beech and chestnut, crossed by two footpaths and a bridleway. Today we'd make do with a couple of A4 black-and-whites which Bewley handed round to us. Sillitoe drew an imaginary line on his own copy.

"So ... you walked from here to here. Tell the court what you saw as you approached the farm building, top left-hand corner of the picture."

Kinsella became slow and measured as he recalled the actual crime. "When I reached this tree here, I heard voices, raised voices, shouting..."

"Coming from where?"

"The bridleway. I stopped, turned and was just about to call out when..."

Sillitoe held up his hand. "You saw three people whom you recognised. Who were they?"

"Freddie Trent, Vic Wesley and Aaron Flaxman."

"You're absolutely sure it was them?"

"Well, yes, I've known them long enough. Aaron head and shoulders above the other two, soppy haircut. Vic was looking pretty sprauncy, actually. Jacket, collar and tie. He'd been to lunch with his wife, I heard later..."

"And Freddie?"

"Freddie looked, well ... Freddie. Same old anorak, same old cords, hadn't shaved for a couple of days."

"And the three of them were heading from the farmhouse, top right of the picture, towards the farm buildings, top left."

Kinsella nodded. "Where the chickens are. Vic on this side, Freddie the other, Aaron in the middle."

"I want you to mark exactly where you were on your copy of the photo."

He gestured for Bewley to hand Kinsella a marker pen and with no hesitation Kinsella put a cross about an inch from the edge of the bridleway, beneath the tree.

"And where were Wesley, Trent and Flaxman?"

Again with no second-guessing, Kinsella drew another cross about three inches from where he'd placed himself.

"That puts you roughly twenty metres away from them. Do you agree?"

Kinsella nodded.

"You have to voice your answers at all times."

"Yes!"

"You said you could hear their voices. What exactly did you hear?"

"Well, it was only bits and pieces..."

"Tell us the bits and pieces."

Out of coy respect for Marion Bewley, Fee and Fairchild, Kinsella whispered the expletives, twisting his lips to soften the impact. " 'Who gave you the fucking right?' said Vic. Freddie kind of parroted him, as usual. 'Yeah, who gave you...' His voice tailed off there because Aaron came straight in. 'You fucking dick, I've struck a deal already! Got us a buyer. Heritage IRA. They'll give us 7 million!' 'Well, we're not helping any IRA murderers,' said Vic."

Kinsella paused while he contemplated the moment which had changed his life forever. He spoke quietly and again his words were slow and deliberate, as if he'd thought about it many times and was still puzzled by it.

"Some kind of instinct must've taken over the moment I heard their voices. Fear, I guess, but I'll never forget Aaron's face, smiling, suddenly reasonable. Then he took a pistol from under his jacket, shot Vic in the head, turned to Freddie, who'd started to move away, shot him in the side. Neither of 'em saw it coming. It was all over..."

He tapped the table twice. Sillitoe gave him a moment to compose himself.

"How many shots?"

"Two, for Christ's sake!"

"What did you do?"

Kinsella smiled, glanced at me for a kind of matey understanding. "I don't remember doing it, but I dropped to the ground, face down in the grass. Then I started praying..."

"There was enough cover?"

"A low bough from the tree I was under, and the grass was..." He held out his hand, eighteen inches above the carpet.

Sillitoe nodded, made some notes and then suggested that we take a ten-minute break. Kinsella tried to take control again and asked if anyone wanted more coffee, whereupon Fee offered to make it.

"Before we break, did you see what Flaxman did immediately after he fired the shots?" Sillitoe asked.

"Well, I raised my head once or twice and there he was, dragging Freddie to the other side of the bridleway. That done, he shifted Vic to this side, into the grass."

"And then what?"

Kinsella shrugged. "He walked off, back towards the farmhouse. Once he was clear I legged it to my car."

"Why did you go into hiding after that?"

"I'd seen what Aaron was capable of. To be honest I wasn't that keen on the heroin thing myself, or selling it to the IRA."

"But you raised no objection?"

"It was too late. The deal had been done, this bloke had been over from Fermanagh and Aaron said he was a hard, nasty bugger. If he didn't get what was agreed we'd all be in the shit."

Sillitoe gestured for Kinsella to answer his next question in the affirmative. "Are you saying that you feared for your life, at the hands of both Aaron and the Heritage IRA?"

"That's exactly what I'm saying."

"Then don't forget to say it in court when you get the chance." He paused. "Right. We'll take that break."

It was quite a decent spring day for mid-August, at least warm enough for Fee to insist that we have coffee out on the lawn. It isn't really a lawn, in spite of the gallons of reviver the bloke who does my garden has thrown at it. It's an irregular patch of grass, green in some places, mangy in others and downright mossy throughout.

I'd taken my coffee over to a clump of hollyhocks and begun picking off dead flowers. Pottering, I suppose you'd call it. More displacement activity than gardening. The 'hocks grew as weeds in most of Winchendon, but had refused to do so in my garden, so Laura had planted some out as seedlings the previous year. She had promised they'd give a show from April to November with their trumpet flowers and powerful colours. True, by the look of it. Not that I really cared if they lived or died, and God knows why they've crept into my account of that day, the ten-minute break. Odd how the unlikely pairing of objects and events works, one helping to recall the other.

Sillitoe came over to me, holding his coffee mug by the rim again, slurping occasionally.

"Hollyhocks," he said. "Magnificent, aren't they?"

I followed his gaze across to where the others were gathered. Kinsella was entertaining the crowd and Fee and Bewley were laughing out loud at something he'd said. Fairchild wanted to laugh but held back. Grogan sat at a distance on a stone bench beside a tub of surfinias, also planted by Laura. After a moment I realised that Sillitoe wasn't taking in the view so much as checking that the others were out of earshot.

"What do you make of it all?" he asked.

"I don't make, I provide. Evidence. You're the guys who make, usually a pig's ear."

He nodded, as if he agreed. His height and large frame suggested a fitness not often associated with lawyers. For the most part, by fifty, they've grown fat on the proceeds of 'humbugging the public and pocketing the fee'. That's the caption to an eighteenth-century cartoon about doctors but, given my relationship with Laura, I've applied it to lawyers. It describes them perfectly.

He stretched and gave himself another two inches, head tilting backwards, looking up at the pillowy sky. "Give me your opinion on the evidence."

"Kinsella's the only witness you've got, which means Flaxman is almost a free man."

He began to cite the other evidence, without conviction. There was the pistol, recently fired, found at the farmhouse, Flaxman's fingerprints over it. I shrugged.

"Where were the bodies found?" I asked.

"Vic, just off a road which skirts the Flaxman farm..."

"What does 'just off the road' mean?"

"In a ditch. He was discovered after that heavy rain. Two feet of water flooded the dip, somebody went to check if anything was impeding the run-off, found a corpse blocking a culvert. Freddie was in a slurry pit on a neighbour's farm, blew up and floated to the top. Went off bang when moved."

"How far from the shooting were they found?"

"Crow flies? Both places four, five miles from Speaker's Wood."

"Was there DNA, forensics, anything at the crime scene?"

"Yes, well, the crime scene wasn't known until three months after the event. Not much left. I mean enough is enough when it comes to a prosecution, but these men had been shot at close range and made a mess of..."

"You'd have expected more."

He nodded.

"Bullets?" I asked.

"They were recovered, yes, 9mm, and before you ask the pistol used was a Luger, found at the farm. Tempting one to say 'bloody Germans again'."

He scissored the air to withdraw the remark, then looked over to where Kinsella was still holding court, only now Dogge was playing the jester as he threw her an old tennis ball, she ran to retrieve it and brought it back. Nothing odd about that, except that Kinsella had taught her in ten minutes what I hadn't been able to in five years. She was dropping the ball at his feet, stepping back to wait for the next throw.

"Look at what I'm working with," Sillitoe went on. "An anti-social, unhygienic Neanderthal. His story may well be true, but who's going to believe it?"

He fixed his eye on the hollyhocks for a moment.

"His derelict state aside," he said, "something about this case bothers me."

That made four of us. Blackwell, if Laura was right, Laura herself, me and now Sillitoe.

"What?" I asked.

"Does Kinsella's evidence sound too prepared?"

"You were the one who asked for detail."

"Yes, but I didn't expect to get it. I thought I'd have to provide it!"

"Coach him after all?" I said, as smugly as I could.

He set his mug down on the wooden bench, took a business card from his top pocket and handed it to me. The name 'Henry Sillitoe' leaped off it in black scroll, with a bevy of phone numbers below it. "The mobile will always get me."

"Why should I need to?"

"Would you be willing to do the Crown Prosecution Service a professional favour, Mr Hawk? Paid for at your usual rate?"

I'd envisaged him picking my brains but not putting me on the payroll. "I'm sorry?"

"Would you go to Grimsby, look over the crime scene, or what the Americans so vulgarly call 'the kill site', and after that 'the dump sites'? See if anything's been ... overlooked or wrongly used in your opinion."

He then asked if I'd mind doing it within the next few days. I told him I'd need to check with Commander Blackwell first but if OCC gave the all-clear, I'd leave as soon as possible. I'd only one question for him. Did he know what my current rate was? He didn't, which was a shame because I didn't either. We left it that his boss and I would negotiate.

For the rest of the day, Sillitoe took Kinsella back and forth through his evidence, occasionally trying to trip him up on the finer details. To no avail. Kinsella was word-perfect.

I tried not to make a song and dance about the proposed trip to Grimsby and, by and large, succeeded. When I phoned Blackwell he said he was 'very happy about the idea'. A cynic might say that he'd been wondering when I'd get round to it.

I told Grogan I was off to the original crime scene in the morning. He nodded approvingly. An image flashed through my mind of Kinsella handcuffed in my absence to every available piece of metalwork in the house, but I let it go.

Fee wasn't so easy to deal with, but I had to get her out of the house for a few days without her knowing the reason. She would've found my irrational fear that a branch of the IRA might descend on Beech Tree in my absence laughable. And even if they did, was I saying that she couldn't handle them? Talk them out of whatever they had in mind? I asked if she would go and spend a couple of days with her brother Jaikie in Chiswick. I was concerned about his relationship with Jodie, I lied, and would value her opinion. That last bit gave her purpose but triggered a volley of questions. What did I think was wrong? Why hadn't she been told about it before? Did The Others know? I waffled...

I was more candid with Laura, the only trouble being that she was candid in return. I called on her at Plum Tree Cottage late that evening and found her trying to revive neglected house plants. The place still seemed half-empty to me, a far cry from its cluttered comfort before it was broken into and vandalised a year previously. Fee reckoned that Laura's failure to replace certain items was a sure-fire indication that she expected to move into Beech Tree in the near future...

"The CPS solicitor, Henry Sillitoe, wants me to go to Grimsby, check a few things out. He's uneasy about certain evidence..."

She smiled. "Any moment now you'll tell me I was right all along. They wanted your help."

I held up a wilted leaf on a plant I recognised but couldn't name. When I let go it drooped again. "It's Kinsella I'm worried about."

"He's filthy but fine," she said.

"I'm not talking about his physical state, Laura, and it's not that I don't believe what he says about the murders." She stopped watering the plants. "I can't work out if he's playing us or if someone's playing him. Maybe both."

"Maybe neither," she said. "He's an odd fish, certainly, and that sets him apart. In many ways he's ... just like a child."

I agreed. And more out of courtesy than concern she wanted to know who I thought might be playing him. With him being the main witness for the prosecution there was only one real contender. The crime squad handling the case.

- 10 -

I'm developing a theory that car journeys get longer in direct proportion to ageing: what was a morning's drive in your early twenties is an absolute slog thirty years later. On top of that the east coast of England has always seemed farther away than most other places in Britain, but I don't have an explanation for that yet. In plain fact, according to Google Maps, Grimsby was 127 miles away from Winchendon and would take me three hours and thirty-nine minutes to reach. Pull the other one.

I took a room in a small hotel in Wragby, one of those Lincolnshire towns more sky than land, like a badly taken photo.

Next morning, I drove to Speaker's Wood via Market Rasen and from there into the Lincolnshire hinterland. Sillitoe had given me a map which pinpointed the ditch where Vic Wesley's body was found. It ran beside a quiet lane, no building within sight, and the field beyond went on forever. Ideal as it was from a killer's point of view, it still seemed a strange place to have chosen.

I'd also been given a couple of photos, taken on the day of the discovery. It had been chucking it down for weeks, evidently, and the find had given local police a dilemma: to move or not to move Vic's remains. They made the wrong decision. They shifted them and the water drained away down the culvert taking with it any evidence, leaving us with photos of an empty ditch and a rotting corpse up on the verge beside it. Useless.

I took a few photos of my own, up and down the lane, across the field, the ditch itself, and then headed for the slurry pit. It belonged to a small dairy farm, the buildings of which I couldn't see from the lane, so again it was a safe place to have dumped Freddie Trent, if you didn't mind him rising to the surface and going off bang, as Sillitoe had put it. As with the ditch there was no evidence of police activity here, past or present. I think if I'd been in charge of the case I'd have taped off both sites until the trial was over, just in case.

Freddie's body had been spotted by a dog-walker, apparently. Her labrador had made a bee-line for the pit, jumped in and then considered himself perfectly disguised, covered in cow shit. Dogge had gone through a phase of it, so I sympathised. I took a few photos, rid myself of the taste which somehow gets into the back of your throat with a strong mint.

To be fair, I hadn't expected to find much of any use at either of the dump sites, so I wasn't disappointed, just mildly concerned. Speaker's Wood was just five miles from both, and Lincolnshire's a big county. Why hadn't Flaxman taken the bodies farther away, butchered them, buried them, burned them? This felt hasty and panicky. And there it was, nagging away at my guts, just as it had bothered Blackwell and then Sillitoe: the feeling that something didn't quite fit.

I headed for Speaker's Farm and parked half a mile away from the main entrance and donned the walking boots. I must've taken roughly the same route Kinsella did, the shortcut through the wood, and I'd expected larger, more impressive trees. Some were okay but most were skinny, crooked apologies for the real thing. With autumn well and truly established leaves were falling, the grass and tall plants on the edge of the bridleway were dried out and skeletal.

The bridleway itself consisted of two parallel tyre tracks with a grass mohican between them, suggesting it was used as much by farm vehicles as by horse riders. Over to my right was the Flaxman farmhouse, a groggy-looking seventeenth-century affair, and more of a scrap yard than a working farm. The high-tech chicken shed was a mile farther on but I could smell it from there.

From the photos I identified the tree which Kinsella had reached just before he witnessed the shootings. I stood beneath it and looked across to imagine what he'd witnessed: three men, three friends, he believed, walking down the bridleway, twenty metres away from him. Talking bits and pieces, Kinsella had said. Acrimonious stuff. Insults, heroin, money, the Heritage IRA, all of it warning him to stay back. Then Flaxman's smile as he shot his two companions. Enough to make anyone take to the hills as Kinsella had done. Not that Lincolnshire has any...

I turned as I heard a vehicle approaching. It was a Land Rover and for a moment I gave way to an odd sense of fellowship when I realised that it was identical to mine.

Then I saw that it *was* mine. I felt for the keys. They were still in my pocket.

The Land Rover slowed down and I could see two men in the front seats, the older one driving, black leather jacket, heavy-framed glasses. The younger had more hair and was trendier, blue nylon zipper and jeans. The driver took his foot off the accelerator and stalled the engine. They got out and, as slowly as it's possible to do without going backwards, they came towards me. The older man was smiling and stretching out a hand.

"Never mind the big hallo," I said. "How'd you get my Land Rover started?"

"It's a skill my colleague acquired in Traffic."

I turned to the nylon zipper. "You'd better not have damaged the paintwork."

"I'm Detective Chief Inspector Carew," said the glasses, a smile wriggling across lips which were too wide for his face. "This is Sergeant Sweetman. And you are ex-DCI Nathan Hawk."

"I already know that."

Again he went to shake my hand. I ignored it, save to suggest that he keep both of his to himself. He held them up like he'd been arrested and assured me they really had come to assist. His colleague looked as if he'd come to have his prostate examined, narrowed eyes, grim set face. He left most of the talking to his boss, who reckoned he was pretty good at it.

"We gather you've come to see where the murders took place. We can show you exactly."

He was relieved that I took him up on the offer. He led me farther along the mohican, eyes down, and stopped when he reached a blue peg marker in it.

"Flaxman was here when he killed them," Carew said. "Vic fell sideways there, bullet through one temple and out the other. Not a great deal to stop it. Freddie turned slightly, took it through his side, fell that-a-way. Bullet stayed inside him."

"You found Vic's bullet where?" I asked.

Carew walked over to a spot between the blue peg and a silver birch. "Two metres from the body, still there on the ground, three months after it landed."

"DNA?"

"We recovered Richard the Third's, 1485, from underneath a car park. Why not Vic the First's, last year, from Speaker's Wood?"

The smart-arse answer was no answer at all. "Is that yes or no?"

"Yes."

I jerked my head at his colleague. "Does he speak or just stand?"

"Sometimes you can't shut him up."

Carew gestured that I should test his assertion.

"Why take my Land Rover?"

"Our car wouldn't have got down the main track. The ruts are two feet deep, dried solid."

It was an accent that had been worked on with the object of losing it. Brummy, I thought, from the little he'd said. He was also fit, but even so I still fancied giving him a playful slap.

I turned back to Carew. "Freddie must have bled quite a bit, chest wound. Where?"

They looked at each other, wondering who should answer the question.

I smiled. "You two wouldn't be making this up as you go along, would you?"

"He fell right there," said Carew, pointing to a dip in the far verge.

"So there was DNA from him too?" He waited for me to answer the question myself. "Don't tell me you never bloody looked."

"We looked and found."

I put a few yards between us by going back to examine the Land Rover's paintwork. It was a beautiful vehicle to drive but had never been much to look at, chipped, dented, well used. I locked and unlocked it with the key to test that it still worked.

"Something else. Here am I asking all these questions and you're just ... answering. All for the love of justice?"

"Commander Blackwell suggested that we look after you," said Sweetman.

"Ah, the man from London, eh? Bloody cheek, muscling in on your territory."

"Not at all. He seems like a first-rate copper."

I never met a policeman who spoke well of the specialist squads. They tended to break up old allegiances, criticise bad habits and generally make the local fuzz resentful.

"What's the thinking as to motive?"

"Money," said Carew. "Fifteen million pounds. We've had crime analysts working on it since March, waiting to see if the heroin pops up anywhere."

"*We've* had? You sound like you own the bloody force."

"Humberside Crime Squad together with Organised Crime Command."

"Caring and sharing, eh? I take it you managed to find the weapon between you?"

"We did, up at Speaker's Farm among a load of crap in the attic room. Aaron said we'd planted it; Joe thought it might've been his father's, a memento from the war; Carrie thought it was a water pistol. Take your pick. Fact is it was an old Luger."

"I wish my kids would do that. Use stuff, then put it back where they found it. Really, all you needed was an eye-witness to make it fit like a glove."

I could see him debating whether to turn nasty or stay friendly. He chose the latter.

"Finding Kinsella was certainly a bonus," said Carew. "We thought he was dead, Flaxman's third victim."

"He'd been hiding out?"

"On the farm. God knows there's enough buildings to choose from and the old man, Joe, was known to be sympathetic..."

"He shot him, for Christ's sake!"

"Fired *at* him. Big difference."

I smiled. "You must think I fell out of that tree. Kinsella may well have thought he was Aaron's next victim, but he hung round the farm for one reason only. He was looking for the heroin."

"Looking but not finding. Best guess on that, I'm afraid, is the Heritage IRA snatched it and as we speak it's being sold on the streets of New York." He pulled out the bottom of his shirt and wiped his glasses. His eyes seemed lost without them, tired and sunken.

"Flaxman moved the bodies in a pickup, right?"

"The old man's Chevy Silverado. Don't worry, it was all there: blood, brains, bits of bone, all in among the chicken shit."

"Why didn't he dump it?"

He frowned. "That bothered me for a while, but you have to know Aaron Flaxman before it makes any sense. Arrogant bastard. Reckoned he was untouchable."

"Known to police, then?"

"Since he was knee-high." He put his glasses back on and tucked his shirt in, then nodded over to the farmhouse. "Decent family, too. The old man always hoped he'd take over the business. Eggs. Dream on."

According to Carew, Aaron Flaxman took a familiar route for kids from well-heeled backgrounds. Expelled from school, he went into small-time crime, breaking and entering, dealing, which involved a couple of assault charges, and then he hit on the big money spinner of ten years ago, supplying non-EU labour to local farmers.

"Is that what the trawlermen were doing when he met them?" I asked. "Bringing in people?"

"We don't think so. The received wisdom is the farmers started getting their own workers in, didn't need a middle man, so Aaron turned to contraband."

115

"And found a mug with some venture capital in the shape of Liam Kinsella?"

He nodded. "I think it was all a bit seventeenth-century in Liam's mind, dodging the revenue men. They certainly made a few enemies, and we're not talking flintlocks and cutlasses. Shotguns and cleavers, more like. We think at least two unexplained deaths are down to Flaxman."

I smiled. "So you won't be sorry to see him go."

"Not in the slightest."

"This gets tidier by the minute."

He shook his head. "Anything else we can help with? Before you go home?"

"Are the wives being charged in any of this?"

Carew said that would depend on the evidence they gave at Flaxman's trial.

"You want them to blame it all on Flaxman."

"I want them to tell the truth."

I climbed back into the Land Rover and Carew came over to the window. I rolled it down.

"You couldn't give us a lift back to the main gate, could you?" Carew asked.

"I could, but the walk'll do you good."

Sweetman came at me with the only thing he had left. "That Smith & Wesson in your glove box. You got a licence for it?"

I laughed. "You'll have to do better than that."

I turned the key, did a rocky three-point turn, and drove away.

And another thing: it used to be that when you arrived at the edge of a town, you pulled in somewhere and checked a local map to find exactly where you were going. Or, God forbid, you asked a local. Now you keep listening to a disembodied voice on a GPS and it takes you right there. I was looking for the postcode which had stuck in Petra Fairchild's mind, DN31 7SY, The Amethyst, and quite reasonably I'd expected to find a stone-built, pokey little dockside pub, weathered trawlermen seated at the bar, with accents so impenetrable I'd need a crowbar to understand them.

But after winding through a wasteland of disused warehouses, separated by acres of broken concrete through which grass and weeds were making their comeback, I arrived at my destination. The satnav had taken me to the estuary side of Fish Dock, more a marina these days than a working dock, with access at each end to the mighty River Humber. A few sad-looking trawlers were tied up there, paint peeling, tar flaking, victims of the pernicious quota system. Alongside them was *The Amethyst*, an old cargo packet with the guts ripped out of her, replaced by a state-of-the-art kitchen, a bar and thirty tables. It was also a food bank for hundreds of gulls, screaming and wheeling as they waited for the leftovers.

I parked alongside a handful of middle-range Audis and Mercs which told me most of what I needed to know about the people on board having lunch. The men would be jacket and shirt, no tie, mid-thirties and monied: the women would be young professionals, dressed in their success with expensive hair and body parts that didn't move. I turned a

117

few heads as I went aboard, heads belonging to the brave couples who were up on deck sipping drinks at wooden tables, defying the onshore breeze and that tang of raw sewage that comes with enclosed water.

As I reached the bottom of the stairs, a man the size and shape of a small planet came over to me. Kristian, his name tag said, and he clearly wished I was three or four people, not just one, wanting lunch. He showed me to a faraway table and I ordered a double scotch in a tall glass with ice to the brim. He checked that I'd meant what I'd asked for and went to get it. As he turned I was able to read the quotation on the back of his black shirt, the company livery. It was a favourite of mine, one that I often use as an excuse for poking my nose into other people's business. 'The only thing necessary for the triumph of evil is for good men to do nothing. Edmund Burke.' Quite a mouthful to get on the back of a shirt, but then it was a big shirt.

A young lad, name tag Rob, brought my drink and a menu. I chose posh fish and chips. Coals to Newcastle, really, but what the hell. He was a skinny kid but the back of his shirt read: 'Always forgive your enemies; nothing annoys them so much. Oscar Wilde.'

As I sipped my drink I sussed out the waitress who seemed to be the chattiest and eventually called her over.

"Yes, sir. Can I help?"

"Tina, hi! What does it say on your back, by the way?"

To my surprise, she knew. " 'A crown is merely a hat that lets the rain in. Frederick the Great.' "

"I like that." Her big smile was still asking if she could help. "Does an Emma Jago work here?"

"No, but there's Emma Wesley."

Some would say I deserved the break; I say I should've done my research, at least dug out some basic info about the trawlermen's wives. It might not have taken me straight to Emma Jago and Emma Wesley being one and the same person, but it would've forced me to check.

No matter. Here I was in the same room as Vic's widow and the questions were forming a disorderly queue. Why had she changed her name, how much did she know about the murders, was she due to give evidence at the Flaxman trial, why had Liam Kinsella sent her a birthday card and was that her walking over to my table, the company smile on her face? It was a hard but well cared for face, black hair tied back to keep it out of the food. The eyes were sharp, intelligent, dead-giveaway eyes, so I banked on getting the truth from her.

"Emma, this gentleman was asking..." Tina began.

"Emma Jago or Wesley?" I said, rising and stretching out a hand.

She stopped, like someone crossing a dance floor and suddenly hearing the wrong music.

"Who are you?" she asked.

For some reason I'd expected watered-down Geordie accents from everyone, but what I'd heard so far were more Moss Side than Tyneside. Apart from the Small Planet, Kristian, who was all-purpose Scandinavian.

"My name's Nathan Hawk and your next question'll be 'What do you want?' "

She gestured for me to answer it.

"Why did Liam Kinsella send you a birthday card and present?"

Kristian was moving towards us, aware of a problem. He in turn beckoned to a bloke behind the bar, who side-vaulted the counter and joined his boss. The waiter Rob went to the kitchen door, opened it a fraction and called to someone named Josh. He turned out to be the chef and he'd forgotten to put down his chopping knife before joining us.

An old Desk Sergeant once told me it was the threat of violence, not the violence itself, that lay at the heart of controlling a situation. It was wisdom based on experience, but was now going to be 'the exception that proved the rule'? Cicero, I think, but not embroidered on anything I was wearing. Trouble was, there was one of me, five of them and rising as a couple of young men left their table and came to join the party.

I reached out and picked up one of those foot-tall, wooden salt grinders from my table and suddenly realised what they were intended for, because they're no bloody good at grinding salt. I held it truncheon-style, slapping the end into my other hand.

"The first one into my space gets his head broken."

The waiter Rob laughed.

"You think that's funny?"

He withered, instantly. The Vaulting Barman looked at his boss for permission to beat the crap out of me but Kristian didn't give it.

"I think you should leave," he said.

"I've only just got here."

"Fucking salt cellar?" said Josh the chef. "You've got to be joking!"

"Thing is, Josh, I know exactly where to bring this down, maximum effect. They used to teach us stuff like that. I doubt if you know how or where to stab me to make any real difference."

He looked down at his hand and seemed surprised to find that he had a lethal weapon in it. He appeared to weigh up the pros and cons of using it, all the while conscious of my salt grinder. Then a voice called into the silence.

"Josh, don't do anything daft, love." It was Emma Jago, arms out, patting down the hot air that had risen. "Please, boys, cool it."

"You heard her," I said, my eye on the knife. "Step back."

It was all the excuse Josh needed to retreat, a pace or two at first and then right back to the kitchen. To this day I think he was more frightened by what he might have done with the knife than ever he was of me. I can live with that.

The Small Planet turned to the troops he'd mustered, thanked them and they drifted away back to the bar, back to their places.

"What do you want, Mr Hock?" said Kristian.

"You to pronounce my name properly. Hawk. Then I want to ask Emma a few questions."

"Are you copper?"

I shook my head. "Solid brass, mate."

"Then you..."

Emma butted in. "Kristian, thanks, but can you give me ten minutes with this gentleman?"

He eventually said, "Call if you need."

As he walked off, Emma sat down opposite me.

"Jago?" I asked.

"Maiden name."

"Not Wesley because of the smuggling charges against you...?"

"Because of my murdered husband," she said, wearily. "I'm sick of people's sympathy. Here I'm just Emma."

"Emma whose back says?"

" 'If the facts don't fit the theory, change the facts. Anonymous.' "

I smiled. "Some copper will've written that. Where's Kristian from?"

"Oslo."

"That's just across the Baltic from Liepaja, where your husband and his crew picked up 15 million quid's worth of heroin."

Her stillness was natural, not forced. "Is it?"

"And you still haven't told me why Liam Kinsella sent you a card and present."

"Because it was my birthday and he knows how much I miss Vic. Liam's a very sweet guy. And brave."

"That's the last thing I'd have called..."

"Listen, I don't know who you are, and I don't much care, but can you imagine the guts it must've taken to turn on Aaron? I hope they hack off his balls and lock him up forever!"

"I've never met Aaron. I only met Liam Kinsella three weeks ago."

The waiter Rob emerged from the kitchen with my posh fish and chips and came over. I leaned back as he put the plate down in front of me.

"Any sauces? Another drink?" he asked, quietly. I shook my head and he turned to go. I called him back. "Sir?"

I picked up a fork, turned over the chips on the plate, stabbed one and said to him, "Eat that."

The request brought out his stammer. "I couldn't, we don't..."

"You don't like chips?"

"It's not that, it's, it's, it's..."

"It's more what Josh has cooked them in, specially for me? Bodily fluids? Take it back to the kitchen, son, tell Josh I'll be in later to push the whole lot, plate and all, down his throat."

His hand shaking, Rob picked up the plate and went back to the kitchen.

I turned back to Emma. "You were the one who brought Flaxman into the firm. You must've liked him to begin with. What changed your mind?"

She shrugged. "I didn't say I liked him; he just had a bloody good idea for getting us out of the red."

"No sign of what he was capable of?"

"He had a temper, yes, but so do I. Reckoned himself as an alpha male but I wouldn't have said he was a killer. Then again, what do murderers look like?" She paused. "Who the hell are you, anyway?"

I reminded her that two minutes ago she hadn't cared who I was. I told her I worked for the man who would put Flaxman in prison for a very long time. She wanted to know my employer's name. I saw no harm in telling her he was called Henry Sillitoe, the CPS solicitor.

"So you're like some ... private investigator?"

"Right. Your sister was married to Freddie Trent..."

She leaped right in, big sister protecting the little one. "Don't go bothering her. She'll tell you the same thing I will, anyway."

"At least tell me her name."

She laughed. "If you don't know that, you don't know much at all..."

"Sarah?"

She flared. "If you bloody knew, why ask?"

"Pure guesswork. Emma and Sarah were two names that often went together, daughters of a certain generation. What are you, early forties?"

It works five times out of ten. "I'm thirty-bloody-four!"

"So she'll be thirty-one, thirty-two? Too much to hope you'll tell me her address. I mean I know she's an ex-teacher, used to do a bit of smuggling on the side, charges pending presumably..."

"Our husbands did the smuggling."

"Heap it all on them, eh, now they're dead? Christ, you'll tell me next you didn't know about the heroin."

She leaned forward and stared at me. "If you're such a clever bugger, look right in my face and tell me if I'd bring in stuff that would kill kids."

"Booze and fags kill. You brought in plenty of that."

She sat back in the chair and looked at me with undiluted scorn. "Don't go all righteous on me. D'you know how many trawlers were registered in Grimsby, 1960, when Vic's dad went to sea? Seven hundred. Today? Eight!"

"All the more fish to catch for those who stuck it out."

"Oh, fuck off! I'm done."

She rose and, despite her anger, checked to see if she'd left anything. She even placed the chair back under the table before she walked off. I toyed with the idea of visiting the kitchen but decided against. I was forgiving my enemy and, according to Oscar, it would piss him off thoroughly.

- 11 -

I gave Grimsby the once-over before going back to the hotel at Wragby. I even took a guided tour up the Dock Tower, iron spiral staircase all the way. A guide who wouldn't have known the head of a fish from its tail gave an exaggerated history of the building and told us not to lean over the edge, if and when we reached the top.

The Humber estuary dominated the view, container ships and ferries to Europe on the horizon. Closer in there was the beach, made of sludge and plastic bottles, with leggy wooden piers jutting out into the water but to no purpose these days. Below me was *The Amethyst*, none the worse for my lunchtime visit, and the dozen or so docks near to it were either marinas for middle-income yachts or plain empty.

I went down again feeling quite depressed and walked into town for the lunch I'd never had. Away from the docks it might've been any one of countless struggling towns in Britain. The big names were there, of course, nipping at people's wallets – Tesco, Marks & Sparks, Shell. High-rise had replaced low terraces, shopping malls had put paid to corner shops, business parks had sprouted where factories once flourished. Christ, I don't just sound like my father, I am my father. Except in one particular. He was a peaceable man, which proves I've inherited at least one character trait from my mother. I was still dwelling on Josh and whatever it was he'd slipped into my posh fish and chips.

While they were alive, Vic and Freddie had a certain amount of privacy, enough to enable them to go smuggling for a couple of years without being caught. The moment they died they became public property. Every detail about them could be found on the internet, and I don't just mean their dirty laundry. Back at the hotel it took me three minutes to find Freddie's, and therefore Sarah's, address. A report in *The Grimsby Echo* told me it was a house in Freshney Terrace, Scartho Top. Admittedly it didn't give a number, but sure as hell there was a photo and the solar panel in the roof marked it out.

I browsed further, one link leading to another, until I came full circle back to *The Grimsby Echo* and a weekly column by a woman called Angelica Carter. The main thing about her was her sympathy towards Emma and her sister, not in a series of journalistic platitudes, but something meatier. She warned her fellow reporters against jumping to conclusions, revelling in the horror, beating the story senseless while forgetting that two young women had lost their husbands suddenly and violently. She spoke in the same vein elsewhere, in the paper, on her blog and evidently on local radio. I logged the name away, or maybe it was the face, the passport-size photo at the top of her column.

Middle-aged, hatchety, glasses, hair permed tight to the head. A script signature after every piece, 'Angelica Carter'.

Scartho Top was south of Grimsby, and 17 Freshney Terrace was in a run of eighties new-builds. It was being lived in but nobody was there today. There was mail on the floor the other side of the wrinkled glass, but with no easy access to the back of the place I decided to wait for the occupant's return.

I leaned back on the Land Rover and sipped a lukewarm coffee, tried to collate what I'd learned yesterday and today. There wasn't much that added to the evidence Sillitoe already had, but I was starting to get the feeling that I'd missed something, that I'd seen it but it hadn't registered. It jagged at me, every half hour or so, flicking me behind the ear like a kid in the desk behind at school. I tried to work on it. Dump site or kill site? I found myself sidetracked, critical of the quick and easy use of those two phrases, their virtual lack of any meaning. Men had been killed, for God's sake, women had lost husbands, parents their children, children fathers, and then they'd been disposed of like so much garbage and left to rot...

I'd turned to get back into the driving seat when a lady who'd been supervising a small child in a front garden, a couple of doors down, called to me in the nearest thing to a regional accent I'd heard since arriving. She didn't exactly call me 'bonny lad', but I'm not sure that I wanted her to.

"If you're looking for Sarah, she's gone to the new house."

"Right," I said, in a 'forgetful old fool' kind of way. "D'you know where it is?"

"Near her dad's in Scotland, I think. My husband helped her load some of the heavy stuff into the van: washing machine, dryer, sofa. Even offered to drive there with her..." She shook her head, puckered face. "Since Freddie she's found it very difficult. Their first house."

I was nodding as if I knew the whole story. "Rest of the furniture...?"

"She'll be back for that. Till then she's asked me to feed the tarantula. Give it a cricket every other day."

From the expression on her face she wasn't looking forward to the task, but it meant she had a key to the house. Could I find a way of getting her to let me in for a poke around? Sarah's sister didn't want me to meet her, so maybe she knew something useful. If she did, though, the police would've known it too. Perhaps I should go back to *The Amethyst*, make up with Emma, then drop into the local nick, fire a few more questions at Carew and his boys...?

I could've carried on re-jigging my agenda till kingdom come in the feeble hope that whatever I'd missed might reveal itself. Instead, I decided to go home.

- 12 -

It was early evening when I drove onto the gravel beneath the big beech and I could've sworn I heard a tensing of muscles from within the house as they braced themselves for my arrival. It was wishful thinking.

Grogan, in an apron, was making supper, following a recipe from *Mrs Beeton's Cookbook*. The woman was flawless, professional and long dead, but he still had a beef with her. This wasn't the way his mother had made shepherd's pie, but she was dead too so he couldn't ask her. Dead or alive, right or wrong, it would be ready in fifty minutes. From the living room I heard Fairchild laugh. I went through to see what was so funny.

They say that if you live with a foul smell for long enough you get used to it, which is probably why the stench of Kinsella hit me afresh when I walked into the room. I'd been away for two days. He greeted me as if it had been a month. Then, with a smile that gave me his own opinion of the town, he asked what I'd thought of Grimsby.

"Never mind Grimsby, what the hell is going on here?"

They looked at me in utter bewilderment with a dash of fear thrown in. I gestured down at Fairchild's laptop open on the coffee table in front of her. She and Kinsella had obviously been sitting side by side, working on it, playing on it, God only knew, and before I could make a further comment Kinsella gave me a jollified explanation.

"Facebook! Petra's been trying to unravel its mysteries for me. D'you have a Facebook account, Mr Hawk? Can I have you as a friend?"

"Petra now, is it?" I asked, quietly.

"That is my name."

I must've looked as if I needed more and with jerky little shakes of her head she told me there was nothing sensitive on her laptop, nothing work-related.

"He asked me to show him how Facebook worked, that's all. Nothing he couldn't have learned in a book."

"Then you should've bought him the bloody book!"

Kinsella stood up. "Hey, listen, I'm sorry, I didn't mean to..."

"Shut up!" I pushed him back down on the sofa.

Fairchild snapped her laptop shut, zipped it back into its case and said, huffily, "The man hasn't even got a computer here, so why you're so pissed..."

"You want the male version or the female one?"

"Unisex."

"This is the second gaffe you've made. You're a fully trained police officer, he's a crucial witness in a murder trial. You posted his mail for him, now you've allowed him access to your computer!"

The raised voices had brought Grogan to the room, untying his apron, trying to figure out what the problem was. I helped him.

"You're more to blame than she is, you bloody fool!"

"What the hell are you...?"

"While you've been arguing the toss with Mrs Beeton, she's been in here showing him how to use Facebook." He was still trailing. "You know what Facebook is?"

"Sort of..."

"Computer access to the outside world."

"Hey, listen, nothing's happened, really, it's just..." Kinsella began.

"I told you to shut up! If I need to again I'll poke you, as they say on Facebook. Both eyes."

He fell silent and all three waited to see what else I had to say. I don't think any of us remembers in detail, but we all knew that I shouldn't have been the one saying it. I was a civilian, for Christ's sake. They were the police, members of an elite squad. I can remember yelling something about Grogan's palpable lack of interest in the case, except when the chance arose to beat Kinsella up or cuff him to the wall. All while Fairchild twitted and pouted in the background, far more interested in the way she looked than in the job she was here to do.

And just as a matter of passing interest, I tacked on, there was no way this filthy bastard could go before a jury as a credible witness looking like he'd just been hauled out of a skip. What had they done about that? Fuck all. I think I flounced off at that point, and ended up with an oversized double, ice all the way to the top.

The shepherd's pie was pretty good, as it turned out. Laura joined us for supper, having stopped off on her way to pick up Dogge from the neighbour she'd been staying with. Kinsella, with his Siamese twin Grogan, joined at the wrist, took Dogge out into the garden after the meal, leaving the rest of us to clear up. As we circled the open dishwasher Fairchild chose a moment to justify her carelessness.

"Okay, letting him near my laptop was a mistake, though I'm not really sure why. Thing is, while you were away I kept him with me as much as I could, to stop him and Grogan bitching. I mean you've both seen Bill lose his rag. The handcuffs, too..."

"What about them?"

"I know you didn't approve and keeping them apart, well, less chance of Bill using them."

Laura was well aware there'd been a contretemps prior to her arrival, but she'd made the best of it and hadn't asked for details. Now she could sense peace in the air.

"I see Kinsella's wearing shoes again," she said, brightly.

"That's because we don't consider him to be a risk anymore," said Fairchild.

"Since when?" I wanted to know.

"Since you told him that Aaron Flaxman would kill him if he got the chance. It's terrified him."

She was filling the cutlery basket in a way that drove me mad. Knives in one corner, forks in another, spoons ... why handle them when they're dirty? Much easier to sort when they're clean.

"So, I need the redraft of that Immunity from Prosecution agreement," she continued. "I've been on to Sillitoe..."

She looked at me, hoping I'd offer to put some pressure on. When it became clear that I wouldn't, she asked what I'd found in Grimsby.

"Nothing extra, nothing different."

"When does the trial start?" asked Laura.

"Two weeks from today," said Fairchild. "You know what still bothers me, though? The heroin. I keep chewing over what might have happened to it, where it could be, did someone take it..."

"It's called future tripping," I said. "According to the local crime squad, the Heritage IRA snatched it."

"So that's it? Gone?"

"I think so. Not that I looked everywhere, of course..."

Fairchild and Laura exchanged a cahoots glance, girls together.

"Are you going to leave us in the dark?" Laura asked.

I smiled. "Mind you don't bump into the furniture."

- 13 -

We met in a pub in Acton called The Rocket which Blackwell knew quite well and said would be safe. It was a long thin place on a street corner, near the railway station. Inside it was grey wooden floors and big sash windows, the woodwork freshly painted, racing green. It could've done with some new furniture; the leather chairs and sofas had paid their toll and the stuffing, presumably horsehair, was poking through wherever it could. It certainly wasn't a copper's pub, nor a lawyer's, but the whisky was the same as anywhere else and nobody queried ice all the way to the top of the glass, which made a change.

Blackwell was already there when I arrived, cradling a single malt. He was dressed as ever, full turn-out, jacket, shirt and tie, creases that cut and shoes that blinded. Most people in the place, including me, had opted for T-shirts that day and the surrounding chatter was mainly about rain. There'd been a three-day run of unusually warm weather which could only mean one thing: a storm was brewing.

Henry Sillitoe arrived ten minutes late, full of apologies. The level crossing had caught him out. The gates had waited for no less than three trains to pass before allowing traffic through. Something really needed doing about that and a letter to British Rail was taking shape in his head...

"To thank them for not letting you be killed?" I suggested.

He smiled. "I suppose so. Solicitor's first recourse, the loaded missive."

He tried to poke back some horsehair before sitting on the Chesterfield, gave it up as a bad job and sank into it. He wasn't a T-shirt and jeans man but the nearest you'll get to it in lawyers of his generation: cotton jacket over a polo shirt.

"Are you chairing this meeting, Commander?" I asked.

Blackwell nodded. "Only one item on the agenda. How did it go in Grimsby?"

"I think you're dealing with a very old problem," I said.

I told them about my visit, missing out the trip to *The Amethyst* and starting with where the bodies were found. The only odd thing about both places was their nearness to Flaxman's farm. I'd have expected a man with Aaron's reputation to do more than just offload his problem in a ditch or a slurry pit five miles from his parents' front door.

Sillitoe, who'd ordered a coffee which hadn't come yet, finally caught the barmaid's eye and mimed drinking from a cup. She waved back and I moved on to Speaker's Wood and the appearance of two members of the local crime squad. A DCI Carew and his side-winder, DS Sweetman.

"Carew?" said Blackwell. "I rubber-stamped his request to assist you."

I didn't like that. "You mean Carew came to you in the first instance, you didn't go to him?"

"Correct, correct."

"He tells it the other way round."

Sillitoe was floundering a bit, the names Carew and Sweetman being unknown to him. I explained that two coppers had stopped by in Speaker's Wood, not because they'd wanted to help me but to check that I wasn't finding out too much.

"I wouldn't say they were directly threatening, but they were anxious for me to pack up and go home." I turned to Blackwell. "Carew's old-school. He'll break the rules and the nearest head if need be."

Blackwell sighed and decided to drink his whisky rather than just hold it. He knew, roughly, what I was going to say next. I spelt it out for Sillitoe.

"This is why I called it a very old problem. Carew and his team have been trying for two years to put an end to Aaron Flaxman. Two years! And everything comes to he who waits. In this case it was two murders and 15 million quid's worth of heroin. Trouble was, there were no witnesses. Then along came Liam Kinsella with a perfect story. They doubtless threatened, cajoled and promised whatever was needed to give him a 'crisis of conscience'. He turned on Flaxman."

Sillitoe nodded, then asked my opinion on the evidence. I said it was the same as when he'd asked me in my garden beside the hollyhocks.

"All I've really got is Kinsella?" he asked.

"What he says may be the truth, but whether it's enough is in the hands of your barrister."

The barmaid brought him his coffee and he thanked her with his smile, thin, immobile and wishing they'd bring back the death penalty for bad service in pubs. She departed from our table with a noticeable shiver.

"So, you've nothing to add," he said, once he'd taken his first sip. "That sounds critical, wasn't meant to be. And why does coffee in places like this look like the real thing but never taste of it?"

"Another letter?" I took a few swigs of my drink and set it down on the table. "I should've said 'nothing *yet*'."

"Meaning?" said Blackwell.

"I don't think we've looked in the right places."

"Where else is there?"

"Stamford Prison. Where Flaxman's being held. I need to talk to him, like I would've done ten years ago."

Blackwell smiled. "Slamming his head down on the table?"

"I might try being friendly this time."

Sillitoe said it was out of the question. The man had been charged. God only knew what his defence would make of me, a third party, walking into Stamford, asking questions, using the answers to further our case.

"Or to shoot holes in it," I said.

That made him even more uncomfortable. He started on about the bureaucratic difficulties, the wrangling, the crawling he'd have to do to set it all up.

I let him exhaust his excuses, then said, "You both think there's something wrong with all this. Let's see if Flaxman knows what it is."

Grudgingly, they both consented.

Out of common courtesy I should have told them about my visit to *The Amethyst* but I knew there'd be questions, aside from the simple one of why the hell I'd gone there. I would've ended up dropping Fairchild right in it, telling her boss that she'd posted a present on behalf of the main witness. I'd have then had to say she gave Kinsella access to her laptop...

"By the way, Henry, have you re-written Kinsella's Immunity from Prosecution agreement?"

Sillitoe play-acted the overworked professional, lost without his right arm, Marion Bewley. "No, I keep meaning..."

"No rush," I said. "In fact, why don't you move it right to the bottom of the pile?"

There were twelve days to go before the start of the trial, with Kinsella due to be called about a week after that. It was cutting it fine to see Flaxman beforehand, mainly because it took a whole week for Sillitoe to get permission for the visit. He'd made the purpose of it deliberately unclear, but that wasn't the reason for the delay. It went up and down the bureaucratic ladder, almost of its own accord, as high as the Ministry of Justice, as low as the Prison Ombudsman, before it was sanctioned. A week is a long time in politics. A British prime minister said that. The man had obviously tried to visit someone in Stamford Prison out of hours.

But at least the delay gave a chance to do some research into Flaxman. He'd been brought up in Speaker's Farm, the only child of an arable farmer. Then the chickens arrived and it turned from a cosy little homestead where you could stop by and get a dozen eggs into a real money spinner. The eggs were free-range, as near as dammit, and the old man, after years of hard graft, had become very wealthy. However, just like me, with my aversion to paying £2.60 for a cup of coffee, Flaxman senior remained a 'cash flow cautious' sort of man.

Flaxman senior had wanted, more than anything else, his son to take over the business. His son didn't want to, endorsing an unpopular belief I'd held for years: the more you give your kids, the *less* they take. Obviously I'm not talking about straight cash. But capital assets that come with obligations and responsibilities? For example, 16,000 chickens?

Fair enough, Aaron hadn't wanted to follow in his father's footsteps, but that didn't give him the right to make the choices he did. By seventeen he was what the local worthies would've called a troublemaker. Fights in bars, and there can't have been many in Wragby to choose from, but Aaron was always a contender. He moved on to burglary, but that didn't provide the one-on-one satisfaction he was after. It was people's belief in their fellow man's inherent goodness he wanted to steal, not their money. His need to be seen as the local bad boy moved him on up to armed robbery. No surprise in that. He'd been using shotguns on the farm since he was twelve years old, so by twenty-four he was a dab hand.

The big event was robbing a jeweller in Lincoln, putting the fear of God into customers, passers-by, staff, even the bloke he tried fencing the stuff to. He was caught because he wouldn't keep a low profile. And his father was sick of bailing him out. He got nine years and did six and, mainly because of estrangement from his parents, he then turned to the labour scam, bringing in non-EU workers for local farmers. It fizzled out. He turned again, this time to smuggling.

A search of his room at Speaker's Farm shocked a few people. There was a computer there, naturally, but what did the officers dealing find on it? A few games, music, some porn like they might've expected? No, evidently Aaron was a bit old-fashioned when it came to women. What they found was a whole host of material about British mobsters, almost a historical collection. It covered people like the Krays and Richardsons, yes, but included lesser-known names like Billy Hill, the Sabinis, Jack Spot. This wasn't a kid who'd seen romanticised versions of these men in films and wanted to be like them. This was a serious student, cherry-picking the best of various crimes. No wonder Kinsella was terrified of him.

- 14 -

A couple of days before the prison visit was due, Fee and Laura took Sheila Bright to the cinema in Aylesbury. All I know about the film is it starred Ben Affleck, so take your pick. It left just me, Grogan, Fairchild and Kinsella at home and it was my turn to cook supper, which meant it was a stir fry. Simple to prepare, quick to make, easy to clear up afterwards.

We started eating in silence, which was unusual. I looked across at Kinsella in my umpteenth attempt to answer my own question. Was he playing us, or was someone playing him? I'd cracked the second part, at least to my own satisfaction. Somebody was. The Humberside Crime Squad, in the shape of Carew and Sweetman. What about the first part, though?

Across the table he was shovelling his food in like someone who hadn't eaten for a week. He realised I was looking at him and raised his head, peered out from behind the curtain of hair.

"I'm going to see a friend of yours tomorrow," I said.

He carried on shovelling. "I didn't know I had any left."

"I'm going to see Aaron Flaxman in prison."

The child in him came through straight away, rice noodles hanging from his mouth, catching on the beard, a prawn on the end of his fork as he stopped dead and looked at me.

"Why?" he asked. He swallowed what was in his mouth and then wiped his lips on the caked sleeve of his denim shirt. "I'm sorry ... I meant why do you want to meet with him?"

"Questions."

"What about?" he asked.

"Well, if we're going to put him away then every little helps..."

At the other end of the table, Grogan was nodding. "I think it's a good idea. Word is, you're a past master at the face-to-face."

Kinsella stood up, his way of countering the rising fear apparent in his face. He clawed the hair away from his forehead and proceeded to walk back and forth in a space the size of a prison cell.

"You really need to think about this, Mr Hawk!" His arms were trembling and, for want of anything to do with them, he hugged himself. "Are you seeing him on your own? In the same room?"

"What's the problem?" I asked.

He leaned towards me, eyes wide, and tapped his head, knocking as if trying to get in. "He's a psycho. He'll pick a fight, no excuse. God knows what he might have on him at the time..."

Fairchild tried to calm things down, choosing now to dish out second helpings of the stir fry. I wanted things to stay up in the air. That way I might've learned why Flaxman's name had sent a balloon up in Kinsella's world.

Sure, I'd said the man would kill him if he ever got the chance, but was that a reason to panic? Right there and then, I meant.

"I'll have him frisked," I said. "I'll do the job myself."

"If you talk to him, he'll know it was me turned him over to the police."

"He'll know that anyway. If by any chance he doesn't, he'll see you in court. You can't go in disguise. And while we're on the subject of your appearance..."

"But it's not just me he'll turn on." He swept an arm round the table. "You, your family, friends..."

"Sit down, Liam," said Fairchild. He turned and looked at her, unsure of what she'd just said. "Sit down!"

She'd called him Liam and there was a wealth of meaning I could've read into that, but at least he did as he'd been told. He pushed his plate aside, then rested his elbows on the table, dropped his head forwards and covered it with his hands. He was sweating, still trembling, apologising. I'd never thought of him as especially streetwise but nor had I believed he was this naive, imagining that contact with Flaxman would put us all in more danger than we were in already. It was straight from another soap opera.

"I'll think about what you've said," I told him. "Meantime I've no intention of confronting him. Why would I need to? He's facing the worst charges a man ever could."

He nodded and calmed a little. "Murder. But is my evidence enough to put him away for it?"

"Chief Inspector Carew thinks it is, Henry Sillitoe thinks it is. Me, I'm not so sure."

- 15 -

I waited up for Fee. She came through the door at one o'clock. After the cinema she'd gone to Laura's house for a drink and a chat. But this was just like the old days, she said, as she squeezed half a glass of red wine out of the bottle left over from dinner. She would go out for the evening with Maggie's and my blessing, return when she felt like it, but there one of us would be, waiting, no matter what godforsaken hour it was.

"What was the chat about? Me?"

She smiled. "Dad, not everything's about you." She sat down next to me. "Jodie Falconer. You sent me off to see her and Jaikie because you had something going on in Grimsby. It was a con."

"Don't tell me you found something wrong..."

"No, Jaikie's fine. I pissed him off a bit by saying you thought there might be a problem..."

"Thanks for that."

"Jodie's fine too."

"The word 'fine' doesn't say a great deal," I said. "Choose another."

She flopped down in Maggie's dad's rocker, creaked back and forth a couple of times.

"Jodie Falconer is one of the nicest women I've ever met. Just what Jaikie needs. She supports him, slaps him down when he gets unbearably up himself." She paused and nodded as she checked the truth in what she'd just said. "And he loves her. They're talking about marriage, Dad. Children. So why don't I feel over the moon?"

This was turning out to be more complicated than I'd foreseen, as most things with Fee did. And she wanted a response to the question. I simply asked if she'd phoned Yukito yet and got my head bitten off in the process. If we were going to talk, she spat, could we at least avoid the obvious? So she'd just broken up with somebody and Jaikie and Jodie were on cloud nine. Christ, it didn't need a fucking psychoanalyst...

"Your baby brother's checking out. If you thought Jodie wasn't good enough for him, you'd step in and see her off. Like you did with Sophie Kent..."

She rocked forward and stared at me. "I had absolutely nothing to do with that!"

"Except that you couldn't stand her and made it perfectly plain. He listened to you."

"But I never said a word! Okay, she was a greedy, grasping, gold-digging bitch and thank God he realised..."

"Fee, you didn't *need* to say anything. And now Jodie's taking your place."

She nodded. "He doesn't need me anymore."

She went over to the sink and threw her wine into it. Some of it splashed back onto her top. She swore quietly and ran a handful of kitchen towel under the tap, removed the stain.

"Things here okay?" she asked.

"Fine."

She pointed at me for using the meaningless word.

"I'd like your opinion on something, Fee. I came back from Grimsby to find Fairchild teaching Kinsella how to use Facebook, using her laptop."

She didn't react adversely, like she was meant to.

"I blasted her," I said. "What's the harm, she said. I couldn't really answer, just knew instinctively that it was a stupid thing to do. Was it?"

She thought for a moment. "Well, in theory, yes. He could memorise her passwords, break into her computer later on..."

I nodded, feeling vindicated. Why had he needed her to teach him how to use Facebook? The man was thirty-two years old. Facebook, Twitter, all that stuff went in with his mother's milk.

She came over to me with a pitying smile on her face. "Come on, Dad, even people his age forget the details of it, specially when they don't use it for a while. Remember you and me...?"

She was referring to the several goes I'd had at mastering Facebook, under her tuition, before getting the hang of it: the difference between profile and page, a timeline, newsfeed, events. And when it came to Twitter, we had to start all over again.

"Why does everyone have an excuse for this guy?" I asked.

"Because we can all see that he doesn't have, say, Jaikie's self-belief. He doesn't know who he is."

I slapped the table and stood up, never mind what time of night it was. "Then let's help him find out. Over the next twelve days I'm going to change that little bastard, make him oven-ready for court."

"Won't he object?"

"I'm sure he will. Problem is, where to start? I mean it's hair, beard, the clothes, the teeth..."

"Start with the hair," said Fee. "Fairchild's mother only lives in Ashendon."

"So what?"

"She used to be a hairdresser."

I was first up the next morning, six thirty, and anyone who knew me would have seen it as a bad sign. A project was about to be unveiled and those within striking distance would have a role to play in it.

Grogan and Kinsella appeared on the dot of seven, the one chirpy and chatty, his other half bleary and bad-tempered. Fairchild entered soon afterwards, the pink dressing gown corseting the life out of her. I set a bowl of porridge in front of her; she loosened the cord, stopped yawning and started eating.

"I've got a job for you," I said.

She didn't like the sound of that. I shouldn't have been the one telling her what to do, but she still asked for the details.

"Phone your mother, see when she can cut Kinsella's hair."

"Now just a second..." Kinsella began.

"It's a haircut, not a circumcision," I said.

"To me it's just as personal..."

"You have it cut by a pro or Grogan holds you down and I do it. Your hair, I mean. And that stupid bloody beard's coming off as well."

He started to argue, appealing to Fairchild. To my surprise she agreed with me, though the language she used was gentler, more diplomatic. If he looked clean and conventional, she pointed out, he'd stand a better chance of appealing to a court. It was all very well being a free spirit, an original, but juries weren't renowned for their love of eccentrics. And he did want Flaxman convicted, didn't he?

I sat in the passenger seat of the Focus, Fairchild driving with undue caution. Grogan was squeezed into the back handcuffed to Kinsella. I'd lent Kinsella a pair of Jaikie's old walking boots which fitted him perfectly and completed the picture of a 'gentleman of the road', as my mother would've put it. He was silent throughout the five-mile journey, probably grieving for his human rights. Mind you, we had most of the windows open so it would've been difficult to hold a conversation.

Ashendon is a brick and flint village at the end of a road that turns into a track which becomes a footpath and then disappears. It lies in a small valley and must once have been a farming community, and a hell of a lonely one at that. The early Victorian buildings, barns and animal shelters, were certainly not grand in their day, but were now highly sought after with price tags to match. If Mrs Fairchild was a hairdresser, then her husband must have had a more lucrative trade. It turned out he was 'in property', another molested phrase covering anyone from Peter Rachman to the Duke of Westminster. Jack Fairchild owned local houses, shops, pubs, factories and had a decent enough reputation.

As we pulled into the yard of the Fairchilds' old barn conversion, the hairdresser came out to greet the policewoman and they embraced almost tearfully. It happened every time, they said, whether the absence had been a few days or several months. Grace Fairchild was clearly her daughter's mother, though the pointed angularity of her body had been rounded at the corners with age and good living. She was an inch or so shorter than her offspring, as most of us are, and it came as no surprise that her blonded hair was immaculately done, a walking advert for her expertise.

When Petra turned to introduce her to the rest of us I saw Grace pause at the task which lay ahead of her as Kinsella emerged from the car. Whether exhilarated by the challenge or wishing she hadn't been so ready to help, I couldn't tell, but she invited us into the house and offered us coffee.

I'm not sure why she turned directly to me and asked if I'd noticed how time flew faster with age, but I agreed out of courtesy. Her observation had something to do with Danish apple bars. They were Petra's favourite and if she hadn't been so busy she would have set to and made some, but she hadn't had time. She would make some today, somehow get them to us. Meantime there were only bourbons, digestives and Jaffa cakes. Could we manage with them? Kinsella said he loved Jaffa cakes, hadn't had one for ages, and his apparent delight at the prospect of them brought Grace's attention back to him.

We were in the kitchen by now, plenty of light from windows on three sides. Grace pulled a chair onto the central mosaic of tiles, gesturing for Kinsella to sit. He did as he was asked, breathing in her expensive perfume as she circled him. All we'd wanted was a short back and sides but given the starting point, a greasy mass of rats' tails, it was bound to be less than straightforward.

"I was expecting something, well..." Her voice dwindled.

"Human?" I suggested.

"Easier to work on..."

"We all were. And, by the way, if he quotes the International Declaration of Human Rights at you, hand me your scissors. I'll cut off more than his hair."

Regardless of the tattered package he was, Grace Fairchild insisted on covering Kinsella with a protective sheet which, once in place, rendered him just another head at the barber's. This helped her maintain an objectivity, I imagine, and over the next half hour a curious thing happened as she unearthed the original Liam Kinsella from the shallow grave of his hair. Though it pains me to say it, a good-looking man emerged. And as she started work on the beard, so the shape of his face became apparent. The only person in the room who wasn't impressed was Bill Grogan, but mother and daughter were pleasantly surprised. I was more interested in this chance to now read Kinsella's face without hindrance. It was youthful, certainly, though pitted by the sores of recent neglect. They would heal.

It was certainly a striking face, long and bony, like the rest of him. The nose and ears were untouched by violence or rough sport and, now we could see them, the eyes were grey and steady. But, along with the mouth, they were the things that betrayed him. They remained still until he moved them for effect, which may not seem worth mentioning, but most people under stress twitch their lips or move their eyes involuntarily. Those who don't are almost certainly controlling their emotions and doing so for a reason that needs to be identified. As for his other talking points, the hair was jet black and mostly in the bin along with the beard. He was beginning to reek of ground-in sweat again, the clothes were still ragged and the teeth...

"Open your mouth," I said.

"Why?" he said, tight-lipped.

I walked over to him, leaned down and he smiled. The teeth had been cleaned.

"When did that happen?" I asked.

"This morning. First time for three months."

In hindsight, alarm bells should have rung, but at the time it seemed like a detail. Besides, Fairchild was already holding up a barber's mirror for him to see the work so far.

"Recognise him?" she asked.

Kinsella looked at his reflection as he might have done a school photograph, recognising but not knowing his own face gazing back. He seemed to force himself to like what he saw, then smiled at Grace Fairchild and thanked her for her handiwork.

- 16 -

On the drive back to Beech Tree, talking above the wind rush from the open windows, Kinsella gave us a running commentary on the virtues of Grace Fairchild. She was warm and friendly, Grace by name, gracious by nature, stylish and non-judgmental, her classiness reminded him of his own mother, her obvious love for her daughter spoke volumes. Generalities, all of them, and as he began to struggle for further compliments I did him a favour and told him to shut up. In the peace and quiet which followed I noticed his minders stealing the occasional glance at him, Grogan with a head turn, Fairchild in the rear-view mirror. Perhaps they were wondering what to expect from this metamorphosis...

I wasn't sure that a simple makeover would alter him at all. Change would imply a move from one position to another, whereas Kinsella still felt like a man in flux, someone who had literally dropped out of the night sky with an undeclared purpose and continued to throw into question my celebrated ability to judge people.

Back home, Fee looked at the work so far, then raised approving eyebrows.

"Promising," she said. "He reminds me of someone. Who is it, Dad? Come on, you're good at this stuff."

And as she snapped her fingers, trying to bring a name to mind, some Hollywood star or other, a bolt of panic hit me, pit of the stomach. My daughter was a beautiful girl, on the rebound from a long-term relationship, and Kinsella was the good-looking enigma such women fall for. He smiled at her, clean teeth and all.

"Let me know when it comes to you," he said.

I'd taken back the boots he'd worn for the trip and made a mental note not to tell Jaikie they'd been lent. He was odd about people's feet at the best of times. But it wasn't just his boots that needed keeping quiet about. Fee decided to search the loft, a cramped space beyond the attic rooms, home to a small colony of pipistrelle bats and family junk. In a box marked 'Jaikie Clothes', which she herself had packed when I'd moved house seven years previously, she found a selection of her brother's cast-offs. She brought them down to the kitchen where Fairchild was boning a chicken and I was preparing vegetables for an evening casserole. Grogan had offered to help us and been declined. He sat in Maggie's dad's old rocker, evil-eyeing his refurbished charge who was basking in the growing effect he was having.

"They aren't so much worn out as out of fashion," Fee told the assembled company. "Being Jaikie's, they're top dollar." She looked at Kinsella. "Before you try anything on, you'll need another bath."

"Of course. Care to join me?" He'd meant to say it with a kind of impish charm but it failed and came out as plain awkward and silly. He winced with embarrassment. "Sorry. Bath. Right."

Exhibit one was a single-breasted jacket on a hanger which Fee hooked over an old cast-iron nail in one of the beams. There was a shirt to go with it and a pair of slacks, even a tie. What did everyone think? Fairchild was enthusiastic and said it would do nicely. Grogan nodded and looked away.

Sensing mistrust from my direction, Kinsella tried to include me in the conversation. "These belong to your son, right? Jacob Hawk, the actor? Will he mind?"

"He won't know."

"Not unless one of us tells him, eh?" He winked. It was another attempt at passing humour but it fell to earth unnoticed.

"There's just about everything he'll need up there," said Fee. "Underwear, socks, trousers ... shoes, Dad?"

Grogan muttered with his usual brevity, "No shoes."

Fee appealed to me as if I might countermand that. I shrugged, but no one got away from Fee that easily.

"So Liam walks into court in a Ralph Lauren jacket, Prada shirt and bare feet...?"

She too was using his Christian name. For me that marked the crossover from formality to friendship.

Fairchild had stopped work on the chicken. "Is it really a Ralph Lauren?"

"No, but you get my point!"

Fee could hear herself becoming short and cranky and she backed off a little.

I thought back to the evening when Kinsella had panicked at news that I was planning to visit Aaron

Flaxman. Two days ago? Three? The fear he'd shown hadn't lasted. Had it been real to begin with?

Given Fee and Fairchild's reactions to the new, improved Kinsella, I was interested to see what Laura would make of him. I'm not suggesting that any one of them would have fallen prey to his good looks and awkward charm as he emerged from his derelict state, but on the other hand he knew how to use both to full advantage.

She arrived at Beech Tree, after a twelve-hour day, to join us for supper and, still in GP mode, asked me how Kinsella was. The lice were history, the nits had left the building, but was the ointment she'd prescribed working? I gestured to where he'd just entered from the living room and was standing in the doorway. I watched her body language as she approached him and could only see the doctor at work. He smiled, hands outspread, inviting her to give an opinion. She swallowed gently, searching for words, then said blandly, "Much better. And the ointment I prescribed has definitely worked."

He counted off his other improvements on the fingers of his left hand. "Cleaned my teeth, had another bath, and the T-shirt and jeans are hand-me-downs from Jaikie."

"Shoes?"

"No shoes yet. I don't mind. I understand their reasoning."

"You're too understanding by half," said Grogan, shoving him from behind, pitching him farther into the kitchen.

"Good evening, Sergeant," said Laura.

He nodded. He was still embarrassed whenever she addressed him directly, especially with a smile. We thought it went back to the day she'd caught him off-guard in just his tattoos and boxers.

Having handled Kinsella, she went to the sink and washed her hands. The rest of us followed suit, mainly to spare ourselves the lecture.

During the week when Kinsella became human again, some other subtle changes occurred in our little commune, the one that surprised me the most being Grogan softening towards his charge. His excuse was that we needed Kinsella to feel secure in the days immediately before the trial and his way of achieving that was to occasionally utter the two words, "You okay?"

"Yeah, thanks, Bill," Kinsella would answer, bewildered by the hint of concern. He was downright flabbergasted when Grogan went up to three words:

"Cup of tea?"

"Please, yeah. Thanks."

"Apple bar?"

"Yeah."

True to her word, Grace Fairchild had made a big tin box of them and her daughter had been over to collect them.

They were good. Grogan and Kinsella would sit together under the big beech, working their way through them, the model of tolerant incompatibility. On one occasion Laura, Fairchild and I were in the kitchen and I caught Laura gazing out at them with a pleasantly bewildered look on her face.

"When you think back to what he was, just four weeks ago," she said, "it's nothing short of miraculous. A triumph of persuasion over pressure."

I glanced at Fairchild, who hadn't fully understood the remark either.

"We've brought him round with argument..." Fairchild began.

"And a few threats," I said.

"Don't fool yourself that if you'd simply bullied him he would've changed," Laura said. "Four weeks ago he was filthy, self-obsessed and anti-social, riddled with lice and covered in sores. Now he's good-looking, charming, confident ... a different man."

Fairchild raised her eyebrows at me, behind Laura's back, and, as usual, when I should have kept my mouth shut I opened it.

"That's just your weakness for seeing the best in people."

They were both taken aback by my remark, the way I'd said it more than the words themselves, and wanted me to expand on it. I said they'd forgotten one crucial aspect of this whole business. Liam Kinsella had turned on his friends in order to gain his own freedom, not because he'd had a change of heart, a moral awakening.

"I think you're being grossly unfair," said Laura.

"P'raps I am, but just consider what he's managed to achieve, to gather round him in those four weeks, all with us barely noticing. He's got his own personal physician, you, Laura, dealing with lice and impetigo. He's got a legal adviser, me, securing his immunity from prosecution. A campaign leader in Fee, fighting for his human right to wear shoes. An armed bodyguard, Grogan and Fairchild, to say nothing of a bevy of housekeepers, cooks, cleaners and bottle washers: advice on what to wear, what to say, how to say it..."

There was a pause before Laura responded, as stalwart as ever but not quite as certain. "You can't have it both ways, Nathan. The CPS needed a witness to a brutal murder; Kinsella turned out to be perfect for the job. All you're doing is criticising the way it's happened."

I told her she was fudging her own argument. The way it happened was just as important as the result itself.

Fairchild was puzzled. "With us barely noticing, you said?"

I nodded. "And I do mean us, all of us."

Laura had been taken in by him, I insisted. She'd sung his intellectual praises to me, bemoaned his missed opportunities. Gallant, she'd called him, because he let her win at chess! His sob stories had been believed, even though they contained no specifics, just generalities that could be seen on television most evenings of the week. Fairchild had said he was just a kid caught up in the justice system, then she'd become his gofer, doing odd jobs for him, buying and posting presents, teaching him how to use

Facebook. Fee had dressed him up like a doll in her brother's Bond Street clothes, when a Marks & Spencer suit would have done him just as well. Even Bill Grogan was now softening, actually talking to the guy...

A defender of any cause to the bitter end, Laura said, "I still think you're regarding our achievements, his achievements, in the worst possible light..."

"Do you? I've known my fair share of turncoats down the years, a few of them women, most of them men, and not one of them possessed a single saving grace."

- 17 -

When I set off for Stamford Prison, I wasn't exactly heading into unknown territory. I'd visited enough prisons down the years. Too many. That sounds like resigned self-importance, but I can't think of one prison I came away from feeling positive or optimistic.

Visiting rooms are sad places, no matter which side of the table you're sitting, your every gesture, every word, overseen by prison staff and CCTV cameras. The inmates want more from their couple of hours a week and know they won't get it, which explains why some prefer to do their time alone, regarding contact with their families as more punishment than privilege. The wives or partners are under sentence themselves; some are trying to push on with their lives, while remaining loyal to the man they've come to see. Others are on the verge of ditching him. No in-betweens.

The prisoners' parents are the saddest to watch. They run the gamut of human emotion from bewilderment to anger that a child of theirs could've been so stupid. Then they turn on the system to find a reason. Unemployment, bad company, bad education, poor housing, that's all before they turn back on themselves with guilt. You don't hear much laughter in a visiting room, even from the kids, who'd rather be somewhere else for those precious few hours. You come away wishing there was another way, but knowing there isn't, especially for the likes of Aaron Flaxman.

Everyone has their own mental image of a prison and Laura Peterson reckons it's one of the four institutional portraits painted into our memory in childhood. The other three are hospitals, schools and churches. When they're referred to we each see our own particular favourite, if that's the right word, then flip the pages of the album to view others. My abiding impression of prison is the Victorian one, a poor man's castle of a place, two turrets either side of a heavy wooden door. If it were to open, out would ride a knight on a white charger, lance in hand, and he would gallop towards an imaginary foe. In reality he'll be a clapped-out prison van, hammering back and forth to the local courts.

People have an impression of the inside as well and Stamford was very close to mine. A central hub with five spokes bracing the rim of a wheel, each spoke being two tiers either side of a concrete floor, joined at the landings by metal joists holding up a safety net. And while the media get most things right, from the look of the place to the echoes, the kerfuffle and slamming doors, there's one thing they'll never capture. The smell. It lingers in the back of your throat long after you've left, being a mixture of sewage, sweat, stale food and disinfectant, none of them more palatable than the others.

I parked the Land Rover away from the main entrance and walked along beside the high brick wall, with its buffers running along the top of it. At the entrance I went through the usual security rigmarole with the Officer of the Day stalling at just one item I was carrying.

"What's in the bag?" he said.

"Chocolates."

Something about my answer appeared to baffle him. "What d'you mean, chocolates?"

"Chocolates," I repeated. "A box thereof."

Bewilderment became suspicion. "Let me see."

He examined the box, took note of the price, then asked why I was bringing Belgian chocolates to a prisoner, especially one like Aaron Flaxman. Looking back, I think that was the point at which my visit started to go wrong. In answer to his question I said I'd tried to get hold of some skunk but my supplier had a school exam that day. He referred to the letter on the desk beside him in which the Ministry of Justice had sanctioned my visit and he decided not to get into an argument. He summoned a young prison officer and asked him to show me into Reception Room C.

It was laid out in the sort of discomfort I'd expected. A single Formica table with a springy metal chair either side of it, a third chair over by the wall. The decor was just as homely. The walls were cream, the floor was grey, the lights were bright. The Officer of the Day kept me waiting half an hour before bringing Aaron Flaxman down from his cell on the remand wing. We didn't greet each other formally, no handshake, no friendly exchange of names. He stood just this side of the doorway and looked across at me.

"I've had to leave a really interesting class because of you," he said. "Transcendental meditation: a search for inner calm."

I asked him if he'd found any and he smiled, lip curled at one side.

"I hear you want to talk to me," he said, eventually. "What about?"

"Murder," I replied. "Vic Wesley, Freddie Trent."

The prison officer who'd brought him in closed the door behind them. Flaxman and I watched as he strolled over to the chair by the wall, sat down, took out a tablet and began to play *Xenonauts* on it. Flaxman pulled out the chair his side of the table, turned it at an angle and sat, one leg over the other, arms folded. I pushed the chocolates in his direction. He reached out for them, removed the cellophane with his teeth and examined the card which described them. He picked one out and started on it, half sucking, half chewing.

He was a big man, mid-thirties, dressed in prison garb, grey tracksuit, white T-shirt. Emma Jago had called him an alpha male. He was a lot further down the Greek alphabet in my opinion, tough on the outside maybe, feta cheese on the in. It was a weird sort of face, everything slightly out of place: the lips too far down from the nose, the eyes too close together, the hairline starting too far back, not receding, just wrong. His hair was thick and parted down the middle, auburn in colour, and at the back someone had put a basin over his head and trimmed away the surplus. They'd steered clear of his big, bushy sideburns.

"Hawk," he said.

He made a gargling sound deep in his throat, the other meaning of my name. Then he swallowed and reached for another chocolate. "My brief said I shouldn't talk to anyone, let alone you. He says you've got a reputation."

"What for?"

"Turning nasty if things don't go your way. On the plus side, you half killed a fellow copper."

I laughed. The power of time and repetition had blown a three-second lapse of judgement on my part out of all proportion. I'd hit the man, certainly, but I did not half kill him.

"I'm a civilian now, just like you," I said. "Tell me what happened that day..."

"Oh, for fuck's sake!" He half stood up, interrupting the prison officer at a crucial point in his game. The officer told Flaxman to sit down, but Flaxman already had done. "I've been through this a thousand times, same words, same look on the faces of those I'm telling..."

"Which is?"

"You're a lying bastard, we don't believe you."

I nodded. "It's a funny old world where everyone thinks you're guilty, except you."

He looked away. "What was the name of it, that film my mother keeps on about? Jane Fondant's dad was in it, turns a whole jury round."

"*Twelve Angry Men.*"

"That's the one."

"I don't think the bloke on trial had your history. Not someone who was born with a silver spoon, then took to robbing jewellers, running labour rackets..."

He screwed up his face in contempt. "What are you? You can't be an ex-copper, there's no such thing."

"Oh, I'm ex alright, but it's the ones still working you need to worry about. Carew and Sweetman."

"Carew's been on my back for years. Anything bad happens on his patch, I'm the first man he calls on. Gives me a sense of ... self-worth."

I shrugged. "See it that way if you want, but they've given two years of their lives to you. If they're out to nail you, they will."

He sneered again. "The voice of experience, eh?"

Still sitting in the chair, he turned it and shuffled it up to the table. He wanted to keep the conversation low, out of the prison officer's hearing and masked from the camera in the corner.

"I don't care if they've given blood," he said. "See, I'm going to win this one. The trial will be over in two weeks, maximum. Why?" He emphasised his first point by placing a clenched fist down on the table, raising his thumb. "First, I didn't kill Vic and Freddie." His forefinger joined his thumb. "Second, the only so-called witness is Liam Kinsella and my brief will have that tosser for breakfast."

So he wasn't worried by anything Kinsella might reveal. On the contrary, whatever he said might help him...

"They've got other stuff," I said.

"Two bullets and some DNA, some off my dad's pickup."

"Narrows it down, I'd say."

He waved the evidence away with a flap of both hands. "Opens it out. The old man has seven blokes working for him; they're in and out of Mum's kitchen all day, begging food. Dad leaves the key in the Silverado, anyone can drive it."

"You do know Kinsella's been offered immunity to testify against you."

He smiled properly. Decent teeth, a lover's gap between the two front incisors. "Well, of course he has, and who could blame him for taking it?"

"It goes a bit deeper than that, centres on his moral objection to the heroin."

He looked at me, almost pityingly. "Moral objection, eh? Did it make his evidence any more compelling?"

"I don't think it was *his* evidence. I'm not saying he wasn't there when you killed Vic and Freddie; I just think there are ways of telling it and they've coached him so well he can recite it in his sleep."

"Who are 'they'?" he asked, reaching for another chocolate.

"Carew and Sweetman, you bloody fool! Aka Humberside Crime Squad. Trouble is, Kinsella's desperate for you to get banged up so he can carry on looking for the expensive haul you and your crew brought in from Liepaja."

He sat back in his chair, arms folded again. "Liepaja? Sounds foreign."

"Denying the stuff ever existed won't help you. Telling Blackwell where it is might do wonders. You know Blackwell?"

"I met him. Didn't like him."

"Met him where?"

"Here. He was on the same kick as you. 'What happened that day, who were you with, where did you hide the scag?' I told him to ease it all gently up his arse."

"You reckoned that would help your case?"

He shrugged.

"I went up to Grimsby, met Emma Wesley," I said. "No big fan of yours. Thinks you should be castrated, then be locked up forever."

He laughed. "That's Emma for you. No prisoners. Except me."

"Listen, however sharp your brief is she can't wipe out your past: what you did to those people in the jeweller's. That got you eight years. Will a jury think you're capable of murder?"

"Previous convictions aren't meant to be dragged up in..."

"It's called 'bad character' and barristers dredge it up whenever they can. Besides, you think those jurors don't go home at night and look you up? It's all there on Google, the manageress who collapsed and you just walked over, the other customer you thumped and got done for GBH."

He put his hands behind his head and stretched out in the chair, in so far as it was possible to do so, and looked up at the ceiling. "I don't know if you're trying to scare me into something or out of it, but either way it's not working."

"And such is your faith in British justice, it'll be alright on the night, eh? Put it this way, then. Where were you the day Vic and Freddie were murdered?"

He addressed a ceiling tile rather than me. "I was at the farm with my parents. It was my mother's birthday..."

169

"So there'd been no meeting arranged, you, Vic, Freddie, Kinsella? Nobody was thinking of going to the police about the heroin? You hadn't agreed a knock-down price for it with the Heritage IRA?"

"What heroin? Come to that, what IRA? Which all adds up to 'what the fuck are you talking about?' "

"So the Irish angle's an invention too? You didn't have a buyer who'd paid you up front? You were just sitting there with Mum and Dad, talking ... what?"

When the conversation shifted to his parents, he sat up straight in the chair again. "Look, I couldn't remember then, I can't remember now. All I know is eventually the subject of chickens came up and the old man tried, for the two hundredth time, to persuade me that I wanted nothing more out of life than to run an egg farm. I told him I was sick of bloody chickens, would he please stop asking."

"What did you buy her?"

"Eh?"

"Your mother. You said it was her birthday."

He laughed. "I take it you've never been to Speaker's Farm."

"Not inside."

"It's a well-scrubbed, well-hoovered rubbish dump. If something breaks, the old man fixes it; if something needs replacing, he buys it second-hand. As for anything that would make life easier, sweeter for Mum, he won't cough up."

"Long pockets, eh?"

"He's a tight-fisted old bastard..."

"Tight-fisted? He wants to give you the business."

He leaned forward across the table, closing the gap between us. "It already *is* my business. Not on paper, but I was the one who forced him into it. Without me there'd be no money for the old sod not to spend!"

I shook my head. "You'll have to explain."

He took a deep breath and puffed out his cheeks before going into the well-worn story. "Fifteen years ago, he needed something new to get him out of a rut. Mum certainly did. For two centuries his family had been growing potatoes, cabbages and cauliflowers. I hate all three! Like bloody peasants they were out there dawn till dusk, digging in the earth, always dependent on the weather, the workforce, London prices. The eternal cry in our house was 'come the spring it'll all be okay'. Meaning the bloody cabbages will start growing. Roll on April! Only that particular April it pissed down for three weeks solid, then froze. Killed off the crop. We lived off anything the old man could shoot, trap or fish for."

"What alternatives did he have?"

"Not many, but some. Mum's brother had just died; she fancied taking over his farm in Cartmel. So did I. At least the view would've made up for being skint."

"Never heard. Where is it?" I asked.

He looked at me reproachfully, as if I'd driven off the best thought he'd had all week.

"Lakes," he muttered. "Anyway, the old man wouldn't hear of it. Born here, lived here, so he'd die here. Then I met this Swedish engineer who'd designed a system for managing free-range birds. The old man went for it and 10 million pounds later, here we are."

He must have realised that narrowing the distance between us had allowed him, maybe even encouraged him, to reveal a more telling side to his personality, albeit one that centred around vegetables and poultry. He'd spoken with a degree of passion; his manner had been so intense, an onlooker might have thought he was blaming me for that lousy spring fifteen years ago. He sat back again and resumed his remote cockiness.

"So what did you buy her?" I asked.

"What the fuck does it matter to...?" He calmed. "New settee, right? The old one was disgusting..."

"Dutiful son, eh?"

He looked at me, pure resentment. "I thought we were talking about my alibi? There isn't one. I had a row with the old man after lunch."

"About chickens?"

"I left, four o'clock, went back home."

"Where's that?"

"Over a shop in Churchill Street, Wragby. It's on the market. You interested...?"

"No girlfriend, boyfriend to back that up?"

"No."

"Well, I come back to saying the defence is rubbish, the prosecution story looks good."

"Well, I say Henry Sillitoe can swing from my balls."

"You know, I came here thinking you might have been a victim yourself, of Carew and Sweetman," I said. "What do I find? Some arrogant git who reckons he's untouchable – Carew's words, not mine. Someone who thinks he'll get off this murder charge for the half-baked reason that no one can prove he was there at the time. You daft sod, they don't care where you were! They just reckon your time has come and you're going down. And the whole thing is overshadowed by 15 million quid's worth of heroin, one of the biggest hauls there's ever been. If you brought that in, then as the father of someone whose addiction nearly killed him, I'm with Emma Jago. I hope they send you down forever."

He waited to see if there was more. Satisfied that I'd said my piece, he did the gargling thing in his throat again, long and deep, finally hawking up. Then he leaned towards me and spat in my face, a mix of phlegm and nougat. It hit me on the mouth and I clenched my lips as a roll call of infectious diseases rushed through my mind, anything he could've picked up in prison from a common cold to HIV or hepatitis C. I remembered for a moment who I was, why I'd gone there in the first place. I reached into my inside pocket for The Map, spread it out on the table. I even lifted a finger to bring it down on a more agreeable place. The Map began to shrivel and then disintegrate...

I stood up, pushed away the table and Flaxman rose to fend off the oncoming attack. He was too late. I had my chair by its back, swung it and caught the side of his head with the legs. It wasn't heavy enough to knock him over and he regained the balance he'd lost momentarily. Life in that room and beyond had slowed to crawling pace so I had plenty of time to plan my next move. I could hear a voice calling from over by the wall. I could see the prison officer approaching. I could hear an alarm bell ringing, voices beyond the door clamouring, none of this in sequence, all in a circle of time at the centre of which I grabbed Flaxman, kneed him in the groin and as he buckled forward I grabbed his hair and slammed his head down on the table, once, twice...

By the third attempt I'd lost my reach and strength. The prison officer had grabbed me from behind in a full Nelson and was pulling me away. Two of his colleagues had entered the room. One of them was backing Flaxman into a corner; the other came over, baton drawn, and jabbed me in the guts with it. He knew what he was doing. I wake at night sometimes, thinking I can still feel the pain.

The next I knew I was in handcuffs.

Twenty minutes after that I was sitting in the prison governor's office, wondering what the hell had happened. The handcuffs had been removed and a secretary had brought me a cup of machine tea.

The governor, Stevens, was a man I remember thinking was too short for the job. He had fine silky hair that wouldn't last much beyond his forty years. His face was pointed, not like Fairchild's, whose sharp angles flattered her, but one whose features, birdlike as they were, denied him character. The Heinrich Himmler glasses were an unconscious attempt to be feared, I guess, but since his job was more administrative than hands-on these days, they'd been a waste of money. He was softly spoken and appalled at my behaviour: the baffled head teacher to my fourth-form rebel.

"I'll have to make a report to the Director General," he said, perching on the edge of his desk. "It'll be up to him whether the matter's taken further."

"Where's further?" I asked.

"Ministry. Charges against you."

"He spat at me, for Christ's sake! I can still taste nougat."

"Tell me what happened."

I recounted most of it, the stuff I didn't mind him knowing, and when I reached the point where I'd lost control I thought that would be it. Man in prison reception room went berserk, beat the crap out of murder suspect, charges pending. Strangely enough, though, Stevens became sympathetic. He wanted to know just what it was like to be at the mercy of myopic anger.

I told him it was a terrifying business, losing your grip so completely that for five minutes you might be capable of anything. I've often been asked to describe it, to say how it feels to lose it. Nobody believes me when I tell them I can't remember the rage itself, let alone banging heads on tables, can't hear or see sounds or movement on the periphery. At best, I recall them later.

I hadn't experienced an episode like the Flaxman one for a while; I'd come close but managed to use all the tricks in my repertoire to keep the anger at bay.

"Those tricks and devices...?"

"The most useful is The Map, only it didn't work today."

"The Map?"

I explained that it was an imaginary map of the world which I always carried with me. When I felt rage taking over – the real thing, not just everyday annoyance – I would mime taking it out of my pocket, spreading it flat, lifting my finger and bringing it down on 'a far more agreeable place'. Not my words but those of the career criminal who bequeathed it to me just before he died. Roy Arthur Pullman. He recognised a kindred spirit.

- 18 -

When I stepped out through the door in the main gate to Stamford Prison I felt what a legion of cons before me must've while asking the same question: what next?

I walked back to the Land Rover, sat in the passenger seat as the surge of adrenaline which had fired my temporary insanity continued to subside. Gradually I would see things more clearly, be able to cut through the confusion of guilt, failure, depression, shame ... all of them easy handles to attach to what had just happened. But like all negative feelings they seemed at that moment to be an end in themselves.

As I sat there, mulling over what I'd done, my first thought was of Tom Blackwell. I'd had no contract with him, not even a verbal agreement, but we'd both come to believe that whatever was wrong with this case, I'd be the one to dig it out, give it a name, put it right. However, I'd returned from Grimsby with nothing more than a suspicion that Carew and Sweetman had bent a few rules. Hubris on my part, then. I'd fallen from the vain height of believing I was King Dick, the first person Blackwell turned to when a tricky job needed doing...

For a moment I flashed back to that one-sided row we'd had eleven years ago when I'd accused him of getting others to do his dirty work. Was this some belated revenge? The thought ran on and went haywire. Somewhere on the edge of the picture was that overweight copper, 220 pounds of heroin, still unaccounted for. Was he hoping I'd find it, or at least point the way? Did Blackwell have plans for it? I stopped. The man was a pain but as stiff and clean as the shirts he wore; his morals gleamed as brightly as his toe caps. If he had been using me it was for all the right reasons. I moved over into the driver's seat, fired the engine and headed for home.

Kinsella was first in line, wanting to know how I'd got on in Stamford. Far from lording it, or saying 'I told you so', he was sympathetic.

"Aaron's that sort of man," he said, quietly. "A tactician with a plan for every occasion. Today he made you lose your rag."

"Will there be repercussions?" Laura asked.

In spite of believing otherwise, I said, "I shouldn't think so. He won't want to spend more time in prison while his team file a case."

She nodded with relief.

"And you learned nothing new," Fairchild said, gloomily.

"He denied everything: the killings, the heroin, the link to the Heritage IRA. But then he would, wouldn't he, as the lady said. Where's Fee?"

Fairchild steered me towards a note Fee had left by the kettle. It was handwritten and overlong, sealed in an envelope for fear of others reading it. The gist was that an old schoolfriend, Tanya Miller, had phoned and invited her over to their house in Oxford. She was married now. Two kids. She might stay over. Was that okay? How did I get on in Stamford?

Grogan brought us back to the main business of the day.

"Flaxman is still without an alibi, right?"

"No family, wife, girlfriend to vouch..." I turned to Kinsella. "Did he have a girlfriend?"

"Only woman he ever smiled at was Freddie's wife, Sarah. And that was on pay days."

"So the heroin ... puff of smoke, so to speak?" said Fairchild.

"According to Flaxman, yes."

The mood was getting heavier by the second. Laura stepped into the breach with a clap of her hands.

"Why don't we turn our attention to blood sugar levels? Supper."

"I don't think you realise what's just happened," I said, rattily. "There was a slim enough chance of getting Flaxman sent down to begin with. By laying into him I've given him the moral high ground. His defence team will use it. The judge, jury will sympathise..."

She waved my assessment aside. "That's you believing you're responsible for everything."

"No! That's me having behaved like a bloody newbie."

Blackwell phoned later on that evening. He'd heard from the prison governor about the day's events and was sympathetic; indeed at one stage he even said words to the effect of 'these things happen'. He said he'd like to come over in the morning to debrief me, bring Sillitoe since it had been his idea, see if we could glean anything useful from what Flaxman had said. Would ten o'clock be all right?

After supper, Laura received a call from Sheila Bright, who'd had a down day. Her chemo was giving her gyp; did I mind if Laura went round to her house for an hour or two and boosted her spirits? I thought it was a good idea.

Laura made an upbeat point before she left. Whichever way things went, Grogan, Fairchild and Kinsella would be out of my house on the due day. The place would be mine again and this little episode forgotten.

I smiled at the versatility of Chinese whispers, their ability to work both ways, up or down. In Laura's mind, what I'd done had gone from being a criminal assault to a little episode. I hoped whoever received the prison governor's report would see it that way too.

I remember precisely where everyone was at nine o'clock that evening. Fee was still with Tanya Miller, Laura was at Sheila Bright's. Fairchild was upstairs having a bath, a long soak. She kept letting some of the water out as it cooled and then topping up with hot. It was one of my father's pet niggles. Money down the drain, literally, he would say, relishing the perfect analogy.

Kinsella was in the living room, watching a football match on TV, yelling occasional suggestions to the players. Grogan was with him reading a book he'd recently bought about cacti: as many pictures as words, but it had inspired him to give more time to his collection once this job was over. We'd quizzed him about his spiky friends on several occasions and got very little. He had a conservatory, evidently, where most of the plants were housed. Small, medium, large? Fee had asked. He'd held out his hand, waist-high, and revealed that some of them were 'up here'.

As Fairchild let the water out of the bath for the last time and a sense of relief brushed past me, Grogan came into the kitchen where I was still wallowing in the mistakes of the day.

"He wants to talk to you," said Grogan from the doorway, his eyes wandering to the bottle of whisky, then the glass. "Alone."

Kinsella was trailing behind him, waiting for the answer.

"If it's okay with you, it's fine by me," I said.

I gestured for Kinsella to sit at the table opposite me. Grogan nodded at him, full of threat, and returned to the living room.

Kinsella was nervous and on a scale of true to false I thought it was pretty genuine. In spite of his new appearance, the frightened little boy was poking through the bravado.

"What is it, Liam?"

There it was. I'd called him by his Christian name for the very first time. I repeated myself. "What is it?"

"You reckon it's my evidence that'll do the trick?"

"If that's a question, I don't understand it."

"Aaron. Depending on what I say in court, he'll be done for these two murders or go free?"

I nodded and he lowered his voice to a whisper.

"You said earlier his brief would have the moral high ground, use it for all it's worth, just because..."

"Because I thumped him? That was me being ... oversensitive. Remember what he did to provoke me. He gobbed in my face."

He clearly didn't think that carried the same weight as my attack.

"You said I'd be dead by Christmas, if he got off."

I poured a single measure over the ice cubes and vowed to make that the last one of the day. "I tend to talk like that. There are still charges against him involving the heroin, remember..."

"But no one can find it!"

I tried to sharpen up but it was too late in the day. What I said sounded as pathetic as it actually was. "True. Listen, I can't change your personal history with this man. Just ... do your best."

"You think my evidence is good?"

"I think you've had help in the way you tell it, but it stands a fair chance."

That bothered him. He stood up and began to pace, small areas, then suddenly sat down again and leaned towards me, son to father. "Will you take me through it again?"

"Your evidence? No."

"So if this maniac goes free and by Christmas I'm dead, it'll be your fault as much as..."

I pointed at him. "Don't you play that fucking game with me. This is what you do in court: you tell them exactly what happened, no embellishment, no alterations, no hesitation.

Otherwise they'll have your guts..." He held his arms out wide as if about to be crucified. "Pull yourself together! I don't mean they'll lock you up for a mistake; they'll just brand you an unreliable witness and Aaron will go free. Tell the bloody truth, Liam."

I'd done it again, called him by his first name.

At lights out, round about eleven, Fairchild put the kettle on for her night-time camomile and manuka honey. Stuff made by expensive bees. Kinsella asked me and Grogan if we fancied a cup of tea. Grogan did, I didn't, and when time was finally called everyone in the house crept off to bed, including Laura; she'd returned by then, looking more exhausted than ever, but having managed to cheer up her protégé. I didn't think I'd ever sleep again in spite of an ice-to-the-brim nightcap.

Fee had texted me. She was still awake and close to getting thoroughly slaughtered. She was staying over at Tracy Miller's. Tracy was married, she re-informed me. Two beautiful kids. In the accompanying photos they looked baggy and unsteady on their feet, but that's how it is when you're under three.

I went up to the cabin, took Dogge with me. One of the clocks on the wall told me it was nine o'clock the next morning in Tokyo. I didn't have Yukito's number on my computer, but Suteki wasn't a difficult firm to locate. It was a long, expensive number to dial, but after a series of buzzing noises a female voice on the other end answered chirpily in Japanese, probably saying good morning and asking how I was.

"Good morning," I said, voice bearing down on the foreigner who didn't understand the lingo. "Do you speak English?"

"Perfectly," came the reply. "How may I help you?"

"I'd like to speak to Yukito Kagayama, please."

Her response was so Western it was almost a pleasure to hear. "I think he's in a meeting but I will check. May I ask who's calling?"

"Nathan Hawk."

"One moment, Nathan Hawk."

I could only imagine the conversation between her and her boss across the office, the look of surprise on his face, but twenty seconds later a male voice said, "Hallo, Mr Hawk."

"Yukito? I'm Fiona's father..."

"I thought you would be. How is she?"

"She's fine. I was wondering if you'd, well ... you'll think I'm interfering, but really that isn't my intention..."

"Nothing is wrong, I hope?"

"No. Well, yes." If he wasn't confused before, he certainly was now. "I think you should come over and see her."

"Would she like that?" he asked, eagerly.

"Oh, yes."

"Can I speak to her?"

"No, she isn't here. She doesn't know I'm calling you."

"I understand. May I have your e-mail address, Mr Hawk? I will let you know when I will arrive. It will be soon."

"Good."

I gave him my e-mail and we said goodbye. It was the most constructive thing I'd done all week. I closed everything down, locked the cabin and turned in.

- 19 -

When I woke the next morning I instantly recalled the previous day and the fact that Blackwell was due at ten o'clock. Laura surfaced and asked what time it was. Seven thirty, she answered herself. She pointed downwards, in the general direction of the kitchen, and said, croakily, "Everybody's late."

"No surgery?"

She shook her head.

I climbed out of bed and put on a dressing gown. "Shall I make tea? Bring it back?"

Again she shook her head as if the very idea of tea in bed appalled her. I went downstairs, switching on lights as I went. I was first into the kitchen. There was no telly on, no coffee made, the dishwasher was still closed. Even Dogge was still asleep under the table. She stretched and came over to greet me.

That's when it began, I suppose, the slow realisation that a catastrophe was in the making. The place was usually buzzing by seven. It was half past. Seven thirty-four, to be exact. I went back up the stairs, met Laura on the landing and she picked up my rising concern, asked what was wrong. I waved her aside, went on up to Grogan and Kinsella's attic room. I opened the door and stared into the

186

sweaty gloom. I remember closing my eyes, as if when I opened them again the picture would be different. Fat chance. Grogan was there; Kinsella wasn't. He'd gone.

I went over to Grogan, gripped him by the shoulder and rocked him where he lay on the futon. He stirred but didn't wake up. He was alive but ... what?

I hurried back down the stairs, saying to Laura as I passed her, "Kinsella's gone. Go see that Grogan's okay."

"Why, what's...."

"Just do it!"

She turned and went upstairs. I hurried back down to the kitchen, looked out through the window and across the gravel to the big beech. The Ford Focus wasn't there. And for no reason I can think of, other than paternal instinct running wild, I could see nothing but Kinsella and Fee, him the maverick charmer, her the woman rebounding from the break up of a long-term relationship. Had she really gone to see Tracy Miller last night? I reached for my phone where it sat charging on a designated shelf...

I must have taken a huge breath, or something, and left the phone exactly where it was, pending a more rational alternative presenting itself. I hurried upstairs to Ellie's old room, opened the door. The bed hadn't been slept in. Fairchild had gone as well. The room was pristine, just as she'd found it a month ago. She'd left nothing behind, not even a tissue in the waste basket.

Back out on the landing, Laura was coming down from Grogan. She had a mug in her hand and was sniffing at the dregs in the bottom of it. "He's okay, but he's been drugged. What's happened, Nathan?"

187

"They've legged it. Kinsella and Fairchild, moonlight flit. Right under my bloody nose."

And as I stood there looking at her frightened face all I could hear was the sound of some infernal domino rally, each tile toppling the next, as the signs and pointers to Kinsella's real purpose over the last month fell face up. He'd never intended to give evidence. All he'd ever wanted was to escape from us and find the heroin. The guy had been playing us after all and it looked as though he'd won.

I showered, shaved and got dressed, all on automatic pilot. Downstairs again, I sat at the kitchen table, halfway between despair and anger, wanting the world to feel sorry for me. My grandmother on my father's side had perfected the art of it, her greatest work being accomplished when she herself was the cause of any domestic upset. Her family would rally round and solve the problem which she had created. More often than not they apologised for somehow having been the root cause. It had never worked for me. And the coffee maker was playing up again, wheezing and spluttering in the corner. Its days were numbered.

I looked up when Laura entered. She was dressed and ready for action. She never dwelled on past events, even if they'd only occurred an hour ago. There was no point, she said. All energy should be concentrated on solving the problem. It's a medical thing.

"So what next?" she asked.

I was still blaming others for what had happened. "You were all so bloody sympathetic towards the guy. You, Fee, Fairchild..."

"What difference did that make?"

"...the head lice, the impetigo, letting him win at chess."

"He allowed *me* to win."

I mimicked her. " 'His good looks, charm and confidence. A new man'? Then Fee playing dress-up, fighting me for his right to wear shoes, Fairchild fetching and carrying, teaching him how to use Facebook, for Christ's sake..."

I rattled on. Back in June the man had been arrested by Humberside Police when he was shot in the leg at Speaker's Farm. I reckoned he thought he'd wind up being charged with importing heroin, so he told Carew and Sweetman he'd seen Flaxman do the killing. Those two amateurs went for it, took his evidence, beefed it up, used it to nail someone they'd been after for years.

"And like a fool I argued the terms of his immunity from prosecution with Sillitoe..."

I took my anger out on the table. Nothing on it jumped as I brought my fist down, so I hit it again. Laura stood over me with a mug of coffee until it was safe to set it down. She said I needed to explain just one thing to her.

"If Flaxman was on remand in prison, why was Kinsella afraid of him? Why hide out?"

"If he was missing, he'd be thought of as the third victim, more grist to the prosecution mill. Meantime, he could poke around Speaker's Farm, try and find the haul."

I stood up quickly. It gives viewer and doer a sense of vigour. I paused and sat down again, saying I was getting slower, thicker, older by the day. I should've seen this coming from the morning he tried to escape. Grogan chained him up, we took his shoes, so the only option he had was to reel one of us in. He'd played on Fairchild's sympathy, her unhappiness with the job and the promise of a share of the 15 million. I looked up at Laura.

"Teeth," I said, quietly. "The one thing he did without making a song and dance about it was clean them."

"So?"

"With breath like he had at the start, he couldn't have got near Fairchild, let alone seduced her." I slapped the table again and this time managed to slop my coffee. "From then on all he had to do was use his good looks, charm and confidence to win her over."

She ignored my provocation, reached into a cupboard for the porridge and, despite my world having come to an end, she proceeded to make some.

"D'you know what bothers me?" she said as she stirred a poultice of oat flakes and water in a bowl. "The fact that you think it's your responsibility. Pure vanity, on your part."

"Laura, it *is* my responsibility. I frightened him off by telling him he'd be dead by Christmas. And without his evidence he probably will be."

- 20 -

An hour later I watched Blackwell walk the gravel beneath the big beech and approach the back door in a way I recognised all too well. This was someone who had yet to be told bad news. He was a devious man but not an especially confident one, and both aspects would be thrown into relief during the next half hour. Sillitoe walked behind him, Bewley the bag carrier trailed. As I rose from the kitchen table they spotted me through the window, yet Blackwell still knocked before entering.

He paused and beamed. "Morning, Nathan, Doctor Peterson, Sergeant..."

He looked round, presumably for Fairchild and Kinsella.

"They've gone," I said.

It was an object lesson in turning hope to despair in a snap. They froze, Blackwell, Sillitoe, Bewley in that order.

"What do you mean?" Blackwell asked.

"What do you *think* I mean? Kinsella and Fairchild have legged it. Together."

He took a moment to process the information, then another to stop himself bursting into tears by the look of it. He walked over to the table, removed the anorak and hung it over the back of a chair which he gradually sat down in. Dressed as ever, he was at least being predictable.

"I'll pour the coffee," Laura whispered.

"Would you like a hand?" Bewley asked.

I turned on her, unfairly. "She's pouring coffee, for Christ's sake, not cooking a five-course meal!"

She flinched and seemed to hold the pose as I explained the circumstances under which I'd discovered Kinsella's and Fairchild's absence and that Grogan had been drugged.

"Is he alright?" Blackwell asked.

"He's upstairs, sleeping it off," said Laura. "I think I know what he's been given. I'll confirm it later."

"Are we sure she went willingly?" Blackwell continued.

I nodded. "Tidied her room before she left."

"What time do you reckon that was?"

"After one this morning. I was up in the cabin till then."

"You didn't hear the car start?"

"It was out on the lane, parked on the grass patch. She must have left it there pending..."

"Have they taken weapons?"

"Cleared out the bread oven."

Blackwell brought his hands up to his drooping head and seemed to catch it as it fell forwards. Sillitoe sat down at last; his henchgirl followed suit, quivering at the tension in the air, the prospect of stacks about to blow. Maybe criminal law wasn't going to be as tedious as she'd first thought.

Blackwell surfaced and began to make plans for the immediate future. The coffee helped to clear his mind and gave us all something to do with our hands.

"First things first," Blackwell said. "I'd like as much of this as possible kept under wraps."

Sillitoe agreed. The trial was due to begin in six days' time. Miracles might happen, Kinsella might be found and re-persuaded to give evidence...

"Grow up, Henry," I yelled. "No one'll ever see the man again. Y'ask me, he never intended to give evidence. All he's ever wanted is the 15 million quid. I know it sounds less every time you say it, but it's still worth going to the wire for."

Laura threw in twopenn'orth from the sidelines, turning to Blackwell. "However much is kept under wraps, Commander, you will be informing Fairchild's mother, I hope?"

Blackwell glanced at me, then away again. True to form he was going to ask someone else to do his dirty work, to break the news of her daughter's disappearance to Grace Fairchild. That someone was me.

Sillitoe was shaking his head. "What I can't understand is the attraction," he said. "Pretty woman falls for absolute misfit. There's the money, yes, but is that...?"

"Believe it or not, Henry, he had a way with the ladies."

Sillitoe screwed up his face as if he'd bitten into a cooking apple when he thought it was an eater.

"Mr Hawk means he was a highly attractive creature," said Laura. "He believes that women like DC Fairchild, Miss Bewley and I are susceptible to such men."

"I thought my own *daughter* was, for God's sake!"

"She'll be delighted to hear that. May I be present when you tell her?"

Sillitoe had got rid of the taste in his mouth and went back to shaking his head. "I shouldn't have asked you to get involved, Mr Hawk. You've been out of the game too long."

Whatever he'd meant by it, it sounded like an accusation.

He held up both hands to fend me off. "The fault is entirely mine. We've been dealing with an extremely clever man."

"He might be smarter than you, Henry, but I'm not done with him yet."

"You just said no one'll ever see the man again."

"I was being emotional. I will see him again."

Meantime, though, Sir James Garrod wouldn't be too happy about losing the only witness they had. Why didn't he think on that?

Sillitoe smiled. Old Jim wouldn't be able to care less; he'd still be paid and had plenty of other work lined up. He glanced sidelong at Blackwell, as if peering round a corner at him. "And, of course, the ultimate responsibility for losing our man lies elsewhere."

"The fault is with these two half-breeds, Carew and Sweetman," I said. "Anxious to make a name for themselves by sending down a local bad boy."

Blackwell agreed that he'd had doubts about their probity from the beginning, but the more he learned of Kinsella, the more innocent they began to look. I called him a bloody fool, accused him of defending his own kind. Besides, we knew sod all about Kinsella. What we did know we'd learned in the last hour.

And so the schoolboy discussion staggered on, from tepid insult to half-hearted accusation, until Tom Blackwell said something that really stuck in my craw.

"Regardless of fault, Nathan, I think you should step back for a while."

I stared at him. It was still a tempting head to grab, especially with all that hair on it, but I held back.

"I agree," said Sillitoe. "And please accept my thanks. There was nothing new to learn in Grimsby; it's hardly your fault that Fairchild and Kinsella have taken off, that the case against Flaxman will collapse, that all that heroin..."

His was a fairly tasty head too. "Not my fault? Then why do you make it sound as if it is? Next thing you'll say is I frightened him off..."

Laura tried stepping in. "To be fair, Nathan, I think Mr Sillitoe is just outlining the problems..."

I stood up. "No, he's not. He's looking for a bloody scapegoat."

I'm not sure if things were about to get physical. I doubt it. Whatever the case, a taxi had just drawn up at the front gate and Fee had stepped out of it looking fragile. It took her an age to reach the back door, which gave us all breathing space. She opened it and just stood there, apparently reluctant to move her head.

"I feel like death," she muttered. "And I've interrupted something, I can tell."

Laura did the explaining, told Fee what had happened.

"And at one point your father rather touchingly feared it might have been you who'd run off with Kinsella."

Fee looked at me. "You really thought ... me and that jerk?"

"I know, it was future tripping. Bad."

Blackwell gently scissored the air to suspend our private discussion.

"First thing I must do is tell Jim, Sir James Garrod," said Sillitoe. "I've no doubt he'll open at the Bailey in the hope that his other evidence will be sufficient."

"And if the case is thrown out?" I asked.

"That rather depends on what the police can discover between now and then." He turned to Blackwell. "Presumably you'll be working flat out...?"

Blackwell said he'd start by going to see Mr and Mrs Fairchild. Then he'd go back to Grimsby and put Carew and Sweetman on the spot, get the truth out of them, assign new blood to a search for Kinsella. All the old clichés.

"What shall *I* do?" asked Bewley, as if expecting to play a major role in the drama. The grown-ups in the room stared at her.

"You can give me your mobile number," I said.

"Why?" asked several people.

"Write it down." I pointed to the blackboard on the wall next to the dresser. It had an ancient shopping list on it which she cleared with the heel of her hand, found the chalk and scratched out her number. That done the three of them left, Bewley with her eyes still sparkling, Blackwell and Sillitoe with eyes dead as haddocks'.

Laura went to the sink and filled a glass with water for Fee. Fee drank it in one and asked for another, then carefully slunk into Maggie's dad's rocker.

"I don't know how you do it, Dad," she said.

"What?"

"Drink like you do."

"I take the glass, put it to my lips, tilt back my head..."

"You know what I mean. Too much. What would Mum say?"

"She'd say get off your father's back."

"Grogan doesn't drink, Jodie Falconer doesn't drink, Yukito doesn't drink..."

"His religion?"

"His liver. He'd like to use it for another sixty years."

The temperature under my collar was rising but I managed to break my train of thought and say, "How the hell did we get onto this?"

"Displacement activity," said Laura, the peacemaker. "We're skirting round the sad news about Petra Fairchild."

"You don't think she's in danger, do you, Dad?"

I shrugged. "She's served her purpose, got Kinsella out of the house, out of Grogan's reach, and provided him with a car, weapons, details about the Flaxman case. She hasn't found him the heroin, though, in spite of asking about it at every turn..."

"She's discovered that it's still out there," said Fee. "Like I told you, she's a difficult one to suss."

I smiled from one to the other and pointed in the direction of the departed Blackwell. "And that slippery bastard has lumbered me with yet another of his chores. Did he tell Grogan he was suspended? No."

"That is their business, not yours, Nathan..."

197

I disagreed and suggested politely that Laura cycle off to the surgery, with mug and dregs, and put a name to whatever they'd used to knock Grogan out. I'd go upstairs and tell him what had happened in the last eight hours. Fee should make some fresh coffee.

"Your answer to everything?" she said.

"*Everyone's* answer to everything. Yours right now, if you know what's good for you."

Grogan needed that coffee too. As we sat on the stone bench he occasionally shook his head violently in an attempt to clear it, to bring back the events of the previous twenty-four hours. Unsurprisingly they were a blur. Laura explained to him, later that day, that it was a typical side effect of the drug he'd been given in his bedtime drink: Rohypnol, the date rape drug.

"If you need an ally, Bill, someone to vouch, remember I was there at the time," I said. "You were right all along. We should have chained the bastard to the wall and kept him there."

"Why would I need help?" he asked.

"Blackwell's kicked us both into touch."

"Suspension?" He stood up, joints creaking, coffee running to his head. When he was sure of his balance he asked what we were going to do about all this, finding Fairchild, Kinsella.

"Nothing," I said.

"We're leaving it there? That little sod, he's taken the piss out of me, out of you..."

"What do you suggest?"

He thought for a moment, unproductively, and again he shook his head. Without being too blokish about it, we were experiencing our first moment of mutual understanding. 'Leaving it there' wasn't an option for either of us. We agreed on something else as well. Blackwell may've had all the right motives for what he'd done, using me, lumbering Grogan with a novice, but he didn't have the expertise to put our mistakes right. The case needed a more ... freestyle approach, less hidebound by protocol. Regardless of his imminent suspension, Grogan said he'd help me ... once I'd decided what to do next.

An hour or so later Grogan received a text from Blackwell, sent from the back of a car heading towards Grimsby. It was apologetic in tone but nevertheless suspended him forthwith. Formal notification would follow in the post.

"Fucking bastard," Grogan muttered, then he went on to admonish the internet as a place for cowards like Blackwell to hide in. I asked him to write his phone number on the blackboard. He scratched out an Oxford number, just under Bewley's.

"Matter of interest, what did you want hers for?" he asked.

"Nice to have first-hand intel when the trial begins."

He nodded and went upstairs to pack.

"Where does he live?" Fee asked, once he was out of earshot.

"He's got a house in Summertown, I think."

"On his own?"

"Blackwell describes him as one of nature's bachelors. Make of that what you will."

She went back to her e-mails, hoping for one from Yukito, presumably, just as I was. I asked a silly question. "You really think I ... put it away too readily?"

She gave me an old-fashioned look. "The word is 'drink', Dad, the answer is yes."

I brooded for a moment or two. "Bill's right..."

"Bill now, is it?"

"...Kinsella's taken the piss, made fools of us."

"What's that got to do with drinking?"

"Both depress me."

- 21 -

Over the next few days I slipped down another cog or two, nothing to do with gears on a Land Rover, everything to do with my frame of mind. I'd lost the only witness in a double murder trial and any likely trace of a £15 million haul of heroin. I tried to look at it the way Laura did: it hadn't been my problem to begin with and certainly wasn't now. The logic of that worked for five minutes at a time, then I returned to being the centrifugal force, the main reason it had all gone wrong. Maybe she was right. Pure vanity.

It didn't help, of course, that there was absolutely nothing I could do about Kinsella, even though I'd implied the opposite to various people: Blackwell, Grogan, Sillitoe, Bewley, Laura, Fee. Since then, Tom Blackwell had told me to step back; Henry Sillitoe believed he shouldn't have asked me to step forward in the first place. Those two views made sense, but again in five-minute bursts, so it wasn't long before I found myself studying the Old Bailey hearings list online to find out when the case against Flaxman was due to start. September 27th, three days on from the depth of self-pity, injured pride and resentment I'd reached. And I'd reached it in my own company. My mood had given Laura an excuse to go to work early, return late, sometimes to Plum Tree Cottage. Her house, not mine. Fee had taken the opportunity to visit her brother Jaikie again, in Chiswick. She'd taken a suitcase with her, anticipating a long stay. Even the bloody dog was steering clear of me.

What I needed was a distraction, Laura said, one that would take my mind off Liam Kinsella and be a target for any residual anguish I felt, and, lo and behold, one appeared in the shape of an e-mail from Yukito Kagayama, the man Fee had broken up with. And I'd got in touch with. Something I was now beginning to regret. His message was brief and to the point.

"Mr Hawk, I arrive at Heathrow, 20.15 hours BST Tuesday. Best wishes to you."

My response was even briefer, though not heartfelt.

"Good."

I knew Fee was at a low ebb and my interference in her private life wouldn't go down well. If I'd simply told her that Yukito was coming to England to reassess their future together she would've packed her suitcase, headed for Nepal and her sister Ellie, or Haiti in a search for Con. The situation needed a subtle approach, but I chose to hide it beneath an elaborate disguise. I did some research centred around Yukito's arrival time, 20.15 on Tuesday, then e-mailed Fee, via Jodie Falconer, her sister-in-law in waiting.

"Fee, I've got a slight problem," I wrote. "Laura's aunt is arriving from Venice on Tuesday, Heathrow, 20.35. Terminal 5. I've said I'll pick her up because Laura's standing in for Sheila Bright that evening and you know how rough Sheila's been. Thing is this aunt's a bit infirm and 'difficult' according to Laura. Would you mind meeting us there? More a safety precaution than anything..."

It was a simple enough request but produced a barrage of questions from Fee. What was this aunt called? Eileen. Did she live in Venice? Yes. Where would she be staying? Plum Tree, with Laura. How old was she, how infirm, what exactly did I mean by 'difficult'? It all sounded like the Fee I knew, which was a good sign, and eventually she said yes, she would meet me at Heathrow, Tuesday, 7.45 in the evening. She was thinking of coming home anyway; she had things to talk about concerning Jaikie and Jodie.

If I'd been her I would've smelled a rat at the first mention of Heathrow, but I'd briefed Laura on the deceit so when Fee checked with her, the following morning, the story about Aunty Eileen checked out.

Tuesday came and I was nervous. An e-mail from Yukito said he was about to board the plane at Narita. I replied immediately, reminding him that we'd agreed not to tell Fee of our plans. He didn't respond.

The day crawled by and much earlier than I needed to I drove to Heathrow in Laura's car, parked and settled in Carluccio's. It wasn't just the pastries I was after. The place offered a long-distance view of arrivals.

Fee showed up bang on 7.45, by which time I had enough sugar and caffeine in my veins to fly to any of the destinations on the board, without a plane. She'd brought her suitcase with her, which meant she was returning to Beech Tree, but as if to make out that she'd never been away she insisted on putting her stuff in the car immediately. As we went to the multi-storey I was jittery, she said. No need. We had plenty of time. Eileen's flight was due at 8.35. She wouldn't clear customs till at least nine.

It wasn't 8.35 I was bothered about. It was 8.15.

Back at Carluccio's Fee ordered coffee and cassatedde and I sat back and watched her drink one, eat the other. I'd found us a different table, with an even better view than I'd had before. I could see right down to the sliding doors marked 'Arrivals'. Fee had her back to them.

"You're still on edge, Dad. It's only an old lady, for God's sake."

"No, it's Jaikie and Jodie," I said.

"What about them?"

"You wanted to talk, I guessed that meant a problem..."

"No, no, just ... more change. I think they'll marry."

I thought we'd had this conversation before. I nodded all the same. "He'd be mad not to ask her."

"Would she be mad to refuse, though? I mean can she cope with him flying off to work with some of the most beautiful women in the world?"

"Or being out of work?"

She sighed over her coffee cup. "Half-empty, eh, Dad, not half-full? Give me just one positive, for a bloody change."

"Good-looking grandchildren."

She shook her head with pleasure disguised as weary resignation. "The vanity of the men in my family..."

"You're the third person this week to use that very word to describe me."

"First?"

"Laura. The second was Grace Fairchild."

204

"Hey, didn't I always say you'd find Petra?"

"No, you said I should give it a go."

She nodded at the top of my head. "No wonder you're losing it, all that hair splitting." She was licking the ends of her fingers now, wondering whether to get another pastry. "Will you recognise this Aunt Eileen?"

"Oh, yes. She's sort of tall, smartly dressed ... bit like her niece."

"You said she was infirm."

"I think she's got a touch of arthritis. I mean, eighty years old? Apart from that, much like any other elderly woman."

"And the 'difficult' bit?"

"Outspoken, spade a spade, doesn't suffer fools."

She smiled. "Dad, that isn't difficult, that's normal."

I pointed down the concourse to a clump of arriving passengers who'd just come through the doors. "There she is."

Fee turned and, like I had done, she focussed on a young Japanese man pushing a wire trolley with a couple of bags in it. She looked back at me. I looked down at the floor. Grey carpet tiles with Carluccio's insignia woven into them. She rose from the table and glared down at me.

"Look at me, Dad, look me in the eye."

I did.

"How bloody dare you interfere in my life?"

I mouthed an apology and expected her to accept it before she walked out to greet Yukito. She stayed put.

"I am sick to death of people trying to shove me around!"

"Who else does it?" I whispered.

"Jaikie." She rocked her head to indicate his nagging. "Why don't I stop slagging the guy off, step back and ask myself if he's the one?"

"Sense."

She head-butted the air in front of her. "What's it got to do with any of you? Was Laura in on this?"

I shrugged. It could've meant yes or no. Yukito was getting closer, still thirty or forty yards away. People in the café were looking at us. Fee gave it one last burst of fury.

"Jesus!"

She turned and walked out onto the main drag, turned to face the oncoming traffic. It was a toss-up at that point. Would she stay or would she go?

Strange as it may seem, those approaching appeared to catch on instantly to what was happening and melted away to the sides, the better to watch this magic lantern show of lovers reuniting. When he caught sight of Fee, Yukito stopped and pushed his trolley aside. He was certainly an impressive-looking bloke. He wasn't tall, but neither was he as short as she'd led me to believe. Full head of black hair, slim, fit, wearing a classy suit. And I'm pretty sure it wasn't my imagination, they really did walk slowly towards each other, pause with a yard or so between them and exchange a few words. Then, without smiling, they stepped in close, he took her in his arms, and they kissed. In public, as my mother would've added. It was the best thing I'd done for about three weeks.

And as I watched them my phone vibrated and moved a fraction across the table. It was a text from Marion Bewley, informing me that all the preliminary to-ing and fro-ing was over, the trial of Aaron Flaxman began in earnest tomorrow. His parents were anxious to meet me.

- 22 -

I've been to the Old Bailey many times down the years, mainly to give evidence, but it's my first ever visit that stands out and against which all others are measured.

My father would take me into London once a week, in school holidays maybe twice, to see the sights, to become familiar with my heritage, the one he'd fought for as a teenage conscript. He believed, without voicing it as such, that it was part of my education, and looking back I can't think of many places we didn't visit, usually just the two of us, without my mother. Perhaps that was the attraction for him, the quietness, the chance to be himself as opposed to living up to her expectations. We took in places as varied as Madame Tussauds and the Tower, the British Museum and Lord's Cricket Ground, St Paul's Cathedral and the Inns of Court, and he was surprisingly knowledgeable about them all. Either that or he made it up as he went along...

The day we visited the Old Bailey, we walked up from the river towards St Paul's and he suddenly took me to one side, twisted his cigarette end under foot and told me that for the next two hours I was to be fourteen years old. Did I understand? Not fully, but it gave me an unfathomable sense of pride that in his eyes I would have no trouble playing two years older than I actually was. The reason for this charade was that then, as now, a child under the age of fourteen wasn't allowed into the public galleries.

As we turned into Old Bailey, the actual street, I was overcome by the building's power which to this day I can't explain. It seemed to stand alone – indeed there was no extension to it then – and it demanded a quiet respect, a kind of fear which my father honoured by speaking in a whisper for the next three hours. I can't remember the case we saw, or the court it took place in. A butcher had been robbed, my father managed to tell me, and two policemen were being cross-examined, but why these bewigged adults were so formal to one another, talked in such stilted language, bewildered me. My father explained later that it was custom, principle, tradition, and where would we be without them? I didn't understand that either. At lunch time we went to a nearby café and I had baked beans on toast and a cup of tea.

On the morning I chose to attend Flaxman's trial, I went into a Caffè Nero on Newgate Street, one I'd used in my police days. It was much the same as I remembered it: large, dusty, big leather sofas and hardback chairs at wooden tables, and on two walls hung black-and-white photos of celebrities who had drunk the coffee and lived to tell the tale. The third wall had the chalked-up prices of what was on offer. They'd gone up since my last visit.

At the counter I asked an Australian barista if he would look after my rucksack which contained my phone, an illegal self-defence spray and keys to the Land Rover. The first two were pure anathema to any court in the world. That would be twenty quid, the Aussie said. To a charity.

Baristas in Need? I suggested. He smiled. I handed him both bag and money and he gave me a card with the number 3 on it, then asked if I wanted coffee. Was that extra or thrown in? It was £3.40. I loosened my collar, despite the fact that I was wearing a T-shirt under the leather jacket.

When I turned into the Bailey, the sense of awe I'd felt as a boy had become more one of foreboding. The quietness I'd recalled still prevailed, broken occasionally by the clang of scaffolding being dropped nearby, voices a hundred feet in the air shouting instructions. Outside the main entrance the press had gathered, not all for the Flaxman trial but mostly. From experience, I could pick out relatives of the accused, their faces betraying a mess of raw emotion, mainly fear disguised as bravado. A couple I took, from their age and self-consciousness, to be Flaxman's parents were dressed in their finest and stood apart, strangers to London if not to courtrooms. I was just about to go over and introduce myself when the front door was opened and we entered at a shuffle. I was last in the queue.

When you step from the pavement into that oppressive little reception area you become an immediate cause for concern. Fair enough, given the Provos' attempt to flatten the place in 1973. But there are ways of voicing that concern, and the guy who came over to me before I'd taken my third step wasn't familiar with the polite versions.

"Yes?"

He was four inches taller than me, ten years younger and completely bald from choice to give himself an edge he didn't really need. He had a complexion similar to my kitchen table: grainy here, a darkened knot there, scarred in several places and scrubbed to a false shine. He was dressed in a black suit, white shirt and house tie.

"I'm here at the request of Henry Sillitoe, solicitor in the Flaxman hearing, court 4."

"Name?"

"Nathan Hawk."

He held up a hand. "Wait."

He turned to his superior behind the desk. The superior was dressed in the same garb; he was older, fatter, and his head was gleaming with sweat even this early in the day.

"You can't," he said.

"Can't what?"

"Sir James Garrod has asked that you be kept out of the courtroom."

"Can he do that?"

"He has done. The judge has ruled."

The last of the visitors had gone through the scanners, leaving just the three of us and a huddle of security cameras watching our every breath.

"I'd like to talk to your head of security," I said.

"He's in a meeting."

"Then will you call Marion Bewley? She's Sillitoe's assistant..."

"No can do. Strict instructions."

"Who do I talk to, then?"

"Me."

"Not good enough. I want the organ grinder, not the monkey."

He rose from his chair. He was certainly flabby but a little more dangerous than I'd first thought. For a start he had within reach all the bells and whistles that would lock the place down and bring armed security running.

"You're becoming abusive," he said.

"You're the reason for that. I've been asked by the prosecution..."

"And I've just told you, that's been ruled against. Both sides have agreed."

"Any explanation?"

"The judge doesn't have to give one..."

"All this is bollocks and you know it!"

He pointed at me. "Language! Your presence would be prejudicial to the case, I've been told, but you're welcome to observe from the public gallery. Out the door, turn left, twenty yards down, Warwick Passage." He paused. "You can go now."

This minion, who hadn't once addressed me as 'sir', was dismissing me. His junior colleague went back to the door and held it open. A ski mask of anger seemed to slip over my head and begin to tighten. The Kitchen Table would be a problem, the sweaty man behind the desk not so much of one: short fist to the nose across the counter, burst open his face. Would it be worth a day in the Old Bailey cells, though, white tiles with mouldy grouting like a lavatory on an old railway station?

I walked over to the desk, heard the door clatter shut and the Kitchen Table walk up behind me. I reached into my inside pocket, at which point they should have leaped on me and tied my arms in a knot. They weren't to know that all I'd take out was The Map. I spread it on the counter, then took out the imaginary spectacles and put them on. The two men stared at me. I wasn't dangerous after all; I was just weird. I closed my eyes, raised a forefinger and brought it down on a far more agreeable place. Winchendon. My own garden.

How anger can turn to sentimentality in a snap, I'll never know. Maybe the two states of mind aren't so very different to begin with. I could see Fee and Yukito, strolling beneath the big beech tree, hand in hand. She appeared to be laughing. So was he. I'd never credited the Japanese with a sense of humour.

I took off the glasses, folded up The Map and returned both to my inside pocket.

"Sorry, where did you say the public gallery was?"

The Kitchen Table replied as if nothing out of the ordinary had occurred. "Out the door, turn left, Warwick Passage. Go in, up the stairs, knock and wait."

"Thank you."

I may even have dredged up a smile. On balance, I think it's unlikely.

Warwick Passage runs alongside the new extension, beneath the court offices. Halfway down there's a doorway, a slab with a tiny window in it. 'Public Galleries', it says on an enamelled plate. The walls nearby are festooned with notices telling you what you can and can't do in a gallery, what you can't bring in. Some of the instructions are contradictory, there to disconcert rather than inform.

I climbed up the stone stairs – Christ, there was even a notice telling me how many steps there were ahead of me – and when I reached the first landing I knocked on the wired glass doors to courts number 4 to 8. I waited and in time a gallery officer, a short, round Scotswoman of microscopic charm, came to the door and asked what I wanted. Court 4, I said. She told me to wait and disappeared. Ten minutes later she returned to inform me that Sir James Garrod was in the middle of opening for the prosecution; I would have to wait till he'd finished before I could enter. 'Wait' was fast becoming the word of the day. It's a word I've never had much time for...

In time the Scotswoman returned and repeated, in a Glaswegian accent, everything I'd read on various notices, then led me to the gallery above the court where Aaron Flaxman was being tried. She told me exactly where to sit, alongside thirty other people crammed into the gods of this second-rate theatre.

Courtrooms are easy to read, once you've been in a few, and this one was pretty basic. The judge sat at the front, elevated. In front of him, lower down, was his clerk, a young black woman, her striking face ridiculed by the traditional wig. Facing them at floor level were the two barristers, pro and con, behind them the instructing solicitors. Sillitoe was leaning towards James Garrod, probably telling him what a marvellous job he'd just done, setting out the prosecution case with so little to work with. Behind them, in the glass-fronted dock, sat Flaxman with his solicitor, a middle-aged Indian. Aaron didn't see me enter. He was more interested in staring out the multi-ethnic jury of seven women and five men who, after hearing Garrod, were beginning to wonder if this was going to be the fun experience they'd hoped for.

Beside them, at a distance, sat the two people I'd rightly assumed were Flaxman's parents. The mother was looking up at me; in fact she didn't take her eyes off me until the defence barrister rose to speak. Her name was Charlotte Thornton, fifty years old and a couple of stone overweight, showing mainly in her face thanks to the black gown. Posh, pedantic voice which delivered a nice line in sarcasm disguised as reasonable argument.

"My Lord, the defence's case can be expressed quite simply. My client, Mr Flaxman, had no motive whatsoever for murdering Frederick Trent and Victor Wesley and furthermore could not possibly have done so because he was not present at the scene of the crimes when they were committed. He was at his parents' house throughout the afternoon of March 12th, that being his mother's birthday, and as your lordship knows I shall be calling Mr and Mrs Flaxman in due course. A lively business discussion ended at 4.00 pm, at which point my client returned home to his rented flat in Wragby. My learned friend has implied that, since neither Speaker's Wood nor the village of Wragby is festooned with CCTV cameras, we have no proof that my client returned home rather than meeting up with Mr Trent and Mr Wesley, murdering them and then disposing of the bodies..."

The judge's body was certainly old, but his brain wasn't. "Miss Thornton, it's your case the jury needs to hear at this time. They've already heard what Sir James has to say."

"I'm grateful, my lord." Like hell she was, but she'd managed to hint at the slapdash nature of Garrod's evidence. She turned to the jury and elaborated. "Ladies and gentlemen, you will discover as we proceed that the evidence in this case is largely circumstantial. Allow me to explain, my lord, with just two examples, the first being the murder weapon itself. The bullets which killed both victims certainly came from the Luger pistol found at the Flaxman family farm. However, the absence of fingerprints and DNA on the weapon raises a number of questions. Secondly, the Chevy Silverado on which the DNA of both victims was found belonged to my client's father. It was a vehicle which at least seven other members of the farm workforce used on a regular basis..."

"I gather this is some kind of farm vehicle, manufactured by Chevrolet," the judge clarified to the jury.

"Precisely so, my lord."

She turned her Arctic charm on the jury again.

"We will not be seeking to present Aaron Flaxman as a saint. He has answered to the law on several occasions down the years, but I submit that a police record does not prove culpability of the crimes we're examining here."

She looked up, not so much thinking time as pregnant pause. The delivery seemed painful to her.

"I shall also be questioning certain members of the Humberside Crime Squad. We have and propose to question two officers concerned in the investigation. Thank you, my lord."

So Charlotte Thornton had more up her sleeve than a bingo wing and, just like me, thought Carew and Sweetman were dodgy. She'd delayed seeding her doubts to the end of her opening. That made it stick in the jury's mind. It hadn't wrong-footed the judge, of course; it had simply dissuaded him from commenting further.

"Right, well, let's crack on, shall we?" he said.

There was a host of witnesses to be called over the next few days – a forensic pathologist, a scene of crime officer, a firearms specialist, all the usual talking heads – but for some reason Garrod first called the copper who'd found Vic Wesley's body in the ditch, ten days after the murder. I couldn't actually see the man; the witness box was directly under the public gallery, and I was sitting right at the back. I could hear him. I could hear his spotty face, his greasy skin, his close haircut all on top of his grim set defiance, as if he himself were on trial. His name was Eric Pine and by a quirk of rostering he and his partner had also found Freddie Trent's body in a slurry, two weeks later.

In Vic's case he'd been called out to a flooded road near the Flaxman farm, donned his wellingtons and found the obstruction jammed into a culvert. It was Vic Wesley's rotting corpse. Like a prat he moved it; the water ran away, taking with it any evidence. Then he called his duty officer, who called the local crime squad in the shape of Carew and Sweetman. There was more, but I'd lost the will to live by the time Pine had told us this in his slow, treacly voice.

I looked round the public gallery, even though I could only see backs of heads and occasional profiles. It was a multi-cultural gathering of thirty people, a dozen of them twenty-year-olds, law students probably, plus an elderly couple there out of interest and some foreign tourists. The woman I was sitting next to was long-boned, her hands told me, and standing up she'd probably be taller than most. That wasn't the only thing she had in common with Laura. She wore the same perfume, some Versace concoction. She fidgeted occasionally, drumming her fingers on denim knees. No one spoke. The Scottish barrel would have rolled on us if we had.

Pine was now describing how he'd found Freddie Trent and Versace put a hand to her face, as if to hide behind it. Freddie was floating face down, the size of a domestic oil tank and just as combustible. Again Pine phoned his duty officer, who passed the information on. Meanwhile, Pine fished the body to the edge of the pit, rolled it over, whereupon it punctured and some of the gas seeped out.

The judge was getting hungry and called lunch after Pine's unchallenged evidence. We'd reconvene at two, he said. We rose at the usher's command and off his lordship went to a three-course lunch in house.

Warwick Passage opens out into a square behind the courts. In one corner there's a small garden, no bigger than my kitchen, cast-iron railings on two sides fencing off four pillars, survivors of the lord mayor of London's original entrance to the courts. Pomp and circumstance reduced to a garden ornament. There's a marble bench beneath them and that's where I went to consider what I'd just heard. Or hadn't heard.

There'd been no mention made of heroin. That was fair enough. It hadn't been found; in strictly legal terms it might never have existed, so couldn't be used as motive. There'd been no reference to Liam Kinsella either, but why should there have been if both sides fully expected him to turn up on the due day? They had his statement; they believed the man himself would follow. That led to the possibility that neither Garrod nor Thornton had been told he was missing. Tribute to Tom Blackwell. He'd wanted the disappearance kept under wraps and it had been. Meantime, at the behest of the Crown Prosecution Service, we had to go through the farce of trying Aaron Flaxman with evidence that a ten-year-old could rebuff.

The thought pitched me downwards, not to any great depth, but to a consideration of the obvious. The truth was the last thing the law was concerned with, today or any other day. The manipulation of it sometimes fell to earth in the right place, but only by chance. From preparation in a police station to solicitor's office, to barrister's chambers, to the courtroom itself, it was always the best liar who won the day. And the bigger the lie, the more likely it was to be believed. Yet how could one plain fact be both truth and lie? The wrangling, the back-and-forth protocol, the use of a private language which only they spoke was simply a means for lawyers to get fat...

I stood up to get away from my self-inflicted gloom and caught sight of Flaxman's parents emerging from Warwick Passage into the autumn sunshine now falling on the square. They were walking towards me, eyes wide as if held in perpetual surprise. I smiled at them; Mrs Flaxman smiled back and walked past. I was slightly bewildered.

"Excuse me," I called out.

They unlinked arms and turned.

"Yes?" Mr Flaxman said.

"I thought you wanted to talk to me. Nathan Hawk."

Slowly their faces cleared and I could see beyond the fear of their son going to prison yet again. They were country faces alright, lined with weather and worry. His was lean, sunken at the cheeks, drawn at the mouth, grey hair under his best cloth cap. His wife was more rounded, face, body, personality, but tell-tale signs of constant hard work were there in the hands, cracked and leathery skin, bones disfigured by hard knocks. They both looked ten years older than the sixty they actually were. He transferred the bag he was carrying to his left hand and cautiously reached out to introduce himself.

"Joe Flaxman. This here is Carrie."

She shook my hand as well, once her husband had let go of it. "Were you in court this morning?"

The woman had stared at me for a good five minutes from her vantage point in the courtroom, but now claimed she didn't recognise me.

"I was up in the public gallery."

"We wanted to thank you," said Joe.

"What for?"

When it came to anything important, Carrie was the one who did the talking for fear that her old man would get it wrong.

"Aaron said you visited him in Stamford," she said. "You told him you thought he was a victim in all this."

I didn't pick her up on the fine detail of the conversation I'd had with Aaron where I'd said he *might* be a victim of Carew and Sweetman. "You do know we had a stand-up fight that day, don't you?"

She smiled, raised her eyebrows, as if reminding me of a secret we both shared. "He tells me everything."

"Listen, we're not supposed to discuss the case so near to the court. Why don't we find somewhere..."

"We've brought a picnic," she said, pointing to the shopping bag.

I gestured for them to follow me.

People used to approach St Paul's Cathedral, stop and gaze up at it in wonder: tourists, out-of-towners, Londoners themselves. They don't anymore, mainly because they don't see it until the very last moment. It doesn't dominate the landscape anymore; it shrinks away from the steel and glass competition around it. Once you're in the churchyard itself, the balance is slightly redressed, but the place never looks quite as magnificent to me as it did when I was a child.

There were sightseers and local office workers aplenty in the churchyard, but winter clothes were taking over from summer ones and suntans were beginning to fade. We found a seat that gave us a distant view of the Millennium Bridge, built from the leftovers of a Meccano set, Joe observed. Of more interest to him was Edward Copnall's sculpture of Thomas Beckett, moments before he was murdered. As Carrie unpacked the picnic, Joe went over to Beckett, reached out and laid a hand on his head.

"No facial features, but somehow you can still see what he went through," he said, eventually. "Going rusty round the neck."

Carrie patted the seat beside her and he sat down.

"Would you like a ham sandwich, Mr Hawk?" she asked. "I've made plenty."

I shook my head. "You came down this morning, from the farm?"

She nodded. "We'll stay till it's over. I said to Joe there'll be lots of places we can get sandwiches, but he's not keen. And he prefers tea," she added, unscrewing the Thermos. "There only seems to be coffee in London."

She passed Joe his sandwich and he started peeling the crust off, throwing it to the pigeons.

"Aaron tells you everything, you said. Like what?"

"Well, the main thing is he's going to get off."

She was smiling again at our shared secret, only I didn't know what it was.

"How does he know?"

Her voice was down to a whisper. "Because Liam Kinsella has disappeared and, according to you, he won't be coming back. You frightened him off."

I stared at the ham sandwich she was about to bite into. Maybe Tom Blackwell hadn't kept Kinsella's moonlight flit under wraps as firmly as he'd hoped. Apart from Fairchild's parents, the only people who'd ever been party to it were Blackwell and Sillitoe. And Laura. The idea that one of them had got in touch with Flaxman to give him the good news was absurd. And that's when I went as cold as Thomas Beckett. There'd been a fifth person present.

Marion Bewley. All ears, in my bloody kitchen, the morning Fairchild and Kinsella did a bunk. Had she been breaking rules? Was she the one who'd passed on the information to Aaron Flaxman, via his solicitor?

I managed to chit-chat through the next half hour, learning stuff about chickens that according to Joe would stand me in good stead if I ever decided to keep some. At one point I tried to veer the conversation off in another direction by asking where they were staying. I expected him to give the name of some tall, narrow apology in Paddington.

"The Savoy," he said. "Nothing to write home about."

I'd forgotten they were loaded, money no object, but here she was clearing up the remnants of a picnic she'd made at crack of dawn. She muttered some generational thing about waste.

At ten minutes to two I reminded them the trial was due to resume imminently. We went through the handshaking again, as if it were a new trick they'd learned. And off they went, arm in arm.

- 23 -

I wandered back to Caffè Nero and retrieved my rucksack, then texted Marion Bewley. I said I'd like to meet her, right there beneath the photo of Al Pacino. Four o'clock. She texted back immediately saying that would be fine.

In the interim I took a long walk along the river and tried to answer a question I'd been asking myself all day. Why was I there? What was I hoping to achieve? If I'm honest I'd have to say it was to find Kinsella and the heroin, and shove both in Tom Blackwell's face. How I could achieve that from the starting point of a trip to the Old Bailey, I wasn't sure, but something had brought me to London that day. It may well have been for comfort, a trip down memory lane, but it sounds better if I throw instinct into the pot. They used to call it 'copper's nose' when I was a kid. Coppers don't have noses these days. They have iPads.

Caffè Nero was busy and Bewley was already there. I joined the queue and when my turn came the barista greeted me like an old friend as I ordered a chunk of carrot cake with a straight coffee. I hadn't had anything to eat or drink for about eight hours. Mind you, I hadn't had any alcohol for five days, but the fact that I was counting probably meant I could've murdered a double scotch, ice to the brim. I drove it out of my mind.

Bewley stood up and cleared a space for my tray as I went over to her.

"How'd it go this afternoon?" I asked.

"Autopsy, cause-of-death stuff. The firearms bloke is sitting over there, under Kevin Bacon." She nodded to a bespectacled man of fifty, dressed for court, reading a newspaper. "He's really hacked off, has to come back tomorrow."

There were other court-looking people in the café, so I leaned towards her and spoke quietly.

"Marion, did you tell Flaxman's solicitor what you heard in my kitchen? That Liam Kinsella had checked out? And that I thought he wasn't coming back?"

"No."

"That I'd scared him off?"

"I swear I didn't..."

I smiled. "I don't believe you."

"I don't care."

I glanced away at the prices board. The coffee I'd just bought was £3.50, the carrot cake £1.50. They'd both better be worth it, I thought, aware that I was allowing the economics of the situation to sidetrack me. Bewley was trying to do it as well.

"How's Fee, by the way?" she asked.

"Do you care, or are you changing the subject? She's good. The boyfriend she broke up with suddenly turned up on the doorstep. Peace and love were restored."

She nodded her approval. "Doctor Peterson?"

"Knackered. A colleague in her practice ... breast cancer. She's taken on her workload."

She breathed out through screwed-up lips. "It is an obscene disease. Aaron's mother told me Sarah had a lump removed, earlier this year." She reached out and tapped a wooden coaster. "The worry never leaves you..."

I looked at her. "Sarah who?"

She frowned. "Sarah Trent, Freddie's widow. You were sitting right next to her in court this morning."

"Versace! Tell me she was only there to see her husband's killer be tried."

"Quite the opposite. She was there because she and Aaron, well, you know..."

"No, I don't bloody know. What are they? Lovers?"

"Oh, no, no, no! I mean I expect they are now, or would be, if he wasn't on remand, but they weren't at it while Freddie was alive."

"You're working for the prosecution, for God's sake, not the defence. So what were you doing talking to Aaron's mother in the first place?"

"Being polite. Are you going to eat that cake?"

I pushed it across the table to her. It wasn't me Carrie Flaxman had been gazing at in court; it was Sarah Trent. Her big sister, Emma, waitress aboard *The Amethyst*, the Fish Dock restaurant floating in all that treated sewage, had tried to keep me away from her.

"Did she come back this afternoon?" I asked.

"No."

"Was she there yesterday, the day before?"

"Not that I recall..."

Was this girl clever or just stupid? Both, maybe. They often go hand in hand.

"Marion, someone should tell you this and I'm as good a someone as any. You're playing with fire."

"How so?"

"I reckon you told Flaxman's defence that Sarah was up in the gallery and they took it from there. Maybe you warned her off yourself."

"Why would I do that?"

It wasn't a place I could raise my voice in, so I settled for hissing. "Don't play games! If Sillitoe can put Aaron and Sarah together in the same room, never mind a relationship, he'll have motive..."

"I swear I didn't."

"And I still don't believe you!"

Not that it mattered to me if she was lying or truthing. In Sarah Trent I had a missing link. I'd been at her house, Freshney Terrace on Scartho Top. Her neighbour was feeding the tarantula; the husband had offered to drive Sarah to the new place.

"Does Sillitoe think the trial will go all the way?"

She shook her head. "No, but he's playing it like Kinsella will show up on the day and spill his guts."

She checked a message on her phone and gasped, then jabbed a quick response.

"Something wrong?"

Her persona had changed completely. She'd arranged to meet her boyfriend outside the Tate at half four, she said. It was already way past! She gathered her things together.

Like my mother used to, she asked me to check, even though she hadn't put much down to begin with. Had she left anything, on the table or under it? I looked and told her it was clear. She thanked me and hurried away.

I made two decisions after she'd gone, each of which had a profound effect on the next few weeks of my life. The first was not to tell anyone about a trip to Grimsby I was planning. Except Laura, of course. And Bill Grogan. And Fee, and thereby my other kids, to say nothing of Yukito. Christ, why didn't I just post it on Facebook and include some photos?

The second decision was to go for a pee.

The gents' toilet was down a wide flight of stairs that took me past black-and-white photos of Ian McKellen, Meryl Streep, Robert De Niro. The stairs bottomed out into another arrangement of tables and chairs, but there weren't many customers down here, for a very good reason. The walls were painted dark red. It would've been like sitting in a giant blood cell.

The gents' was posh but anyone who was desperate for that pee needed full control of their bladder as they negotiated a heavy outer door, then a turn down a corridor, past other doors to cupboards, another turn and then the final door, again heavy, sealed at the edges. Inside there was grand porcelain, befitting a smart hotel. Lavish. Mirrors that didn't tell the truth.

When the peeing was done I stood at one of the sinks and ran the brass taps. The man looking back at me in the mirror was ten years younger than he felt. He was trying to tell me something, almost mouthing the words. You cannot save the world and you certainly can't do it single-handedly. I avoided his eyes. Find the heroin? Maybe. Find Liam Kinsella? Possibly.

I heard the outer door open and thud shut and a few seconds later the inner door open and break that slight vacuum. Someone entered. Then somebody else. In the mirror, by one of those tricks of reflection at the bevelled edge, I could see them multiplied, stretching away into infinity. Carew and Sweetman. I turned, straightened up, hands still wet, and went over to the dryer, not just to dry my hands, but in the vain hope that I could rip it off the wall and use it as a weapon if necessary. Nobody said a word over the hum of the hot air. When it stopped, Carew looked at me, that worm-like smile wriggling across his face.

"They don't make karseys like this anymore. You know what I like about it? No cameras. That would be the final assault on privacy, watching a man take a piss."

He took a few steps towards where I'd placed my rucksack. Without taking his eyes off me he picked it up and threw it to Sweetman.

"You can't say we didn't give you a chance, Mr Hawk."

"To do what?"

"To do nothing. Now we hear you've frightened off our only witness and that defence tart has 'profound misgivings about our testimony'. Who gave her those, I wonder."

The dryer was bolted to the wall with a real purpose. Sweetman had my rucksack and had found the spray. He took it out and smirked. "You travel light. Not even that old Smith & Wesson."

"Yeah, next time I go for a piss I'll take a Kalashnikov."

"Nah! Places like this you need something small you can reach quickly. Other than your cock."

To be fair to myself there wasn't much I could've done, so I fell back on a well-worn last stand. "I'll make a mess of one of you, count on it..."

Carew laughed. "The old ones, always the best, eh?"

Sweetman threw the rucksack aside and approached. I'd go for his face, I thought. Fingers in his eyes, pull down. I knew a bloke who taught women to do that in his self-defence classes. He had a percentage figure for how successful it was. I couldn't remember it. What I could recall was Jaikie saying to me, over a year ago, that I should stop getting into fights I couldn't win, and in Sweetman I was facing someone who knew exactly what he was doing. I reached for his face; he flicked open both my arms, jabbed me in the hollow of my throat. He grabbed me by my wrist, kicked away my leg and I keeled over.

Lavatories like the one at Caffè Nero are bad places to fall in – urinals, porcelain basins, stone floors – and once I was down they resorted to old-fashioned bludgeoning. I rolled over, covered my head as best I could, took most of the kicks in my back and sides. Then Sweetman reached down, grabbed my collar and dragged me to the door. He opened it, put my head between the edge of it and the jamb and was about to slam it shut when he paused. He'd heard the outer door open, voices, at least three. He looked at Carew, who must've signalled a retreat. Sweetman went; Carew followed and at the door bent down to say, "They told us you were always a lucky bastard. Next time, eh?"

He pulled the door open wide and left, allowing it to swing back and pincer my head. The leather jacket, up round my neck, went some way to cushioning the blow.

I've occasionally considered what my last thoughts in this life will be and as that door swung towards me I had a preview of the real thing. I'd always imagined it would involve my children, my wife, some photographic moment catching us in memorable pose, at a table in heated debate, out on a beach somewhere, even at Maggie's funeral, grief-stricken but solid as a rock. Not a bit of it. The last thing I saw and heard before I went unconscious was my father. He was standing over me, roll-up fag in hand, saying it was a bloody good job I'd never got round to buying a new coffee maker, I wouldn't have got my money's worth.

I must've been unconscious for about five minutes and came round to find a young barrister type crouched down beside me, his face a blur, then sharp, then out of focus again. He and his companions hadn't moved me; they'd simply wedged the door open with my rucksack and played everything by the first-aid book.

I groaned, which translated meant I wasn't dead, and he told me to lie still. The paramedics were on their way. He called to his companion, "Charlie, take over, I'm bursting."

Charlie kneeled down, readjusted my head minimally and we both heard his friend sigh with relief at one of the urinals. The third guy was evidently out on Newgate Street, waiting to flag down the paramedics. Distraction. The poor sod's bladder must've been full to the brim, but it really was his problem, not mine. I tried to stand up. Charlie advised against it. I asked him where I was. People think that's just a line from a film, but I've heard it twenty, maybe thirty times for real. First thing you need when you come round is bearings.

"Caffè Nero, Newgate Street," said Charlie. "You've been assaulted."

And only then did I remember what had happened. I made another effort to stand up. My head was already thumping, saying that tomorrow it would feel even worse. My guts, my sides, were freshly kicked, and in twelve hours' time I wouldn't be able to move them. Did that matter? Yes. I was heading off somewhere.

"Grimsby," I said to Charlie.

He gave me a puzzled, 'poor old sod' look. "Take it easy."

The paramedics arrived and took over from the three barristers. Dressed for combat, reflective jackets with pockets everywhere, trousers you couldn't wear out, boots you could kick a door down with, they stuck their dials and meters all over me. The readings said I was alive. I'd tried to tell them that myself. I finally got to my feet, against their wishes. I swayed for a moment as my balance adjusted and using the walls I staggered out into the blood cell and took a break in a passing chair. The conversation with the paramedics was bitty and broken.

"We're going to take you to a hospital," the girl said.

"You've broken a couple of ribs," her colleague added.

That was something else I could've told them. I was torn between playing along with their good intentions and heading for the stairs, up them and away. I tried to get to my feet and flopped back in the chair. Then the police arrived. I stood up and left. I made it to the entrance, and what puzzles me still is that while they were asking what had happened, how and who, they were helping me to leave. They should've held me back.

Out in the street I hailed a taxi with a low wave. One of the coppers even opened the door for me and helped me in. He explained to the cabby roughly what had happened and, just because a copper was saying it, it was believable. If I'd been on my own, the guy would've driven straight past, and who could've blamed him? No cabby needs a beaten-up, legless drunk at six in the evening, drizzle in the air and the light fading.

"Marylebone Station," I said to the driver. "Easy round the corners."

- 24 -

I knew the next few days would be difficult. In thirty years I've never made much fuss about getting kicked in, mainly because I've been reluctant to dwell on fights that I've lost. Obviously Laura and Fee deserved an explanation about my condition, but I wasn't looking forward to the overdose of sympathy it would bring.

When I reached Haddenham Station I called Laura and asked her to come and pick me up. It must've been my faltering voice that aroused her suspicions. Why a lift, she wanted to know. Had the Land Rover I'd driven off in that morning died? Exactly, I said. She didn't believe me and went into action, telling me to wait. Wait as opposed to what, I wondered.

Ten minutes later she drove into the circular pick-up point at the station and spotted me on a bench, face and head beginning to swell and discolour by then. I stood up slowly, ready to fend off her gushing concern. She looked at me clinically, then wearily, and said, "You've been in a fight, for God's sake."

Back at Beech Tree, sympathy from Fee came in the shape of a direct attack.

"Dad, what the bloody hell were you doing?"

"I keep telling you, I was having a pee, these two blokes..."

Tired of my evasiveness, she chopped her response into single words. "I know. What. You. Were. Doing! Who were they and why...?"

I waved her aside. "I'm going to sit here in your grandfather's rocker for the rest of the evening, like the old git I feel. Meantime, get off my back. Yukito, how are things?"

"Things?" he asked, unsure of what I might be implying.

Fee rattled off something to him in Japanese, then turned to me. "He's fine."

"He can answer for himself," I said.

Yukito gazed at me, no doubt wondering if this was how things worked in our family: I would get into fights, my daughter would have a go at me, my doctor friend would be on hand to deal with any injuries.

"Fee is right," he said, quietly. "I am fine."

That meaningless word again.

Laura stepped into the breach of silence. She'd been rummaging in her doctor's bag for something and had finally found it.

"Arnica," she said. "It's a homeopathic gel for bruises, the ones you'll wake up with tomorrow."

"Quackery."

"Lift up your shirt." She groaned impatiently at the expression on my face. "I want to see the damage to your ribs, then I'm taking you to A and E for an X-ray."

"No! They'll try and keep me in overnight. Tomorrow, I'm going to Grimsby."

She paused in her examination of my chest and her eyes roamed my battered face.

"To do what? Frighten the children?"

We did go to A and E that evening and spent less time there than most people do on account of Laura knowing the doctor on duty. The X-ray revealed two cracked ribs, no broken ones. There's no treatment, Laura and the doctor told each other, just painkillers and rest. My ribs would be themselves again in two months.

In spite of that favourable diagnosis, I did spend the next three days confined to barracks, not purely on medical advice, but due mainly to difficulty in moving. The muscles in my back and chest seemed to burst into flames every time I reached out, coughed, ate, drank, swallowed or spoke in more than a whisper.

In a quiet moment one evening, when Fee had taken Yukito up to The Crown to get Annie McKinnon's opinion of him, Laura said to me in her own sympathetic voice as opposed to her medical one, "Thank God for the call of nature, eh? They could've killed you if it hadn't been for those three young men. It would've... you know..."

We were in the living room at the time, watching some medical documentary, young doctors in Sierra Leone. She'd muted the adverts halfway through.

"Upset you? I'm glad to hear it."

"What I mean is ... well ... love's the nearest word. Don't ask me why."

The last sentence was either an apology or self-defence. I wanted to say the feeling was mutual, but couldn't bring myself to do it. She didn't push me.

"Liam Kinsella," she whispered instead. Her face said she wanted me to pull out of the whole affair and concentrate on getting fit again, but her voice asked, "So, what next?"

"Grimsby."

She winced and was about to protest.

"I'm going to ask Bill Grogan to come with me," I said. "And I'm taking the dog."

She was pleased about Grogan, puzzled by Dogge and asked me to explain.

"She's a drug squad reject, but that doesn't mean she can't sniff out a dragon when called upon to do so."

It still didn't make much sense to her. I hadn't wanted it to.

When I phoned him, Bill Grogan came as near to being excited as I'd ever heard him. It was still only two words.

"Great idea!"

All I'd said was I was planning a trip to Grimsby, the crucible of all our troubles, and would he accompany me?

He drove to the house that same afternoon in a white Fiat 600, a begging dog sort of car, ten sizes too small for him. I watched him squeeze himself out of it, then turn to me.

"What happened?" he said of my face.

"A fight. I lost."

We shook hands and I ushered him into the house.

He sat in his usual place at the kitchen table, rising when Laura entered to greet him.

"Sergeant Grogan, how lovely to see you again. How have you been keeping?"

They shook hands and he said he was extremely well. My guess is he was re-living the day she'd seen him in just his boxers and tattoos. In the silence which followed she gestured for him to retake his seat.

He stood up again when Fee entered and his eyes went straight from her to Yukito and back again. His expression was unreadable and I wished I'd checked on his family background, just enough to find out if a favourite grandfather had ever been in a Japanese POW camp. Prejudice is nearly always inherited and a week in Grimsby with a victim of it might be tiresome. Fee pecked him on the cheek, told him who Yukito was. Yukito bowed, Grogan muttered "Hi!" and sat down again. Then somebody made coffee.

As we drank it, Laura coaxed out of Grogan that he was on indefinite suspension, certainly until after Flaxman's trial and no doubt beyond. He stooped to a brief outburst of self-pity, oddly expressed but keenly felt. He'd been a copper for fifteen years, he said. Never a foot wrong. Queen's bleeding Police Medal. And for what? In the end, shrimp, prawn or lobster you get served up on a plate. Headless, legless, shell removed...

He stopped himself and apologised.

"Any news of Petra Fairchild?" I asked.

"I've heard on the grapevine they're both in France."

"So she fell, hook, line and sinker..." Laura muttered.

He nodded. "Comes from being stuck in the same place too long. Stockholm syndrome in reverse. Jailer falls for prisoner."

Laura wanted to know how her parents had taken the news. As far as Grogan knew they were devastated on just about every count: running off with a villain, dereliction of duty, not even saying goodbye. The last didn't surprise him. She'd have risked them talking sense into her.

"But she's not in danger, as far as anyone knows?" Laura asked.

He shrugged. "Who's to say? And Blackwell's right. I didn't see it. I should've done. And maybe I should've been kinder to..."

I intervened and told him the decisions Fairchild had made were hers alone. It was true, but he didn't believe it.

Fee couldn't resist embarrassing us all, it seemed. "Were they actually banging away in our house, Dad?"

I deferred to Grogan for an answer.

"They had time alone, if that's what you mean. We had a kind of roster, she took the days, I took the nights..."

"So the answer's almost certainly yes," said Fee. "The idea of it, though, until recently at least..."

She shuddered. The silence which followed called for a complete change of subject

"So what have you been up to, Sergeant?" asked Laura. "I mean I know it's only a fortnight since we last..."

"Decorating. The flat. Barley twist."

"A kind of beige, if memory serves," she said. "My mother used to say you can depend on beige..."

"I'm bloody sick of it," he said. "And we've only done half. That's one reason I jumped at the Grimsby offer, guv."

So I was guvnor now, was I? I'd started off being 'old-school' and 'way past it'. But it was Fee who'd spotted the most interesting word he'd used so far: the 'we' in 'we've only done half'.

"Why go for barley twist if you didn't like it?" she asked.

He paused, conscious that he was about to seem disloyal. "Viv chose it. My partner. How did we get on to paint, for Gawd's sake? Wherefore Grimsby, Nathan?"

He listened with a permanent frown on his face as I explained that Carew and Sweetman had attacked me, the day I attended Flaxman's trial. But it wasn't revenge I was after. I wanted to follow a hunch.

He shifted in the chair. He wasn't deadly keen on hunches. Did mine come with anything concrete? I told him about Sarah Trent. He wasn't bowled over by that either. I resorted to the 'you and me' treatment, forefinger wagging back and forth between us, the professionals.

"Bill, you and I know that 'follow the money' isn't just a handy mantra. It works every time. There's 15 million pounds' worth of heroin out there. If we can find that we can find Liam Kinsella, France or no bloody France."

"You think he's got it?"

"No, but I think he *wants* it. No disrespect, Bill, and no hard feelings, but with or without you I'm going after it."

"And the hunch part?"

"Freddie Trent's widow. This Sarah. She and Aaron were 'close'. So close she came to the trial. Didn't stay."

He nodded his way through what I'd told him, made his decision. "Fair enough."

"Thing is you'll have to do the driving. I mean we'll take the Land Rover..."

He said it wasn't reliable and nodded out through the window to the white Fiat 600. Viv's car. We'd take that. I asked if it had a back seat. The answer was yes, but why?

"I want to take the dog. She's ex-drug squad."

"Long time ago, Dad," Fee chipped in.

Grogan shrugged. If I wanted the company, let her come. I reached across the table to shake his hand, turning the sudden rush of pain into a smile.

"First stop, Speaker's Farm, the Flaxmans' place."

He pointed out that Joe and Carrie Flaxman wouldn't be there. Weren't they at the Old Bailey every day, dossing down at the Savoy? I nodded. He smiled at the possibility of some good old-fashioned breaking and entering.

I sat back again and turned to Yukito. "How are things, Yukito? God only knows what you make of all this..."

Fee started to translate into Japanese but he raised a hand to stop her.

"Things are fine, Mr Hawk. I hope you catch your man."

- 25 -

We left for Grimsby early the following day and were instructed many times by Fee and Laura to look after ourselves and the dog, to drive carefully, to keep in touch and not to get into fights. I've occasionally wished I was a child again, and by the time Grogan turned into Morton Lane I felt like one.

We returned to being adults when Grogan asked in a faraway, detached manner, "Brought anything?"

I nodded. "Smith & Wesson, had it for donkeys' years. You?"

He said he'd brought a Glock. In spite of all the bureaucracy surrounding his suspension, no one had asked him to surrender his firearm.

"And a baseball bat," he said. "In the boot."

I laughed. "Baseball bat?"

"Well, rounders really. You never know."

We must've seemed an odd couple, trio if you count the dog, two large men in the front seat of a Fiat biscuit tin doing no more than sixty miles an hour, at my request. We didn't talk much, with Grogan being taciturn by nature and me reacting to every bump in the road. He was at his most vociferous when any vehicle overtook him. 'Fucking wanker' was the usual epithet. When he found himself stuck behind someone doing forty the insult changed to 'doddering old tosser'. Apart from that, silence.

It hardly needs saying that nothing 'relevant to my inquiries', as police jargon has it, occurred on the overlong drive to Grimsby. Relevant isn't the same as memorable.

We were approaching Lincoln on the A46 and were both feeling peckish so Grogan pulled onto the battered gravel front of an eating place, the kind you see in American movies. Isolated, with large swinging signs, the name in neon capitals. It was called Polly's Diner and the clientele were mainly lorry drivers going to and from the east coast. It was nothing fancy, my father would have said. A good-value place. And dogs were welcome, another sign proclaimed.

The lady who ran it, no doubt Polly herself, was just as I'd imagined her in the minute or so before we met. She was in her fifties, blonde, with a large bust which wasn't an overt selling point though she obviously knew its value, otherwise she wouldn't have dressed so tightly. The decor, the tables and chairs were cheap and cheerful, the menu aimed at shortening the customers' lives: pies, chips, a few veg, stodgy puddings, tea in large mugs. We went for the homemade chicken and ham pie.

After she'd taken our order, Polly glanced over at us in spare moments, probably because we didn't quite fit. When she put the plates down in front of us she tried to dig deeper, starting with an observation about my bruises. I'd been in the wars, she said. Fell over, I replied. Where were we heading? The coast. Where had we come from? Oxford.

What was the dog's name? Dogge. I think that's when she cut her losses and went back to her other customers.

Once more I took up the challenge of conversing with Grogan. Politics, current affairs and family were nonstarters. Any talk about the job would have depressed him, so I fell back on decorating.

"Bit of a win for you, this."

"How so?"

"Well, we accomplish what Blackwell couldn't in a million years, our reputations are restored and Viv'll do the rest of the decorating." I smiled to indicate that a joke was coming. "Or will she leave it till you get back?"

He stopped eating and I could read his face immediately. He was challenging me, all but saying if I didn't like what came next I could tie it round my neck and jump.

"He," he said. "Viv is a he. Nurse at John Radcliffe. Vivian."

He carried on staring, searching for any sign of that old copper's raised eyebrow, the hand-me-down prejudice, the squad room contempt we both knew so well. He didn't find it.

"It just kind of ... happened," he said. "We don't talk much about it, just get on with our lives. Busy lives."

This may sound overblown for such a commonplace revelation, but when someone tells you their biggest secret they don't just share it with you, they give you a key to their very soul. You can either use it or lose it. I planned on leaving mine right there on the table at Polly's Diner. That doesn't mean I knew what to say next, so I just kept looking back at him, hoping he'd move the conversation on, claw some other subject out of the air. But this was Bill Grogan, listener more than talker. Then, luck of the devil, one fell at our feet.

The door to Polly's opened and a couple of boiler-suited blokes entered, one in his thirties with an unnecessary beard, the other ten years older, unmemorable. I'd seen two Bowker lorries pull onto the gravel a few minutes earlier. These guys must've been the drivers. They were well known to Polly and her face lit up as they greeted her with pecks on the cheek, flirtatious remarks and laughter. She took them over to their usual table.

But all that was peripheral to what had really grabbed my attention. Dogge, who'd been lying under the table, stood up soon after they entered, nose twitching from side to side. She approached the younger of the two drivers, wagging her tail. He was flattered.

"Hallo, doggy! What are you? Girl or boy?"

"Girl," I said.

I went over to him as he stooped to make a real fuss of her. She sat down, turned and looked at me. I called to Grogan, "Bill, get over here."

I turned back to the driver. "I have to tell you, mate, it isn't you she likes, it's the weed in your pocket. Least, I hope it's just weed."

He tensed up, guilty as hell, then suddenly remembered his right to have in his pockets whatever he damn well wanted.

"So what if it is?" he said.

"So nothing. Enjoy your lunch."

Grogan looked down at Dogge and smiled. "You can't teach 'em new tricks, but they don't forget the old ones, eh?"

We arrived in Wragby around seven that evening and took rooms in the hotel I'd used before. We turned in early, had a full English breakfast at eight the next morning to set us up for a day's sailing close to the wind.

As we made our way up what could loosely be called the driveway to Speaker's Farm, Grogan did his best to avoid the ruts and cuts made by the heavy August rain. The ground was dry now, hard and axle-breaking, the surrounding trees bare and skinny, and when the house itself came into view it did so all of a sudden, as if we'd flicked through a slideshow and arrived at some post-apocalyptic amphitheatre.

We drove into the yard and got out. I'd only seen the place this close up in photos and I suppose we'd taken a risk in just bowling up. After all, someone might've been house-sitting, or a worker from the chicken farm could've dropped in. There might even have been a dosser living in one of the outbuildings. However, the absolute stillness told me the place was deserted. Grogan looked round, from the barn to the grading shed, grain store to the house itself, and his reaction was much as I'd expected.

"Fuck me!"

The words echoed back to us, bounced off one of the buildings.

"Place talks back," I said. "How shall we do this, Bill?"

"A better question would be '*what* are we doing?' "

I still hadn't got a satisfactory answer for that, or at least one that went beyond a hunch.

"Dunno. There's no heroin here, that's for sure. If Kinsella didn't find it, if Carew and Sweetman haven't..."

"Then why should we?" he said, flatly.

"That aside, I'll stake five years off my life that by the end of the day we'll know where it is."

He wanted to call me a fool, or so I interpreted the stony face, but instead he took a deep breath, clenched his fists and waited for further orders. I suggested that we work together, take the dog with us and start on the outbuildings since the doors to all of them were already open to some degree or other. We began at the grain store, a place the size of a village hall and bang opposite the back of the house.

Against the will of its rusted hinges, Grogan hauled open the massive door to its full extent and leaned it back against the outside wall. Inside it was gloomy rather than dark. He cast around for a light switch and found one above the lintel. The forty-watt bulb gave us everything it had.

"Mean old sod," said Grogan, building a profile of Joe Flaxman.

"Careful with his money," I defended.

We split up. Grogan took the left half, I took the right and we edged our way between the artefacts in that petrified museum. Most of the exhibits had been made long before either of us was born.

An old Ferguson tractor had been driven skewiff onto a flatbed trailer to make room for an early combine which dominated the building. Central to Grogan's side was a disc roller, rusted to immobility, bedecked with an array of hand tools, scythes, ploughs, an old bailer. Dogge worked back and forth between the two of us and the only thing that grabbed her interest was the largest rat I've ever seen. She chased it under an old cart where it went to ground. I've never been good with rats, all to do with their watchful silence, then sudden rush in all directions.

We had to shift some of the smaller objects. I pulled aside an old hand plough, for example, only to have it virtually disintegrate in my hands. Grogan lifted part of a spiked harrow, threw it onto another pile, collapsing it with the extra weight. More rats. It took us an hour to find nothing.

In a way it was dispiriting, not that we had any right to complain. If we didn't know what we were looking for, what made us think we might find it?

"One of those places you push from the front," said Grogan, looking at the grain store from the doorway. "You run out of room, you pile the front stuff on the back and start again. Must be a hundred years' worth of scrap metal here, an absolute bloody fortune."

I reminded him there was an even larger fortune in free-range eggs a mile down the track and that was one reason all this had been left unsold.

We crossed the yard to the grading shed, stepping over broken slates from its roof. The double doors stood wide open and seemed to flutter in the occasional breeze. Just inside, a small Peugeot stood beside a beaten-up Toyota pickup.

"I thought he had a Chevy," said Grogan.

I nodded. "That's in a police warehouse, West London. Evidence."

We didn't need a light here thanks to a ten-foot hole in the roof. Crooked slates hung at the edge of it, ready to fall and guillotine the unsuspecting intruder. A vent, dead centre of the roof, gave us the only noise we'd heard thus far, apart from those of our own making. Two pigeons who'd been using it as a home clattered in panic and took off into the woods.

At one side of the building stood a vegetable grading machine, powered once by electricity, long since decommissioned. The channels down which potatoes, turnips, carrots and the like had been hustled to their doom were covered in dust, bird and bat droppings, leaves which had sought refuge from the autumn gales. Against the far wall stood a row of hoppers on stilts, beneath which sacks were once filled and fastened. There was a device for boxing up the more fragile stuff: cauliflowers, broccoli, cabbages, anything that needed to look well cared for on supermarket shelves. Beside it was a stack of folded cardboard containers, saturated and held in place by the rainwater which had leaked in from above.

We checked everything, from machinery to old tyres, old engines of disembowelled vehicles, even a clapped-out motorbike and sidecar, but the place had nothing to give us other than a history lesson.

As we met in the middle I could see that Grogan wasn't so much disheartened as resigned to our lack of progress. It was a feeling we both knew well, but he was the more philosophical about it. From casual examination to fingertip searches, evidence is difficult enough to gather at the best of times. On this occasion there were just two of us and an elderly dog.

We were interrupted. Dogge heard it first and since this wasn't her territory she merely pricked up her ears, no bark, no growl. A vehicle was approaching. I glanced at Grogan, gestured for him to stay back, and went out to greet the driver. It was the postman.

He was a short man in an orange anorak, health and safety taking precedence over style and comfort. To my initial surprise he didn't seem to notice our Fiat parked dead centre of the yard. He got out of his van and strolled over to the back door of the farmhouse, a fistful of mail in his hand, earphones dangling and whatever he was listening to giving his walk a dislocated rhythm. He shoved the mail through the letterbox and turned. That's when he saw me.

"Morning," I said at my most friendly pitch.

He stopped dead and pulled out the earphones. I explained my presence there.

"We had a letter from Mr Flaxman about some of the antique machinery. We buy and sell it. You don't know where he is, do you? Only this was the day we arranged..."

I held my bewilderment at Joe's absence long enough for the postman to say that Joe was in London.

"O-oh," I said, long and surprised.

He nodded. "His son's in court."

"Nothing serious, I hope?"

"No, no."

This was community spirit at work, neighbourhood watch keeping the intruders at bay.

"So you don't know when he'll be back?"

"Not today."

"I wonder if he got my letter. Does he get much mail?"

He was sidestepping back to his van. "No more than most."

I wanted to ask if any mail came for Mr Flaxman Junior, from Timbuktu, Never Never Land or possibly Ireland, but I couldn't bridge the gap between antique machinery and wanting a pointer to 15 million quid's worth of heroin. Besides, even if this guy had known anything, he wouldn't have told me. He replaced his earphones, got back in the van and drove off. Worst case scenario then was that he'd tell his mates about two middle-aged men he'd seen up at the Flaxmans' place. They didn't look like antique dealers so much as ... antique coppers. One of them had a bruised face.

Grogan came over to me. "Nice try, guvnor. The barn next, eh?"

The barn was the least cluttered of all the outbuildings, which wasn't saying much. The place had once been used for stabling, the far side divided into stalls, the walls hung with tackle: head collars, harnesses, something called an evener, Grogan explained, for spreading the effort when two or more horses were linked together. The actual machinery here seemed less neglected than stuff elsewhere. There was a tractor, a digger, an old planter, all three in working order, I reckoned.

Grogan had found the light switch and an old chandelier hanging from a cruck beam lit up the place, revealing stone steps built into the wall and leading up to the attic. This was where Joe Flaxman had confronted Liam Kinsella and as the latter had made a dash for freedom, he'd shot him. He'd aimed wide and put four pellets in Kinsella's leg, then knocked him senseless with the butt of his shotgun.

We sent Dogge up the steps to the attic, which we peered into from the hatch. There was no light there, no switch for Grogan to find, but she made her tour and came back apologetically. Nothing there of any interest, not even a rat.

Out in the yard again, Grogan found a second wind, renewed enthusiasm for the job in hand, prompted by a chance to show off his alternative skills: house breaking.

Walking round the outside of the place, we could've broken in at any one of half a dozen points. We chose a set of French windows, not unlike some my parents had installed back in the sixties, the very latest in swank. Grogan examined the handle and turned to me, disappointed. The least he'd expected was to use a penknife or to elbow a pane of glass, he said. Instead he slapped the central point where the two doors closed on each other and a pin on a chain the other side fell out of its hole. The handle turned, the securing rod dropped and we entered as if we owned the place.

The house was a psychoanalyst's nightmare, denying all attempt to clinically describe those who lived here. I could see straight away that Carrie Flaxman wasn't a hoarder but a sentimentalist. There were none of the piles of frayed and fading magazines which characterise the former, no stashes of coupons, no mountains of wrapping paper. Instead every item might have told its own story, linked its keeper in a flash to some event or person she wanted to recall.

In the room we'd broken into not one object matched another, even when it might have been expected to. The six chairs at the table were all different; the candlesticks on the mantelpiece didn't match. The serried ranks of ornaments were a mix of old china and modern resins, even plastic: no theme, no preferred colour, nothing that would pin their owner down as a so-called type. Even the curtains weren't a matching pair.

And so it was in every other room downstairs, yet in spite of its unashamed chaos the place was spotlessly clean, not merely flicked over with an occasional duster. I'd expected the same lack of care we'd found in the outbuildings, where at least rust and dust gave the contents a uniformity.

The pictures on the walls gave little away. In some of the photographs there was a family likeness passing down through the generations on Joe's side. There was nothing of Carrie until the wedding photo. Before coming to live here, it seemed, she hadn't existed; on the day of her marriage she walked through the door, founded a dynasty and began to chronicle its history with junk.

The house was arranged on three floors with a ballroom of an attic turned into a storeroom. Much-loved furniture gleamed in readiness for a possible return to use. Boxes, clearly marked, seemed ready to spring open and their contents – china, glass, tableware – pick up where they'd left off. Meanwhile, the beams and floorboards creaked under their weight.

The middle floor contained the bedrooms and bathrooms. The latter were a mix of ancient and modern; copper and plastic pipes jostled with cast iron, even some lead.

Aaron's room was the only one that offered relief from Carrie's belief that everything had a value and a place. A pine desk was set beneath the window, bearing a clear indentation where a computer had once been. That was in West London now, along with the Chevy and the Luger pistol.

The walls were covered in posters creating a homage to famous gangsters, just as Blackwell had told me. Strange, though, that when put together in the same room the most evil men in history lost their power to terrify. I wondered what they talked about when the door was closed and darkness fell. What did Bugsy Siegel say to John Dillinger, Al Capone to the Krays, Charles Richardson to Pablo Escobar? Grogan reckoned they discussed who should play them in the movie of their lives. That aside, he shuddered at the notion of parents who allowed posters of thieves and murderers to adorn their offspring's walls.

The Luger pistol, the bullets from which killed Vic and Freddie, had been found in a cupboard in the corner of the room, along with a host of other militaria. We agreed that it was an odd murder weapon of choice, all too easily traced back to the Flaxman farmhouse. And from what we'd heard, what we'd now gathered for ourselves, anyone could have gained access, roamed the house at will, taken and replaced a Luger pistol with ease.

But for all our agreement, for all the thorough search we had made, we'd discovered nothing of use. The same went for Dogge; indeed the outright cleanliness of the place had bored her and yet, not wanting to let us down, she had trudged dutifully from room to room in anticipation.

The kitchen was where we ended up. It's where I always end up in situations domestic or professional. The room was a boiled-down version of the rest of the house. Some of the objects were virtually new and must've been the stuff Aaron bought for his mother's birthday: a new cooker, fridge, television, settee. Hanging from hooks along a low beam were mugs of all ages, not a single one matching another; stacked plates sat awkwardly in a pile, not being from the same set; the cutlery gleamed, each item trying to outshine others in the drawer. Some of the pots and pans had been handed down over centuries, others were Le Creuset's latest.

The central feature was an oak table which bore the marks of eighteenth-, nineteenth-, twentieth-century wear. The chairs around it were original ladder-backs, all shapes and sizes, but each one the genuine article.

On one corner of the table sat the mail, divided into three piles: brochures, letters, brown envelopes. I scooped it up and slumped backwards into the green velour settee, which immediately began to devour me like a Venus flytrap with its prey. I switched on a powerful reading lamp on the table beside me and started skimming through the envelopes. Grogan went to the front door to collect this morning's delivery and returned with quite a bundle, three or four days' worth.

"Strange, nothing here for Aaron Flaxman," I said of the post.

"He doesn't live here, guv," Grogan pointed out.

"No, but I still get letters for my kids delivered to Beech Tree: old building society accounts with five bob in them, invitations to old school stuff..."

He nodded down at the pile I'd flicked through. "Someone comes every so often, sorts through it. That's weird. Nothing here either..." He threw today's post down on the sofa beside me. "Pity there's no milk in the fridge. I fancy a cuppa."

"Black coffee?" I suggested.

He shook his head.

"So who is it, Bill? Who comes to check the mail? I nominate Sarah Trent."

"You said she'd moved away, no known address."

"She hasn't gone to bloody China!"

The sofa was playing hell with my back, had me almost in a squat. I slapped the cushions on either side of me, raising some dust. I reached out and Grogan hauled me to my feet.

"Ex-teacher, so she's not stupid," I said. "I'll bet she also checks his flat, his Facebook, Twitter, e-mail accounts, just to see which way the wind's blowing. So far there've been no hitches. Nobody's on to the heroin, nobody knows they're an item."

He was still po-faced about it, thought I was making a drama out of a few details. "And that gets us no nearer to the drugs or to Sarah, never mind Liam Kinsella."

I turned back to the sofa. The dust I'd raised from slapping it was still in the air, hovering in light cast by the reading lamp. I froze. It was one of those moments you wish would last. Grogan must've thought I'd slipped into some hypnotic trance.

"What is it, guv?"

I'm pretty sure I smiled. "Four hours ago I said by the end of the day we'd know where the heroin is."

"Five years off your life..."

"So I die at ninety-seven, not a hundred and two. It's in a sofa!"

He glanced down at the one I'd been sitting in.

"Not this bastard, or Dogge would've gone barmy, but the one it replaced. Aaron stuffed the heroin inside it. Six cushions, each one jam-packed."

He nodded, as if only just catching up, but in fact he was ahead ... future tripping.

"I feel a search of local rubbish tips coming on," he said, soberly.

"No! It went from here to Scartho Top, 17 Freshney Terrace. Only now it's moved on, to Sarah's new house. Wherever that is."

- 26 -

It was two o'clock that afternoon when we sat down to a meal at The Wragby Arms. Grogan ordered spaghetti meatballs but questioned why Italian food was on the menu in such an English pub. The answer came out to chat to his customers in a quietish moment. He was an Italian chef from Salerno and enquired what I thought of the ossobucco. I told him.

Grogan and I discussed our next move, whether and when to include Blackwell in forthcoming events. Grogan was against it, his reasoning petulant and vengeful. I didn't admit to such feelings, of course, but if that was what Grogan wanted I'd go along with it.

In a moment of ragged thinking he suggested that we go to *The Amethyst* and harry Sarah Trent's new address out of her sister. Almost as he was saying it he spotted the flaw. Emma would get straight on to Sarah and the sofa would be spirited away. If it was still there. If it ever had been. If it was stuffed with heroin. My absolute certainty of two hours previously had ... matured into logical probability.

We went back to the hotel and phoned Marion Bewley. The trial was grinding on, she told me in a return call. The expert witnesses were gone; Sillitoe had just questioned the owner of the shop above which Aaron lived. The CCTV had shown Aaron leaving the flat the day of the murders, but not returning, at least not when he claimed he did. Charlotte Thornton, for the defence, had then lured the owner into admitting the camera had been on the blink for several weeks previously. Could anything it recorded be considered reliable? Was he in breach of his own insurance policy? Would charges relating to dodgy evidence follow? I asked if Sarah Trent had been seen in court since that first day. She hadn't.

I took a bath and, since Laura had slipped a lifetime's supply of arnica into my travelling bag, I applied some of it to my fading bruises. I put on fresh clothes, jacket, collar, tie, as agreed with Grogan, and went down to meet him in the bar. The irony of our rendezvous didn't escape me. He was teetotal, I wasn't drinking at the moment, and yet the police habit of doing business in bars was a difficult one to break.

Grogan looked ... different in his double-breasted jacket, shirt and tie, as opposed to anorak and sweater. He might've been the president of a rugby club, a town councillor about to do battle ... or a retired police officer. I kept my thoughts to myself.

Darkness took its time falling on Scartho Top: something to do with its height above sea level and nearness to the North Pole, Grogan said, unconvincingly. A strip of blue-grey light backlit the horizon, throwing what there was of it into relief and casting a cold twilight across the landscape. It was ideal. As a backdrop to awkward questions, fading light has always been preferable to full sunshine.

We drew up outside number 17 Freshney Terrace, which was clearly empty. An estate agent's board said it was for rent. I pointed towards number 23, where the lady I'd spoken to lived.

We left the dog in the car and walked up to the front door. I thought of Jaikie as I fumbled with my one and only prop, a leather folder case: to tuck or not to tuck under my arm, that was the question. I dangled it by one corner and rang the bell.

Anne Draper quickly placed me when I asked how she'd got on feeding the tarantula and from that point on she treated me like an old friend. She shuddered. That spider was only the size of a fifty-pence piece, she said, yet she'd dreamed about it ever since, devouring the house, the whole terrace, then marching down to Grimsby for more. She beckoned us in.

"Sarah came back to collect it, then?"

"Oh, yes, she loved it. Tilly," she added wryly. "Tilly the tarantula."

Her husband appeared at the living-room door, polo shirt over an extensive belly, trousers held up by braces, socks but no slippers, three days' growth on his chin. What was left of his hair was slicked straight back over his head. He wanted to know who we were before Anne invited us all the way in.

I reached out to shake his hand. "I'm John Ferris; my colleague here is Peter Andrews. We represent a firm of heir hunters."

"Like on the television?" Anne said.

"Exactly."

If it's been seen on telly and there's money being given away then ninety-nine percent of the general public will swallow it whole.

"You'd best come in," said Eric Draper. "How much are we due?"

I laughed. "I'm afraid the subject of our search is a Mrs Sarah Trent, an ex-neighbour of yours."

He took the disappointment philosophically and we followed him into the chintzy living room, memorable for a carpet whose swirls seemed to constantly rise from the floor and lasso those who walked on it. His wife offered us tea and went off to make it.

Over the next ten minutes I learned more about Eric Draper than I've learned about any human being in such a short space of time. We had landed on the doorstep of a man starved of people to bore and became hostages to his life story, starting with his childhood and schooling, moving on to his apprenticeship as a welder, then a life in the motor trade which had wrecked his body. There'd been numerous operations: a new knee, replaced by an Indian surgeon in Manchester; double hernia repaired by a Scot; bad back, physio from a Taiwanese girl, very pretty but didn't say much. Couldn't get a bloody word in edgeways, I thought.

His wife entered with the tea. Anne Draper was a neat, precise woman, no more than five feet tall and seemingly unaffected by her marriage to a self-obsessed bellyacher who knew the nationality of everyone who'd come within ten feet of him. She wore her honey-coloured hair close, like a mob cap, probably to keep her head warm. Her skin was reddened by weather and I put that down to her part-time job as a lollipop lady. I'd seen her stop sign and peaked cap out in the hall. She poured tea, adding an invitation to help ourselves to sugar and the biscuits.

"So, how can we help, Mr Ferris?" she asked.

"We wondered if you knew Sarah's current address."

She looked at her husband in the way she'd probably done for thirty years, checking their combined knowledge.

"I'm afraid we don't," she said, sadly.

"Mr Draper, you offered to help her move some of the furniture, I believe."

He nodded. "In spite of my back. Still, you don't go lifting engines out of cars without paying a price..."

"Love, that's true, but Sarah never said where she was going, did she?"

Was that a genuine or a rhetorical question, I wondered.

He thought for a moment, through the pain of past injuries. "Her dad's place, I think. Cornwall, Yorkshire, somewhere like that."

"Didn't you say she had a friend with her, the day she went?" his wife prompted.

He sniffed. "Latvian lad. There's been a rush of them in these parts. Nobody seems to say anything..."

Grogan thought he should join in, for credibility's sake if nothing else. "He was hired help, then, not someone she knew?"

"Right."

"Strange that she didn't take you up on your offer," I said.

"To be fair, I think she knew I'd had problems. Back, double hernia..."

His wife smiled over the bone china. "I've since heard that her father, Gareth Jago, lives in the Isle of Man." She lowered her voice to a whisper. "Tax."

"What bloody tax?" her husband said with disdain. "Man had no money. Always on the scrounge, always fishing."

"A bit of a parasite, you mean?"

He looked at me as if I'd gone mad. "No. Fisherman. He had a thing for salmon."

"You can take the man out of Grimsby, but you can't take..." I began and stopped.

"You know what I think?" Eric said. "I reckon that for all his faults Gareth Jago put his foot down, moment Sarah and that Aaron Flaxman got lovey-dovey. It's what I'd have done."

His wife sighed and corrected him. "You might've tried, love, but she's a grown woman."

"She's a bloody kid..."

"But romance was in the air, then?" I said to Anne with a smile.

"More of a crush, really. All over and done with now."

I turned to Grogan. "I don't think we need take up any more of these good people's time. Thanks for the tea, Mrs Draper."

"You're welcome." She pointed at me, as if a light had suddenly been switched on. "You do know she's got a sister, don't you?"

"Really?"

"Emma Wesley, Jago as was. She's head waitress on *The Amethyst*. It's a restaurant in one of the docks, an old battleship converted..."

"Cargo ship," her husband said. "Bloke who runs it's a great fat Norwegian bugger."

"And there's the pot calling the kettle," Anne quipped.

"Well, thank you for the information." I turned to Grogan, reproachfully. "We've somehow missed the sister, Mr Andrews, possibly because of the different surname."

I stood up and reached for the leather document case. "The van, Mr Draper, the one Sarah hired to move her furniture. A local firm, I imagine. Can you remember the name?"

He tugged at his braces, stretching out his self-importance. "I can. Sheraton. Don't let the name fool you. The owner's a Bangladeshi called Rahman."

Mrs Draper saw us to the door and I turned and thanked her again.

"Drop in again if you think we can help you more, or if you just fancy a cuppa."

"Certainly will."

We made our way to the car in silence and were both settled and strapped in before one of us spoke.

"That was quite a performance," said Grogan. "Runs in the family, then."

"The ability to bullshit, you mean?"

"I meant acting."

"So did I."

Sheraton Motor Hire was based on a new business park just outside Grimsby on the A180. At the front there was a man-made lake, almost perfectly round, the excavated earth plonked down beside it, like a giant poached egg. A few dismal trees stood guard, bent towards the west by the prevailing wind off the North Sea.

We'd dressed down for the visit, back to normal. Grogan was in sweater and anorak, me leather jacket and T-shirt. I hadn't packed a jumper and was regretting it. Grogan offered the observation, "You should've brought a pullover, guv." It wasn't worth responding to.

Sheraton Motor Hire was busy, with it being early in the day. There were twenty or so vehicles standing on the tarmac, all shapes and sizes, none of them shouting too loud that they were hired: just the company name on the doors with a phone number below it.

Inside, the front office was pretty standard: white walls, grey carpet tiles and a chrome and black leather sofa. Beside that was a glass-top coffee table bearing some car magazines and the local paper. On the other side of the panelled counter sat a woman of forty called Jackie, according to a name plate. She was trying to look younger than she was. Her hair was a shade too black to be real, her face heavily made up, mascara like a panda. She'd put on weight lately, or simply bought clothes that she planned on slimming down to. Meantime, they wrinkled slightly at her stomach. None of that prevented her from handling customers with knife-like efficiency, one eye on her computer, the other on those who had just walked in through the door.

She smiled at us and I asked if we could speak to Mr Rahman. She reached under the counter and pressed some kind of intercom through to his office, I imagine, before asking the nature of our business. We were anxious to trace a van rented from this firm in the first week of September, I said. In spite of my smiles and frankness she kept her finger on the intercom. I nodded at Grogan and lowered my voice. It was the only place we could think of that he could have left his briefcase, I told her.

"We've had nothing handed in," said Jackie.

"I pushed it well under the seat," said Grogan. "I mean if my head wasn't screwed on, well, you know..."

Jackie didn't know and waited for the rest of the sentence.

"...I'd have left that in your van as well," he said.

"If you'd like to take a seat..." she began.

Sajid Rahman appeared at the door through to the workshop and took over. He was a baggy-looking man in his mid-forties, with real black hair and eyes to match. His face was puffy, the skin rough as if pitted by some childhood epidemic.

"Can I help you gents?" he said.

"Hope so," I replied.

Jackie lifted a counter flap as Rahman beckoned us to follow him.

The workshop was small but alive, three or four mechanics calling to each other, yelling along to music from a local radio station. Rahman's office was a partition in one corner, glass and plasterboard, and was furnished with a single desk, two chairs, a telephone and a portable computer. Nothing else, not even a carpet: no files, no records, no proof that he'd ever been there, should proof be called for. He offered us the chairs and perched on the desk.

He smiled, something he did with untrustworthy ease. "You didn't leave no briefcase in one of my vans, mate."

"No, no, we didn't," I replied.

I'd made a quick judgement. The best way to handle this guy was to give him a version close to the truth. It throws some people off balance, usually liars, and Sajid Rahman was as tricky as they come.

"We're ex-coppers," I said.

I felt Grogan flinch.

Rahman remained as smiley as ever. "So?"

I lowered my voice to a paternal level. "We're trying to trace a young woman. Her disappearance is worrying an awful lot of people."

He laughed. "You don't look like the worrying type, mate."

There was a slight pause. My eventual response surprised Grogan, surprised me as well. The demon on my shoulder was urging me to take Rahman's head and introduce it to the desk. A louder voice said we were close to getting the information we needed.

"The van was hired on the third of September, probably used over..."

"She in trouble?" he asked, the smile suddenly gone. "She used my van for dodgy business?"

"No, no, moving furniture to a new house."

"And she forgot to give you her address?"

"I'm sure it was an oversight, but yes..."

He nodded and weighed up his options. The smile returned, though not quite as readily as before. "So?"

"We're just wondering if she told you where she was heading or if you keep mileage records."

"We check everything that concerns us, mate." He held up a fist and raised fingers as he counted off the points. "State of the vehicle, petrol in the tank, mileage before, mileage after." He spread both hands and explained. "Some guy drives five hundred miles a day, five days? I don't care where he goes, but I should pay the wear and tear? Fuck, no!"

"So you can't tell us where she went, but you could tell us the round trip mileage?"

He let his head fall to one side. "Sure I could, but I ain't heard no reason to do that."

"How's about fifty quid?"

"Sounds promising."

Grogan stood up. His eyes were roaming the room, focussing on various points as he went. I'd seen it before. It was a sign that he was about to lose control, and Rahman must've felt the same vibe. He tapped on the glass and a series of calls went across the workshop, directed at a young man, white, bald and the size of a buffalo. He ambled towards the office.

"Two hundred quid," said Rahman.

"Hundred and fifty," I said.

He smiled and nodded, then turned to the window and waved the buffalo back to work. The situation became a little tense again as I checked my wallet. I was about sixty quid short of the agreed price and turned to Grogan, who just looked at me.

"Gents, no problem. I take a credit card, you get a receipt for services rendered. We all know where we stand. Follow me."

We went back to the front office where Rahman took my credit card, then asked Jackie to bring up the details for the first week in September.

"A van," I said. "Second, third, fourth of the month."

Her hands flashed across the keyboard and ten vehicles were listed on the screen, seven of them cars. Three vans.

"The Transit," said Rahman. "The other two are runarounds, postman size."

"What name did the lady give?" I asked.

"Mrs V Smart," said Jackie. She saw the simple irony at the same moment I did, only she thought it was amusing. "Mrs Very Smart. I like it..."

"Not smart at all," said Grogan. "If you want to stay under the radar, you don't get clever."

"Your PIN number, please," said Rahman. "Then press enter."

He pushed the card machine towards me. I could've been at a restaurant, a filling station, a Waitrose checkout and any second now he'd ask if I wanted cashback. I entered my PIN, kissed 150 quid goodbye and took back my card.

"Miles on the clock when hired," said Jackie, writing the figures down on a slip of paper, "8,742. On return, 9,146. That's 404 miles driven. I'll do you a receipt."

What we needed was a ten-year-old, not just to do the cutting and pasting required but the maths thereafter.

On the way back to our hotel we stopped off at a Martin's. Grogan stood beside me as I chose four Ordnance Survey maps to cover the land north, south and west of Grimsby. I then bought a small roll of Sellotape for sticking them together, a roll of parcel string, a small deck of thumb tacks, a twelve-inch ruler and a hard pencil. It all came to about fifty quid. My investment in finding Vic and Freddie's murderer was increasing and I wondered if I'd ever see a return on my money. Grogan wasn't helping. The look on his face was asking what he'd done to deserve this.

"Bill, for fuck's sake, could you be a little more optimistic?" I muttered as we stood in the queue to pay.

"I haven't said a word."

"That's kind of the point."

"Sorry. I'm hopeful. Very."

Our relationship was turning into a bad marriage, the kind where one partner wants a fight and the other refuses to be drawn.

Back at the hotel we went up to my room and laid out the four maps on the floor.

"Sod it!" I said. "We didn't buy scissors. We need to cut the edges off the maps."

He said he had a tool in his bag that would do the job and popped next door to fetch it. He returned with what he called a multi-tool, an object which owed its design to the Swiss army knife. This creature was far more elaborate, though, and could saw, screw and drill anything that crossed its path. He found the scissors on it and went to work. When he'd finished we Sellotaped the edges together and ended up with a pretty acceptable map, the size of a hearthrug. We tackled the maths.

"What's the scale on this thing, Bill?"

He picked up one of the trimmings.

"One in 250,000," he said. "Two point five kilometres per centimetre." He chose the moment to vent some of his frustration. "In the last five hundred years, every time we fought the bloody French we won. How come we use their measurements?"

I nodded at his iPhone. "What's 202 miles in kilometres?"

In time he said, "325.087488. See what I mean? It makes things twice as complicated."

I closed my eyes to keep the basics from drifting away. "Three hundred and twenty-five divided by two point five. That's..."

I lost the thread.

"One hundred and thirty centimetres," his phone told him.

"Cut me a piece of string ten centimetres longer."

He measured out the parcel string with the ruler I'd bought. I tied one end of it tightly around the pencil, looped the other end round a thumb tack and pressed it right through the heart of Sheraton Motor Hire. We measured the Heath Robinson device to exactly 130 centimetres, winding any surplus string round the pencil. He then drew a circle while I held the thumb tack in place.

"Mind if I ask why I've done that?" he said.

"Is there anywhere on that radius that rings a bell?"

"Eastwards, you're out into the North Sea. Most of the west covers the Irish Sea. Above that, the Scottish borders; below it, the South Coast..."

"I want names."

"Bristol, Southampton, Bournemouth, Dover. Northwards, Dumfries, Kielder Forest. Can't see a young couple starting a new life in those places..."

He took a moment to correctly phrase the point he wanted to make.

"Nathan, this may be the bleedin' obvious, but we're measuring as the crow flies, 130 centimetres. There's no such thing as a straight road to anywhere. And what if she took a detour?"

"Take twenty kilometres, eight centimetres, off the string, draw me another circle."

Again, he wound the string to length and I asked what he'd got.

"You're still in the North Sea one side, Irish the other. You just make Wales and south you hit London, for Christ's sake. North you nick the Lake District."

"Do it again, another twenty kilometres."

We ended up with five concentric circles, meaningless names of towns, forests, national parks, and a sense, rising from the pit of my stomach, that I'd been mad to believe such a crude device would bear fruit. In spite of knowing its risks, we fell back on Grogan's original idea, a trip to *The Amethyst* to obtain from Emma Wesley her sister's address. Maybe we could cajole her, frighten her, sweet-talk her into secrecy, into believing it was all for Sarah's own good. We folded up the hearthrug map and cleared away the paraphernalia.

Grogan drove slowly to Fish Dock, presumably because he didn't want us to get there. We drove in silence which he was the first to break. He turned and smiled at me.

"I never had the ears for that."

He was referring to the pencil which I'd tucked between head and ear and forgotten. I removed it, dropped it into the side pocket of the car door. Then I took it out again and looked at it. I'm not claiming some kind of sixth sense or third eye, not even an exceptional gift for joining up dots. Even less do I know how the brain is wired when it comes to memory. I've always considered it to be a series of jagged lines, twisting, turning, sometimes going back on themselves, and if that sounds too rich a way of alluding to what happened next, too bad.

All I know is I kept looking at that pencil and for the next minute or so became the victim of a childhood flashback which, even as I tried to reject it, I knew was taking me somewhere useful. It involved a holiday in Keswick, world-famous for its mountains, lakes and ... pencils. I was nine years old and my parents could barely afford the break from their growing business in North London. On the very last day my mother took me into a local shop and bought me a tin of coloured pencils, a dozen in all. I didn't use them for a month; I just opened the lid ten times a day and looked at them. Eventually she persuaded me to draw with them, pictures that would recall our holiday in the Lakes. On our trip to *The Amethyst* I could

273

see those pencils lined up in perfect order, I could see the first picture I drew: mountains, a lake, trees, a few birds in the sky...

"Bill, pull over, will you?" I said.

He was more than happy to do so. We bumped up onto a verge. He even switched off the engine.

"That second circle you drew, you said it nicked the Lake District. Type into your GPS, Grimsby to Cartmel."

"Why there?"

"It's the only place Flaxman ever mentioned. I'd never heard of it, so I asked him where it was. The look he gave me, I thought it was reproof for cutting into a childhood memory. It was fear that I knew something he didn't want me to."

Grogan tapped my request into his GPS. "What's Cartmel to the Flaxmans?"

"A family farm, belonging to Carrie's brother. They could've taken it over at one point. Carrie wanted to, so did Aaron. Joe vetoed it."

He showed me the screen, the heavy blue line of the route between Grimsby and Cartmel, a zig-zag of 185 miles. The spare seventeen, taking it to 202, could easily be accounted for with to-ing and fro-ing, Sheraton Hire to Freshney Terrace, turns off the motorway for a break, getting lost...

"This farm, you think they inherited it?"

"No idea, but take another five years off my life, I reckon we're getting warm." I waited. "Say something."

He said he liked it, mainly because it wasn't inspired 'or any of that crap'. What I'd done was listen to Aaron, words

274

and tone, then read between the lines. He fired the engine, made a U-turn and drove back to the hotel.

- 27 -

I'm sure the drive from Grimsby to Cartmel is a pleasant
one, but for Grogan and me it was spoiled just before
Scunthorpe when Marion Bewley phoned in a high old state
of excitement.

"Guess what!" she said. "It's over! He's done it!"

"Who's done what?"

"Aaron Flaxman, he's got off!"

I'd been expecting it, of course, and from the barrage of
detail she gave me I could picture what had happened. The
judge had got a whiff of Garrod's big problem, namely that
he wouldn't be able to produce his main witness, Liam
Kinsella. So, in the spirit of old school friendship, judge and
barrister had met over dinner the previous evening, the cat
had been hauled out of the bag, and his lordship had just
given his ruling. Aaron Flaxman no longer had a case to
answer and was therefore a free man. He could leave the
court and go about his business. I reckoned the bureaucracy
of it, a bit of a celebration with his parents, would take a
couple of hours maximum. Then he would drive north, to
somewhere roughly 185 miles from Grimsby, where he'd
slump back in that old sofa full of heroin, drink in one hand,
new girlfriend in the other, and they could plan how to
spend all that money.

I thanked Bewley and asked one more favour: would she get Carrie's maiden name for me? Twenty minutes later she rang back with the surname Ellison.

We had another hundred-odd miles to go and Grogan stepped on it. Any arguments he had were with the disembodied voice of his GPS, which became chattier once we'd turned off the motorway forty miles short of our destination. I had my own grievances. I'd expected mountains to rise up before us, lakes to run beside us, rivers, bridges, forests and dry stone walls to take their places in the backdrop of my childhood recollections.

Nearer to Cartmel, I admit, the landscape began to rise and fall, but in a typically Northern way. The weather raised then dumped our spirits at will. When the sun came out from behind great continents of cloud, I was almost glad to be alive; when it disappeared behind furling rain clouds I returned to the present.

Cartmel is a beautiful village, and full of character I'm sure. Retail character. Gift shops here, delicatessens there, pubs turned into restaurants. We avoided it. Instead, without discussion, we drifted around the edge of the village and pulled up opposite a pub called The Pig and Whistle. It stood, boasting its Victorian origin, beside real homes, fifties council houses, laid out beside a triangular green. There was even a Spar supermarket nearby giving the place credibility.

That aside, I sometimes wonder if breweries pay old men to just sit all day at a bar to give an establishment character. The old boy we were about to meet, and whose name I didn't bother to ask, fitted my theory perfectly. He was stocky and powerful, like a pit pony, and well into his eighties, perched on a bar stool nursing the remains of a pint and reading the local paper. He turned to look at us when we entered, made it clear that he didn't like us or any other stranger who came through the door. Grogan nodded at him and he turned away again. He was definitely our man.

We ordered two coffees and a couple of cheese and pickle sandwiches, and as we waited for them I went over and tried to engage our new acquaintance in conversation.

"Afternoon," I said.

He turned, nodded, and turned back to his pint and paper again.

"I wonder if you could help us?" I said.

"Might," he replied.

Difficult to judge his accent at that point in the conversation but it turned out to be a local one, all squashed vowels and dropped consonants, several words running together to save breath.

"We're looking for the old Ellison farm," I said.

This was more to his liking for some reason and he turned fully towards me. He was dressed in a collarless white shirt, frayed at the edges, charcoal waistcoat, black trousers and boots. Plenty of undeserved hair, white near his scalp, yellow at the ends. "Jack Ellison? He's dead."

"Yes, I know..."

"What you want his farm for, then?"

I immediately turned myself into a tourist on a sentimental journey. "I used to stay there as a boy."

He looked at me, sideways. "But you can't remember where it is?"

"I can see it in my mind's eye, can't place it."

He sniffed and washed his contempt down with the remains of his beer. I signalled the barman to pour him another.

"He were a miserable bastard, Jack Ellison. Not surprising, given his luck. Lost his entire flock to the black."

It was obvious I didn't know what 'the black' was.

"Liver disease. Runs right through 'em, quick as knife ... or did then. Broke him. Sold up. She didn't help."

"Who?"

"His wife. Never lifted a bloody finger. Left him for a chimney sweep."

All I could think of to say was, "Poor man."

The old boy got stuck into the refill I'd bought him and must've thought he owed me something. "Out the front door 'ere, turn right towards Howbarrow. Three mile."

"What's the name of the farm?"

"Can't remember that either?"

I shook my head. "Weird, I know..."

"Stratton. Stratton Farm."

I snapped my fingers. "Of course, Stratton! I've been trying to get it all day!"

"Well, now you've got it."

I thanked him and he turned away for the last time, back to his paper.

I went over to a table where Grogan was making light work of the cheese and pickle doorsteps. The coffee wasn't bad either. He flicked his eyes at the old boy and I nodded.

Stratton Farm was the picture-perfect retreat from life itself. It lay on the downward tilt of a fell, overlooking a small valley across which a flock of sheep were evenly scattered, chewing their way towards the late-autumn sun as it came and went. The farm buildings, the house itself, were all of local stone, more Lakeland here than back in Cartmel. The slates on the roofs were the size of breadboards, still gleaming from the last shower of rain. All of it was upstaged by the view which Aaron Flaxman had told me would've 'made up for being skint'. He was right. Ten, twenty miles distant were the peaks of my childhood drawing, purple, grey, green, and just the tip of a lake like a shard from a broken mirror. There were even V-shaped birds in the sky.

This was no working farm, however, and it certainly wasn't the run-down wreck Jack Ellison might've left behind him when he went broke. Money had been spent here and I had to keep reminding myself that the Flaxmans were wealthy people. If, as I was beginning to suspect, Aaron had bought this place recently, for his own use, for his and Sarah's, then he'd thrown a heap of money at it, either drug money or egg money. Even the name plate on the wall at the roadside was quality, if a little garish, the words 'Stratton Farm' in elaborate scroll on a large piece of oak. The gravel on the winding drive down to the house was fresh and clean.

"We need to discuss this," said Grogan. He had paused at the main gate, which stood open.

"I say we just knock on the door, take it from there. If there's a sofa full of smack inside, the dog'll go barmy."

"Then what?" he asked with a smile. "Citizen's arrest?"

I replied as I usually do when stumped for a decent answer. "Piss off."

He stayed put, the engine still idling.

"We call Blackwell, make a deal," I said. "Get you back on the payroll."

He scowled. "Do we have to call him?"

" 'Fraid so. D'you know what we're doing, Bill?"

He guessed it was a trick question. "Yes and no."

"We're future tripping. Drive down to the house."

He signalled and turned in through the gateway.

The place was deserted in the sense that no people, no dogs, no vehicles were to be seen or roused. If Sarah Trent had set up home here, as I'd so promisingly deduced, then she was out. Out shopping, out for a walk, out for tea with new neighbours? I doubted all three. But the place was definitely lived in and, it bears repeating, by someone with a bob or two to spare, obvious even from the outside. A pair of brand new garden seats, solid oak, were set on a stone slab patio to the side of the house overlooking the view. At an angle to them was an oak table. All three items had a four-figure price tag. I knew this because I'd looked into buying one of the seats myself. And passed. Half a dozen stone tubs were dotted around, not just the terracotta jobs that flake and break in the first frost, but antique, heavy-as-hell containers with elaborate carvings. Laura would have loved them, newly set out as they were with winter flowers, miniature box trees surrounded by pansies and cyclamen.

We stood like lemons in the porch at the front door and for the third, fourth time banged a cast-iron face of William Wordsworth against an elaborate striking plate. With a hint of righteous delight, I thought, Grogan pointed at Dogge, who had found a patch of sunlight and was preparing to curl up in it. "Not exactly going barmy, is she?"

"I was exaggerating. She needs to be close to the target."

Why the hell I was defending her abilities I've no idea, except that part of me feared we'd come all this way just for the view.

"Get that gizmo from the car, Bill."

I'm not sure he thought there'd be much point in breaking into the house, but he was willing to give it a go and went for the multi-tool. We walked round the house looking for vulnerable points and discovered the only viable one was a cast-iron latticed window with frosted leaded lights. I assumed that a downstairs toilet lay the other side of it.

It took Grogan a minute to identify the kind of catch holding it shut and another minute to release it with a stiletto-like arm of the all-dancing, all-singing gadget. He seemed disappointed that it hadn't presented more of a challenge and criticised the window for being old and useless.

As the less bulky of the two of us I was the natural choice for climbing through the window, and with Grogan steering and shoving I entered, swam across the top of a cistern, down onto the lid of a toilet seat, into the room itself. My body's bruises objected but once on my feet I went through to the hallway and unlocked the door. Grogan ducked under the lintel, Dogge followed him, and from that moment on we spoke only in the sign language of burglary.

I pointed at him, then myself, then the dog, and towards the church-like door that led through to the rest of the house.

Money. That was my immediate impression of the room we entered. Expensive carpets, antique furniture, a top-of-the-range sound system. Heavy, chunky brass at the fireplace, the latest in wood-burning stoves despite the underfloor heating ... and a sofa and two chairs, leather, pricey and almost certainly new. Dogge walked past them without batting an eyelid. I pointed at the kitchen.

On entering it I began to price it straight away, or rather the cost of it screamed out at me. A full range Aga, handmade fitted cabinets, refurbished floor tiles, an antique table almost too good to sit at. I reached £35 thousand in twenty seconds, by which time it was clear, from Dogge's reaction onwards, that there was no heroin here.

Searching the rest of Stratton Farm was in marked contrast to the morning we'd spent at Flaxman's parents' place. There was nothing superfluous here, no junk, no chips or scratches on surfaces, indicating that the place had barely been lived in. The loft was completely empty.

We left the house exactly as we'd found it, not a footprint or paw print to say we'd ever been there. I was concerned that once outside Grogan would become sanctimonious, shrugging 'I told you so', but he was quite the opposite. Something of the old copper had stirred in him, brought to life perhaps by a resounding crack on his head from one of the upstairs beams, and now I could see in his eyes a trace of the illogical doubt our profession thrives on. He said the place was far, far too clean.

He walked across to the only outbuilding there was, a long low run of animal shelters now used for middle-class domestic life: a garage for two cars, a tool shed, a place for the spare freezer, which of course we looked in. It contained little besides a box of tuna steaks and some frozen veg.

Out on the front gravel again we stood, each with our thoughts, mine a slightly fraying belief that I could crack this case when others couldn't, Grogan's more optimistic. He left me and took a stroll round the sloping garden. I say 'garden' when it was a couple of acres of tufted grass between fading bracken and, at the bottom, what had once been a stone-walled sheep pen. He peered over into it, then turned and called.

"Nathan, you'd better come see."

What he had found, though hardly a trophy to wave in Blackwell's face, vindicated my bullish belief that I was on the right track. I'd arrived too late, maybe, but I'd been right. On one side of the sheep pen were stacked the composting remains of gardening: clippings, trimmings, leaves. There were even a few vegetable stalks and eggshells from the kitchen. But in the centre of the pen there'd been a bonfire, no longer warm, simply a pile of ash. In the white and grey remains were a hundred or more blackened brass studs, the kind used in leather upholstery. Grogan prodded the ash with a stick and flushed out a wheeled castor. The sofa, which almost certainly had once contained an overweight copper's worth of heroin, had been burned to dust.

I walked away, back up the incline. Grogan followed. The dog kept her distance. After a moment or two, Grogan tried to give our fruitless search some dignity.

"It's a find, guv," he said, brightly. I looked at him. "No, really..."

"It's a pile of ash, Bill. No wonder those bloody sheep look so happy."

He stood back, mouth slack in disbelief. "You really think she set fire to 15 million quid's worth?"

"Why not, if she didn't know it was there?"

He shook his head. "He's a lot smarter than that. And so is she, I'll bet. Know your trouble, Nathan? You're unwilling to think of women as evil bastards. That's sexist. You ask your daughter..."

I told him he was half-right. I was unwilling to think of anyone, male or female, as downright evil, though God knows I'd met my fair share of villains, from petty thieves to murderers. They'd given me my suspicious nature which I constantly fought against and lost.

Grogan sniffed and said there was no need to get so bloody saintly about it, just accept the facts. Aaron had killed two blokes and got away with it; Kinsella had lied his way to immunity, buggered off with Petra Fairchild, who'd turned on her own kind, dereliction of duty. As for Sarah Trent, he reeled off a list of charges that would be thrown at her, ranging from stuff under the Drug Trafficking Act to aiding and abetting, illegal importation, conspiracy, shielding a known criminal...

The list went on but his voice had been overtaken by a distant hum that in time became the sound of an approaching vehicle. It was miles away and with no discernible breeze it was the only noise in the otherwise silent landscape. Why it should've put me on alert, God only knows. Grogan stopped listing charges. We glanced at each other and waited, waited some more and eventually a silver tank of a vehicle, a Volvo 4x4, turned in at the gateway. The driver stopped, got out, a woman with long blonde hair beneath a pink beret. She turned to close the gate behind her and that's when she noticed the Fiat biscuit tin, then us.

And she made a *faux pas*. She toyed with the idea of getting back in the car and driving off again. Jaikie would've called it playing the end before the beginning, the mistake many an actor makes of appearing guilty before he's even been asked a question. The rest of us call it giving the game away.

She realised the futility of trying to evade us, closed the gate and then drove down the rest of the drive. As she got out and slammed the door, the resemblance between her and her sister Emma was unmistakable, but I'd been wrong on one particular detail. Her age. She wasn't thirty-two, thirty-three as I'd assumed that day on *The Amethyst*. She was a good ten years younger than that. A stringy girl, not so tall that she would crack her head on the beams in her new house but tall enough for my late wife to have called her a lucky bitch. She was wearing a gilet over a denim blouse, jeans and fur ankle boots: dressed for the winter to come. She leaned the top half of her body to one side as she addressed us.

"Good morning, gentlemen."

"Sarah Trent?" I asked. "We've met before."

She opened her eyes wide, almost coquettishly. "Really? I don't remember."

"Aaron Flaxman's trial. Public gallery."

She looked down at the fob in her hand and picked out a door key. "You must be mistaken."

I assured her that I wasn't. I would recognise her perfume anywhere. The remark spooked her a little.

"What do you want?"

"I'll start with you and Aaron. When did you two get together...?"

I'd been distracted. Dogge had walked over to Sarah and sniffed her fur boots. She then lifted her head to get her bearings, went to the Volvo and walked round it. At the tailgate she stopped and put her front paws up on the rear bumper, sniffed again in jerky breaths. She turned to me and sat down, tail swishing across the gravel. Sarah looked at me in badly played bewilderment.

"Open the tailgate," I said.

"I most certainly will not."

She locked the car remotely, stepped back and took out her phone. She began to flick through her contacts. God knows who she planned on phoning, but she was thwarted by there being no signal.

"Don't let's piss about, Sarah. Let's do this thing properly."

"What do you mean? What thing?"

Grogan went over to the Volvo and peered in through the back window.

287

"Peat-based potting compost," he said. "Six, seven bags of it."

"From the garden centre in Cark," she said, fiercely.

I glanced over at the stone tubs, recently planted out, then down at Dogge, still wagging her tail.

"Drug squad reject," I explained. "They never gave me a list of what she could sniff out, but I'm damn sure potting compost wouldn't have been on it. Open the car."

She considered her options for a moment or two and realised they were limited, especially when Grogan took out his multi-tool and selected one of its more vicious-looking limbs. She pressed the fob again and he lifted the tailgate. Dogge jumped in immediately and was about to go mental over her discovery. I put the slip leash on her and pulled her back to earth.

There were in fact eight compost sacks in the back of the car, bright yellow, pictures of flourishing plants on one side, instructions on how to achieve them on the other. Each had been emptied carefully and refilled with wrapped blocks of heroin, the sacks taped up with transparent gaffer tape. She'd been driving round with 15 million quid's worth of heroin in the back of her car. Plain sight.

"Now what?" she asked.

"Like I said, we do things properly. You invite us into the house, we try to make it as painless as possible."

"Are you police?" she asked.

I pointed at Grogan. "He is, I used to be."

She thought about that, then looked me straight in the eye.

"You can take one," she said.

"I'm not a gardener."

I couldn't tell what was going through her mind as she walked over to the front door. She displayed no sign of panic, so I reckoned she was planning her next move. She'd tried bribing me and it hadn't worked. Next in the long line of manoeuvres would be an assortment of explanations: elaborate, tearfully delivered and ultimately ludicrous.

"Mind your head," she said to Grogan as he ducked under the lintel at the front door.

It was an oddly caring thing to say, from which I deduced she still hoped to get us on side. Grogan leaned forward and took the key out of the door, turned to the car and re-locked it, then pocketed the fob.

We followed her through to the kitchen, where she behaved as if we were friends who'd just popped round for tea. She filled the kettle and plugged it in, opened a biscuit tin and started on a chocolate digestive, told us to help ourselves. As she reached up to a beam for three mugs on hooks I picked up her phone and she dropped one of the mugs trying to snatch it back.

"That is outrageous!" she said, with some of the family flare showing through. "Give it back."

"We'll compromise," I said. "I'll switch it off if you tell me when Aaron's due."

"I haven't the faintest idea what you're talking about." I began to flick through her text messages and she changed her mind. "Tonight. Late."

"How's he getting here?"

The kettle was boiling. Grogan eased her away from it and reached for another mug.

"Tea bags?" he said.

She glanced over at a caddy on a window sill.

"I said how's he getting here?"

She was beginning to accept her position and answered sulkily. "Driving up."

"From Speaker's Farm?"

She nodded. I switched off her phone and placed it high on the corbeling beside the chimney.

"We'll wait," I said. "But you won't mind if we gather up all the knives, all the heavy objects, put 'em somewhere safe? Meantime, you could answer a few questions, if you felt so inclined."

"I don't," she said.

I went through to the utility room to fetch an empty laundry basket and a dustpan and brush. I swept up the remains of the broken mug while Grogan collected potential weapons that Sarah might have used against us. She twitched from one to the other of us with a mixed bag of facial expressions, still wondering if she could retrieve her lost cause.

At one point Grogan went out to the Volvo, moved it into the carport and then hid the Fiat behind the buildings. He returned with three tuna steaks, but while he was away Sarah tried, albeit half-heartedly, to bribe me again.

"I don't know what 15 million divided by eight is, but the offer still stands."

"Nearly 2 million," I said.

"Change your life forever."

"I like it the way it is."

She flicked a strand of hair back over her shoulder and smiled. "Are you married? Do you have children?"

I smiled back. "Sarah, I used to interrogate people for a living. You've only seen it on telly. Asking nice questions isn't the way to win them over." I walked over to her and she went rigid. I leaned forward and nodded. "Versace."

Without Mrs Beeton to interfere in the proceedings, Grogan knocked up a pretty decent meal. He pepped up a weary-looking cauliflower, whipped up a cheese sauce and, as he placed it on the top shelf of the Aga, he gave us the French name for it. Cauliflower cheese, I called it. With tuna. We finished eating at three thirty, so it could still be called lunch, but it meant we had six hours to kill before Aaron arrived. It's a long time and Sarah did the expected squealing when it came to toilet breaks and the like. She got over it. She didn't have much option.

Grogan was the most relaxed of the three of us, possibly because he thought he was on the winning side now. He'd brought his book on cacti from the car and sat in a kitchen chair reading it, marvelling at the photographic plates, occasionally trying to enthuse me about spiky columns of green which flowered occasionally. One that he planned to see before he died was a cactus called *peniocereus greggii* which flowered for just one night with a fragrance beyond belief.

I passed the time trying to squeeze information out of Sarah, who responded by not giving me any.

"I thought you'd be older," I said.

"Did you? Sorry to disappoint."

"Don't apologise. It'll mean you still have a life ahead of you when you get out of prison."

She smiled away the comment.

"How come you got involved with a man like Aaron Flaxman?"

"You think it's just money?"

I nodded. "He ain't George Clooney."

"That's true. George Clooney's taken, of course."

"So were you, by Freddie. What is it? Excitement, danger, or is ugly the new beautiful?"

She said Aaron was one of the gentlest men she'd ever met, which I countered by suggesting she must've known some right bastards in her time. Her father was one, she said; Freddie was another. Grogan looked up from his book.

"Your kind of bloke, then, is he?" he said. "He's turned you into a heroin importer; he's murdered two friends, one of them your husband, the other your sister's."

She stared at him. He shrugged and went back to his book, leaving me to explain that just because charges against Aaron hadn't stuck it didn't mean he was innocent.

"You don't know anything," she said, calmly.

"I know this. He'll get sixteen years for that much heroin. You'll get six. Institutional revenge. With my help, though, you could walk away from it."

She turned away, ending the conversation.

- 28 -

Just before midnight the house phone rang and Sarah made a move towards it. I held her back and the call went to message.

"Sal, it's me. Your mobile's out of range. Or, naughty girl, you haven't paid the bill. Like we said, I'll be there two o'clock." He paused. "I love you."

The dialling tone on speaker sounded harsh against the words he'd used, the way he'd said them. This wasn't the Aaron Flaxman I'd met at Stamford Prison, the wide-boy who'd spat at me, the villain Carew and Sweetman had been after for two years. This was any man returning to the woman he loved.

I outlined the next couple of hours with particular reference to the last five minutes of it. We'd go into the living room, Sarah would sit on the sofa, Grogan would position himself behind the door. I would hover and keep the dog from joining in the fray.

It was gone two in the morning when, through the gap in closed curtains, I saw headlights approaching, carving up the night sky, taking an age to reach us. At the top of the drive the Chevy Silverado paused, engine still running. Aaron jumped down from the driver's side, opened the gate and turned in. He paused again to close it behind him. As the Chevy made its way down the drive it triggered security lights, one on the outbuilding, another high up on the front wall of the house. He switched off headlights and engine and hurried towards the front door, some kind of holdall in one hand, a bunch of gesture roses in the other. He opened the front door, stepped into the hall and called out, "Sal ... Sal, where are you?"

And that's when she gave it the only thing she had left and screamed out:

"Aaron, run! Turn and run! Go, go, go!"

But all that did was hasten his entry into the main room. He barged open the heavy door, saw me ten feet away standing over Sarah. He came forward and, as bag and roses dropped to the floor, so Grogan slammed the door, stepped forward and punched him in the stomach so hard that he seemed to lift up on the end of his assailant's arm before collapsing into surrounding furniture, bent rigid with agony, no breath inside him with which to scream. Grogan kneeled down and cuffed his hands in front of him. Sarah made a move towards him but I held her down on the sofa. There was absolute silence, even from the floor, lasting no more than ten seconds. It seems longer when you're wondering if someone's just been killed. Then Aaron groaned.

Grogan hauled him to his feet by the lapels of his jacket. He looked him in the face, daring him to spit, maybe, but more likely wondering what on earth a girl like Sarah Trent saw in him, the squinty eyes, the low-set mouth, the hairline starting way back on the top of his head. He pitched him backwards into one of the armchairs and told Sarah to keep away from him.

I went into the kitchen to phone Blackwell, who had rented a flat in Grimsby. He answered blearily and I apologised for waking him.

"No, no, I was still up," he lied. "How are you?"

"I'm fine," I said, recalling the word's lack of meaning. "Well, more than fine, really."

He waited, expecting me to elaborate with a request, a complaint, some idea of how much I was owed for safe-housing Kinsella. What I actually said came as a bigger blow than the one Grogan had just given Flaxman. He repeated the information several times as it filtered through to his consciousness. In time he asked, "When you say you've got the heroin...?"

"Tom, why don't you drive over and see for yourself?"

"Where are you?"

"A farmhouse near Cartmel."

"Cartmel, Cartmel."

"No, just Cartmel. I'll explain everything when you get here."

He was beginning to wake up. "Jesus, if what you say is true I should have Aaron Flaxman arrested. If he gets wind of this he'll take off..."

"He's here too."

"He's there?"

"Don't start all that again, Tom! Get some backup organised. The address is Stratton Farm, three miles out of Cartmel on the road to Howbarrow."

"What's the postcode?"

"Oh, for fuck's sake! Ask a policeman."

I hung up the phone. I won't say I'd enjoyed unsettling Blackwell with momentous news. I won't say I *hadn't* enjoyed it either.

In the living room, Aaron was speaking with difficulty. Between them, Grogan and Sarah had explained the events of the previous eight hours and, just like his girlfriend, Aaron seemed unwilling to accept them at face value. It might be hindsight on my part, but as the conversation went on I sensed that something else was on his mind besides his ruined plans and bleak future. Maybe it was guilt, or a sense of karma, that he'd just been acquitted of two murders.

I looked around the room. "Nice place," I said. "Not bought with drug money after all. Just eggs."

"Bought it for my mother more than me. Came up for auction last year."

"It'll be worth a whole lot more by the time you get out of prison. You can work out when that'll be. The CPS have guidelines for judges, depending on the role you've played." I turned to Sarah. "Yours would be deemed a 'lesser role', providing your brief was canny. Three years, out in eighteen months. Aaron, yours'd be a 'leading role' and for Class A drugs that's sixteen years. How old will your mother be by then? I spoke to her, you know, at the Old Bailey."

"She told me."

"She said you knew you'd be acquitted because I'd scared off the only witness. She thought I'd done it on purpose."

He looked at me and either smiled or winced; I wasn't sure. "Poor old girl, always believes the best in people. I got off because I didn't do it."

"So everything Kinsella said was lies, not just half a story beefed up by Carew and Sweetman?"

"I told you at Stamford, Liam was saving his own arse. I'd have done the same in his position."

I think that was where I heard a tiny bell ring in the distance of my mind. 'Tinkling' isn't my kind of word, but that's what it was doing. Something akin to doubt must've shown in my face.

"You haven't worked it out, have you? Go back to your CPS guidelines. I'm not the one who'll do sixteen years. Liam will, if they ever find him."

It was more of a handbell now, like the one the teacher used at school at the end of playtime – loud enough for everyone to hear. Aaron explained haltingly that it was Kinsella's idea to bring heroin up from Afghanistan to Liepaja, across to Grimsby. He even had a customer, ready and waiting. The Heritage IRA. Kinsella? Irish name? Irish connections?

"So you nicked it," I said. "Greed or altruism?"

"Bit of both, really."

"You stuffed it in that bloody sofa, bought your mother a new one and for the last however long it's been driving round in the back of a bloody Volvo!"

"Almost poetic, isn't it?"

But at that moment it wasn't the heroin or the journey it had made that was clanging in my head. It was the murder of the two trawlermen.

"So you killed Vic and Freddie..."

"No."

"You nicked it and killed them, win all around as far as you were concerned. Fifteen million and a new girlfriend...?"

Sarah stood up, too quickly for either Grogan or me to prevent her.

"He couldn't possibly have done it!" she said.

"Why's that?"

Aaron tried to silence her. "Sal, no..."

"He was with me when they were shot. Or rather I was with him, in his flat over the shop."

From the way he groaned and slumped back into the armchair, this was the one piece of information he hadn't wanted to become public knowledge, let alone court evidence. I'd been told somewhere down the line he was an oddball of old-fashioned values, his police record notwithstanding, and Sarah was a married woman, albeit one with charges for smuggling pending. He'd wanted to protect her reputation. Even if she'd come forward with the truth, nobody would've believed her. Where was the proof? No CCTV showing her entering the flat. Aaron had made sure of that.

The bells were slow and deliberate by now, tolling the question I already knew the answer to. If Aaron didn't kill the trawlermen, who did? If, as he'd just implied, the driving force behind the heroin was Liam Kinsella, then he was the only person I could think of with motive to kill two of his colleagues. Perhaps they'd objected to expanding the smuggling business into drugs, but they would never have dreamed he'd kill them to get his own way.

Any more than I would've done. And did. But surely I must've entertained the idea somewhere along the line, seen the signs and, what? Ignored them? Or had Kinsella been so clever as to hide his real purpose from me, from Carew and Sweetman, Tom Blackwell, Sillitoe? No, not clever, just bold enough to live a huge deceit. The bigger the lie, the more readily it's believed.

I turned to Bill Grogan. "I've had a fucking murderer living under my roof for six weeks and I let him go."

- 29 -

Tom Blackwell didn't arrive until six o'clock and did so in ostentatious style. Two cars and a van, all with blue lights pulsing, four uniformed coppers and three lads from the Humberside Crime Squad, all of them pissed off at having been dragged from their beds. God knows what he'd expected to find, but I watched them emerge from their various vehicles and take up covered positions in the yard like something out of a bad film.

As I opened the front door I heard the tensing up of men on a mission, saw firearms raised and aimed at my head. Blackwell, like some First World War general, was standing in full view, defying danger from the enemy. I called out to him.

"Bit over-the-top, Tom. It's one man, restrained, and his girlfriend."

He ordered his men to stand down, gestured two of the crime squad blokes to follow him, and walked over to me.

"You can never be too sure," he said.

I suppose he was right, with the reservation that the whole county and beyond now knew that a contingent of police had swooped on Stratton Farm. They would invent reasons for it and blow them out of all proportion.

He came into the living room with his two minders and looked down at Aaron, who smiled challengingly. Sarah looked down at the floor. Grogan simply turned his back. I pointed through to the kitchen, led the way and closed the door behind us. The crime squad duo stayed in the living room.

"Who's the girl?" asked Blackwell.

I looked at him. "Sarah Trent, Freddie's widow. You've never met?"

"No."

When I explained the dynamics of her love affair with Aaron, he drew the obvious conclusion. "Gave him motive to murder..."

"Leave that to one side, just for a moment."

"Where's the heroin?"

"This is my conversation, Tom. It'll be one-sided, just like the old days."

He perched on one of the bar stools at the island and gestured for me to rant away.

"You knew there was something out of kilter with all this. That's why you involved me. You were right to do so and it's always been in your nature to delegate work. The heroin was one of the biggest hauls there's been in the UK and there were two murders to go with it and we've all handled it like a bunch of two-year-olds. Carew and Sweetman? I thought they were bent to begin with. They're not. They're just stupid, too anxious by far to put away some local oik who'd got rich; classic old-fashioned, old copper resentment. They got their teeth in like a pair of

Staffies and then right at their feet fell a man so unbelievable they believed him."

"Kinsella?"

I nodded. "He was hiding in plain sight, behind a mask of filthy hair, greasy beard, tattered clothes, smelling like a pig, with lice, impetigo, gunged-up teeth. Christ, I'm even wondering now if he got himself shot by Joe Flaxman on purpose. These people go to extraordinary lengths, they thrive on taking risks..."

"What people?"

"He's psycho, Tom, only we call 'em sociopaths now in case it hurts feelings which they don't actually have. But Christ, do they know how to work a crowd! Anyway, his story about witnessing the murders needed work, but that was no problem to an old-timer like Carew. Not that Kinsella ever intended to give evidence. All he ever wanted was to find out where that egg-omaniac through there had hidden the heroin."

"And where is it?"

"Not so fast. You want to catch Kinsella? Speak."

"I want the right people brought to justice..." he began.

"Don't go all poncy on me. The answer is yes. Look good on the old CV, eh? 'The man who stalled a 15 million drug deal and caught a double murderer, all on the same day.' Just think of it, Tom, in years to come. Commissioner, then Sir Thomas, then Lord Blackwell of Guildford-Guildford..."

He looked at me, steady gaze for once. "I don't mind having some piss taken out of me. Your trouble is you don't know when to stop. What's in all this for you?"

I thought about my answer for a moment and decided to make it truthful. "Vanity, mate. The restoration thereof. Liam Kinsella played me for a mug and I intend to hand him to you on a plate."

Much as he doubted my claim he couldn't really afford to ignore it. "How do you plan on doing that?"

"Best you don't know the details."

"Just so long as there are no problems, procedural ones..."

"Tom, you'll find a way round them. You're the arch-mangler of the system. Aaron and the girl. Remand or bail?"

"Remand for that amount."

"Can you make the amount ... smaller? Tell the press they were arrested for 'a quantity, we expect to find more, much more'?"

"I haven't even seen the stuff, yet!"

"One more thing. Grogan..."

"He'll be reinstated."

"I don't think he wants that. But he'd like to leave with a clean record and a full pension."

"Fair enough."

And, without being too generous towards the man, he then showed his true decency which came from having lost his son.

"If Kinsella's everything you say, where does that leave Fairchild?"

"His victim."

"I meant dead or alive?"

I shrugged. "No idea. The heroin's outside, by the way, in the back of a Volvo 4x4. Eight sacks of potting compost."

He nodded and stood up. "I'll give you one month, then we go public with the size of the find."

He headed back to the main room, paused at the kitchen door and turned to me.

"With regard to the murders, there is the slight matter of proof..." he said.

"Evidence? That's your job."

"Proof," he insisted. "Prove to me, one to one, that Kinsella's our man. Give me a starting point I can work from. I'll take care of the evidence."

He waited to see if I'd understood his meaning. I thought I had, but he made doubly sure of it. For the sake of his own conscience he'd need to believe that Kinsella was the killer. I'd spent more time with him than anyone. Surely I'd discovered something that would put Blackwell's mind at ease? I nodded.

He went out into the yard, over to the carport and, through the window, I saw him and two of his men examine the back of the Volvo. One of them even performed the classic taste test on the contents of one of the sacks and nodded. I made myself a quick cup of tea. Five minutes later I heard the language of official arrests being made, Aaron protesting that it was all his idea, Sarah breaking down into tears...

It was midday when Grogan and I left Blackwell and his crew to seal up the house and deal with his prisoners. We'd grabbed a few hours' sleep before leaving and now drove in silence. I broke it once to mention that Blackwell had agreed to his reinstatement, if he wanted it. He nodded, which I took to be his way of thanking me.

Twenty miles later I asked if he fancied staying up in Grimsby with me for the next couple of weeks, helping out.

"Helping out how?" he asked, as fired up as a fridge.

"The place we're going, the woman there's got her own Mandela United Football Club."

He took his eye off the road for a moment and turned to me. "What?"

"People around her who get stroppy."

"Who's the woman?"

"Sarah Trent's sister, Emma Wesley, or Emma Jago as she prefers."

"Restaurant?" he grunted.

"*The Amethyst*. Old ship in the Fish Dock. Don't eat the food. You might not like what's in it."

He nodded again. "I'll stay. Why, though?"

"We're going to catch Liam Kinsella."

He smiled, even dared to look at himself in the rear view mirror. "I like it. How?"

"Bill, do you need an answer for every bloody question...?"

"You mean you're still working on it?"

I smiled back at him. "Actually, I'm not. I know exactly what I'm going to do."

We arrived late at the hotel and 'skeleton staff' was a very fair description of the skinny lad on the desk, half-asleep until we entered, then rattling with nerves as he gave us our keys.

Once in my room I attended to some domestic bits and pieces. I e-mailed Fee and said she'd be holding the fort for another couple of weeks, a classic approach as far as she was concerned. Put her in charge as opposed to asking a favour. At Plum Tree Cottage, Laura was still up, to my surprise, and was more curious than Fee had been about the extended stay in Grimsby.

"How are things going?" she e-mailed back.

I'm ashamed to say that my answer was "Fine."

- 30 -

Next morning, Grogan was already in the breakfast room by the time Dogge and I had struggled downstairs. He'd ordered kippers, saying that he never had them at home because they stank the place out. And most hotels you went to served up those prissy little fillets, not the real McCoy. He hadn't had a decent pair of kippers for...

He broke off, apologising for the lapse into a private obsession. I went for the scrambled eggs on toast, more as an analogy for what we'd done to Aaron yesterday than because I wanted them.

We drove down to the Fish Dock and parked. There was a fair old breeze coming off the North Sea, clouds scurrying inland pursued by weather from Siberia, Grogan claimed. Snow soon. Whether his weather forecast made sense, I've no idea. He stood by the car, as if it were his only link back to reality, and gazed around at the sheer abandonment of the place. He had a comment, naturally.

"Fucking government. Before we go in..."

He wanted to ask questions about *The Amethyst*, presumably, but I set off towards the gangplank. He called after me.

"Nathan, this Mandela rugby club..."

"Football."

"...will I need anything?"

I walked back to him, thinking it was probably best that he knew what we were up against. The owner was Norwegian, built like a balloon but quiet, formal, polite. The barman was an aggressive little sod with a knack for vaulting over the counter, the chef was dangerous and the customers loyal, didn't like strangers.

He went to the back of the biscuit tin and took out his rounders bat. He turned away from me and slipped it down the inside of his trousers, left thigh.

"Just in case," he said.

"Bill, a favour. Let me do the talking."

He looked at me and smiled. "What makes you think I'll suddenly burst into conversation?"

The Amethyst was being laid out for lunch and as we reached the bottom step the ever-expanding Kristian came over to us, all smiles until he recognised me.

"Good morning, Mr Hawk. No offence, but I would rather you did not..."

He let the rest of the sentence articulate itself.

"And I would rather I did," I replied.

I raised a hand at the Vaulting Barman, who had stopped setting out bottles for the boozers' noon rush.

"Sorry," I said to Kristian. "That was a bad start. Combative. I'd like a word with Emma, if you'd be so kind as to inform her that I'm here."

"She is mustering the waiters. We have a new girl." Since I didn't respond, or budge, he eventually went on, "I will ask her. Who is your companion?"

"This is Sergeant Bill Grogan."

Grogan nodded and Kristian rolled across to a door beside the kitchen. The embroidered words on the back of his shirt read, 'The one way to get rid of temptation is to yield to it. Oscar Wilde.' Where food was concerned, Kristian had yielded to the point of defeat.

A minute later, Emma appeared and strode over to us, arms swinging with purpose. She stopped and looked at me. "Yes?"

"Is there somewhere we can talk?"

She wasn't keen on the idea but was curious to know what had brought me there. She asked Kristian if we could take a corner table for five minutes. I corrected her. It would be fifteen. He gestured to a faraway table and she led the way to it. 'Oh, what fresh hell is this? Shakespeare. *Hamlet*,' said the back of her blouse, prophetically, but of equal interest to me was Grogan's slow descent into one of the chairs, given what he had down his trousers. He managed it and leaned back, away from the conversation Emma and I were about to have.

"You know Aaron got off?" I said.

She pursed her lips, deliberately, not naturally. "I also heard it was your fault."

"No. It's because he didn't murder your husband or your brother-in-law."

"Who did, then? The Man in the Moon?"

I said her question was partly the reason for my visit here today. I'd like us to talk things over. How was she, by the way...? I must've sounded like a doctor, oozing sweet reason before I told a patient they had some life-threatening illness which only I could cure. I cut to the chase.

"You know Aaron and Sarah are an item?"

The lips went back to their normal position on her face as she leaned forward, both elbows on the table. Whatever she was about to say, I got in first and told her they'd both been arrested.

She closed her eyes. "What for?"

"The heroin."

I fancied I could see her mind clattering away behind the eyes, wondering how best to protect her younger sister while wishing she'd never been born.

"They've kept it at a farmhouse in Cartmel which Aaron bought," I went on. "She will be prosecuted for her part in it."

"If there's evidence..."

"There's plenty. Including us finding it."

She stood up suddenly, gripping the edge of the table to maintain her balance. "I didn't like you the first time we met! Now, even less!"

The Vaulting Barman had heard her temper surge and stopped work again. No doubt he had some sort of weapon under the counter – barmen usually do – but whether it would match up to a rounders bat was a lab test I didn't want performed just then.

"I say you should hear me out, Emma," I said. "Aaron will do time as well, though not as much as you'd like. Importing the dope wasn't his idea." I turned to Grogan. "How long do you reckon?"

True to my request that he let me do the talking, he raised four fingers.

"I agree. Four years, he'll be out in two. So you might as well draw your horns in, welcome him into the family."

She went into some kind of deep breathing routine to absorb that. When she'd finished, she re-took her seat at the table and over at the bar the bottles started rattling again.

"Did you love your husband?"

"What sort of question is that?" she asked, quietly.

"Would you like to catch the man who killed him?"

"I dream about it. Whoever he is, I'd like to ... like to..."

She grabbed at the air in front of her and twisted it, struggling to think of the worst thing she could possibly do.

"With Aaron you hoped they'd hack off his balls and lock him up forever."

"Way too good."

"So the answer's yes, you'd like him caught."

She was back fighting again. "And you, Mr Clever Bugger, you know who it is?"

"So do you. Liam Kinsella."

Her reaction was a slow build to slamming a clenched fist down on the table, turning the heads of early customers, halting the work behind the bar, bringing Kristian into view.

"I knew it!" she hissed. "All that consideration, all that niceness. I bloody knew it!"

"No, you didn't," I suggested. "But like me, when the penny dropped, all the other coins came hurtling down the chute and added up to more than you thought. Kinsella brought the heroin in, killed Vic and Freddie and tried to have it pinned on Aaron."

Emma sat back, nursing the side of her hand as the blood returned to it. She was still angry, but in a minute or two that would change to feeling stupid for having been taken in.

Grogan reached out to the table beside him, passed Emma a napkin. She dabbed her eyes, careful not to smudge the makeup.

"I'll get some drinks," he said. "We have coffee. What do you want, Emma?"

"VAT." She nodded at the Vaulting Barman. "Tell him an Emma special."

Grogan rose and went over to the bar.

"This is the difficult bit," I said. "Well, easy, really, but difficult too, if you know what I mean."

"Of course I don't. Nobody would."

"How well do you know Angelica Carter?"

She didn't know Angie well, she told me, but in the end she was the only reporter she would speak to about the murders. Emma knew that empathy might just have been her journalistic front, but somehow it never felt phoney or intrusive and they'd remained in contact ever since.

Carter hated the way the police had treated Emma and her sister. Because they'd been involved in the smuggling, the police had left them to the mercy of a baying press who'd become creative with the facts and careless with verification. Carter had written a piece about that as well, slagging off the boys in blue. I liked the sound of her.

Grogan returned, carrying a tray, two coffees and a tall glass with vodka, something fizzy and a chunk of orange clinging to the rim. He set them down in front of us. Emma took a grown-up swig, making me wish I'd asked for whisky, ice all the way...

"What's Angie Carter got to do with all this?" she asked.

"I'd like to meet her."

"Phone her up."

"No, I want the four of us together. First I want you to think hard about what I plan to do..."

"Which is?"

I held up a hand to fend off questions. "If it works, you and your sister could walk away from all this, you from the smuggling charges, her with almost nothing for the heroin. You agree, Bill?"

He nodded, even though he'd no more idea what my plans were than Emma had.

"If it fails?" she said.

"No harm done. Only to your reputation."

- 31 -

I'd expected, maybe even hoped, that Emma would live in a terraced house close to the docks with all the romance of a once-flourishing industry around her. The noise, the bustle, the smell, the oversized characters, but it wasn't to be. Not only had my imagined setting ceased to exist, but once the smuggling business had taken off Vic had bought a bungalow to the west of town, in a cul-de-sac called Montgomery Drive. It had been a birthday surprise for Emma and she'd played the game of being delighted with it. Secretly, she'd preferred their old terraced house in Nelson Street, she told me, and was pretty sure Vic did too.

Inside, the bungalow was efficient rather than homely, modernised to the point of sterility, but I was glad to see that it had two bedrooms and a substantial garden. Easy access from all sides...

Emma had taken some persuading to go along with my plans and, in fairness to myself, I hadn't put undue pressure on her, merely mentioned that I intended to catch her husband's murderer and only had a month to work with so I'd be grateful for an early decision, yes or no. She'd got back to me with a yes, twenty-four hours after our visit to *The Amethyst*, and the day after that Angelica Carter arrived at Montgomery Drive nine o'clock sharp.

She was a well-preserved tall woman, probably older than she looked, but I put her at fifty. The photo she used at the top of her weekly column in *The Grimsby Echo* needed updating but by and large it was faithful. Blonde hair, tight to her head, and a face with few expressions other than indignation. Thin lips, I noted, and the twitchiness of someone who had recently stopped smoking and turned to the dreaded e-cigarette. She asked Emma if she minded her using it and produced from her bag a penny whistle of a thing whose role in life was to load her up with nicotine.

She and Emma talked quietly together in the kitchen for a few minutes, as if Grogan and I didn't exist, and then Carter walked through to the lounge and introduced herself. She couldn't quite abandon the journalist's way of doing things and was full of questions for the first ten minutes. Gradually she showed signs of falling in with my plans and at the tipping point I reminded her there would be a cracking story at the end of it, an exclusive if ever there was one.

"If it succeeds," she said. "What if it doesn't?"

"No harm done, surely," I said.

Emma looked at me. "Only to my reputation, you said."

"And mine," said Carter. "People don't trust journalists at the best of times..."

Grogan, so far my considerate stone in the corner, thought it was time he spoke. "What makes you think it won't succeed?"

She laughed. "What makes you think it *will*?"

"Because all Liam Kinsella ever wanted was the heroin. Fifteen million quid. He's gone a hell of a long way to get his hands on it, committed two murders ... possibly a third, a colleague of mine I should've taken better care of. Why would he stop now?"

She turned fully towards him. "This colleague of yours...?"

He smiled and gently cut the air with one hand. "Later, maybe. If and when."

She turned up her nose and went over to the mantel above the mock fireplace. There were several photos in wooden frames standing on it and Carter looked down at one. She'd seen it before, I imagine. It was of both sisters at a party with respective husbands. Vic was the larger of the two men, powerful and pissed, with his wife twisted into him away from the camera, held by his one-arm embrace. He had a glass in his free hand and was saying something to the photographer. Emma was laughing and so was Sarah, barely out of her teens, but Freddie on the other end of the line-up was there under sufferance, loathing the party itself, or having his photo taken, maybe both. He was tall and wiry with one of those unmemorable, mask-like faces. Like Vic he was dressed in a suit, Sarah beside him was wearing a skimpy hat, so it might have been a wedding, and it's my imagination, of course, but I felt I could sense the strain between him and his young wife.

Carter wasn't looking for inspiration in the photo; she had simply removed herself slightly in order to weigh up her options. She turned back to us.

"Okay," she said. "I'm game."

"Couple of questions?" I said. She nodded. "Will the editor be a problem?"

"Sometimes I wish he would be. I love a good fight. The CEO of the group's no trouble either." She smiled. "I know more about his private life than I really want to, but it comes in handy sometimes."

So, how would she pitch it? Slightly offended, she told me she'd been a journo for thirty years, in which time she'd become pretty good at it. Was there anything else I wanted to know?

Actually, there was. Did she have the contacts, the influence, the power to reach that I needed? I didn't ask.

- 32 -

I decided it would be best all round if Emma moved out of her bungalow for the duration and, partly because she didn't like living there anyway, she readily agreed. She went off to visit a friend in Spain with strict instructions not to confide the real reason for her visit.

Before she left she made up beds for us. I took her room, Grogan was in the spare. She left notes about how to use the oven, what to do if the shower suddenly cut out and how to manipulate the key in the back door to lock it. She drove off, early morning, and Grogan put the biscuit tin in the garage and locked it. It was then a matter of waiting three days for *The Grimsby Echo* to hit the stands, as they say.

Grogan was more relaxed about the delay than I was, partly because he'd found some obscure satellite channel that was re-running a series about desert wildlife which included cacti. I spent the time shopping for food, cooking it and walking the dog. There were fields nearby and very few neighbours, most of whom had been driven indoors by the approaching cold front.

The three-day wait felt like a fortnight, but it gave me time to dwell on Liam Kinsella's affront to me, his belief that he could play me for a fool and win. Virtually every word he'd uttered within my hearing was stuck in my head, its meaning, tone and context defying me to find what Blackwell had asked for. Proof. Not evidential proof but enough for him to feel comfortable about pursuing the case against this principal witness turned prime suspect.

It was the second day of waiting and I'd risen early, made coffee, eaten some out-of-date cereal I'd found at the back of a cupboard, and by eight o'clock, with no sign of the kraken in the spare room awakening, I decided to go for a walk with the dog. I went to the front door and opened it to discover that, true to Grogan's weather forecast, snow had fallen. It was disappointing snow, the kind I recall from childhood being just a centimetre or two deep and in no way fully covering rooftops, cars or distant fields. Might just as well not have bothered falling. A drop of sleet, my father would've called it, before promising that real snow was just around the corner.

It had turned even colder, though, so I went back to Emma's room and in the bottom of a chest of drawers found a sweater, probably one of Vic's. I donned it, put my jacket back on and stepped out again into the snow. Disappointing though it was in childhood terms, it was still enough to be wet underfoot and I wondered if Emma had kept any of Vic's boots. As a trawlerman he must've had a few pairs. I went back indoors and, sure enough, in the hall cupboard found some wellingtons, too big for me but what the hell. I put them on and set off again.

As I reached the front gate the door behind me opened and Bill Grogan stood there, fully dressed, though not for winter.

"You alright?" he said.

"Yeah, why wouldn't I be?"

"Lot of to-ing and fro-ing, that's all." He looked round. "Snow. Told you there would be."

"I never doubted you. Fancy a walk in it? There's another pair of boots in the cupboard."

He clearly wished he hadn't been so concerned about me and, stroking his chin, eventually said, "Alright. Give me five minutes to shave. Haven't had a chance to since we got here."

He went back inside and closed the door behind him. And there they were, lined up in perfect carelessness, a dozen or so words that would condemn Kinsella out of his own mouth. Far from being brilliant deduction it was a matter of 'all things come to he who waits', or in my case he who is forced to wait. Either way I turned and hurried back up the path, opened the door and leaned in.

"Bill!"

He came out of the spare room, electric razor in hand. "What?"

"Put that bloody thing down!"

It must have been the urgency in my voice that made him do as I'd asked and he placed the razor on the hall table, awaiting further instructions.

"Come back to the front door. Stand there on the mat. Don't move."

"Yeah, alright, but I mean..."

"Do it."

He stood where I'd asked him to and I strode twenty deliberate paces which took me down the path, through the gate and out into the road. I stopped, turned and looked at him. He had his arms out wide as if he were being crucified and wanted to know why.

"You *sure* you're alright?" he asked.

"Fine."

Angelica Carter e-mailed me a copy of the piece that same evening, not for my approval, but headed 'FYI'. The item looked even better on the front page of *The Grimsby Echo* the next morning.

It was halfway down, not garish or attention seeking, but unmissable. The headline read:

MURDERED MAN'S WIDOW CHARGED WITH SUPPLYING HEROIN

The piece went on to say:

Emma Jane Wesley appeared in court yesterday, following the raid on a house by police in the Grimsby area on Wednesday.

Wesley, 36, of Montgomery Drive, Great Coates, is charged on two counts: supplying heroin and possessing heroin with intent to supply. She was remanded in custody ahead of a further appearance at Grimsby Magistrates' Court next week. Wesley is the widow of Victor Wesley, who was murdered alongside Frederick Trent in woodland near Wragby last March.

I came back from the local shop with a copy of the paper and showed it to Grogan. He read it and nodded, then echoed my only concern: doubt that Angelica Carter had the contacts and the reach I hadn't cared to ask her about.

I needn't have worried. By lunchtime the following day, the editor on the local ITN news bulletin had broadcast an item about Emma to his audience of 180,000 people. Admittedly he harked back to the unsolved murders, with footage of the highly distraught Jago sisters. The piece was repeated later that evening, by which time the BBC were delivering their own version on their twenty-four hour news channel. It jumped easily from there to the local BBC news.

As I'd hoped, it wasn't big enough, or gruesome enough, to warrant a press corps camping out on the front lawn in Montgomery Drive, although there were a few rings at the doorbell. The dog barked; we ignored them.

By Sunday it was on page five of a national tabloid and featured on a TV discussion programme which earnestly chewed over the plight of middle-aged housewives who were turning to drug dealing. The state of the economy was blamed.

Carter phoned me on Sunday night, largely to boast that she'd achieved what she'd set out to. She also promised that, should nothing come of this pebble she'd chucked into the millpond, she would run an article suggesting that the paltry amount of heroin found at Emma Wesley's house was just the tip of the iceberg. I said I didn't think it would be necessary, but thanked her for the idea. Ever the journalist, she reminded me that I'd promised to let her know the moment anything newsworthy happened.

"I've been researching you," she said. "Quite a tally, thirty-seven murders. Just out of interest, though, why did you hit that fellow officer? How hard and who was he?"

I laughed. "You're breaking up, Angie," I said, and ended the call.

From that point on we went into a kind of limbo. I'd hoped that Grogan and I might get to know each other better as we sat in that bungalow, virtual prisoners of our own making. Admittedly it was only a week but I came away realising that whereas he'd learned a great deal about me, I was as much in the dark as ever about him.

He was one of those curious people who barely acknowledge their past. He'd been brought up in London, born to parents late in their lives. No siblings. Educated at a school nearby. Joined the police at eighteen. This abundance of information was the result of me trying the usual conversation openers only to find he had a knack of closing them rapidly. In contrast he possessed the invaluable skill, at least in terms of our chosen profession, of getting others to talk. Maybe I did so in order to fill the silence, but the result was just the same: within the space of seven days Grogan had a full picture of my upbringing, my marriage and each of my children. He became party to my strengths and weaknesses, but as he did so it was always with deference to my superior rank. I was the officer, he was the company sergeant.

We spelled each other in terms of waiting. He would take eight hours on point, while I shopped, cooked, walked the dog, slept. I would take the next shift while he watched television programmes about far-off places he wanted to visit.

At night we turned in early, ten o'clock sometimes, having exhausted our mutuality. What I didn't realise at the time was that his silence was due to something he'd mentioned just once, in front of Angelica Carter. He felt guilty about Fairchild. He should've kept a better eye on her.

Thursday evening was no different to any of the others. After dinner I e-mailed Laura, mainly to find out how things were going between Fee and Yukito. She replied that Fee was blaming me for holding up her plans. She'd decided to return to Tokyo with Yukito. Each had made promises to the other: Yukito would give Fee more of his time; she would give him, dare I say it, less of hers. She'd had a gradual revelation, she confided to Laura. With Ellie having found her true soulmate in Terrific Rick and Jaikie on the brink of marrying Jodie, it was time for Fee, like any mother, real or elected, to let her charges go. Yukito had dropped everything concerned with his business and followed her to England, a declaration of love if ever there was one. No mention was made of the part I'd played in this, which meant I must've performed with a degree of subtlety. There was no mention either of our wild card, Con...

I remember thinking, as I drew the curtains, that it was a particularly dark night, and that fact ensured that I slept just below the surface. Dogge heard it first. A noise in the kitchen. She rumbled her concern and I opened my eyes immediately, whispered for her to be quiet. The bedroom door was ajar, and dark though the house was I could see out into the hallway, kitchen appliances throwing their LED light, reds, greens, into the space. Something altered the intensity of it, for just a second, and then it returned. Someone was in the house and had probably entered via the back door, the locking of which Grogan and I hadn't fully mastered.

I slipped out of bed and stooped for the Smith & Wesson which I kept on top of the bag beside me. I laid a hand on the dog, her instruction to stay put, and moved to the door, stood at the hinge side of it for what seemed like an hour but could only have been moments.

The door opened a little further and Liam Kinsella tip-toed in. He walked over to the bed. As far as I could tell he wasn't carrying a weapon. He didn't think he'd need one. He leaned down over the bed and said quietly, "Emma ... Emma, wake up."

Receiving no answer, he leaned forward and prodded the ruck I'd left in the duvet.

"Emma, Emma, you've a visitor..." he said, in a normal voice.

I slammed the door, mainly to wake up Grogan, then reached across to the light switch and turned it on. Kinsella spun round. We were both blinded for the moment but I was the one holding the gun, aiming it straight at his chest. He stood there, eyes seemingly frozen in their sockets.

Eventually, he spoke, breezily, almost matily, but surely without realising what he was saying.

"Hi! How you doing?"

The door burst open, though it didn't need such rough treatment. Grogan entered, dressed as I was, boxers, T-shirt, socks.

"Man wants to know how we are, Bill."

He went straight over to Kinsella, threw him to the floor, turned him and applied the handcuffs. He then frisked him in that position for anything he might be carrying, but, arrogant to the last, Kinsella had thought he could get what he wanted just by talking.

Grogan hauled him to his feet, by the collar of the black tracksuit he was wearing, and leaned towards him.

"We're fine," he said.

Grogan handcuffed Kinsella to a central heating downpipe in Emma's kitchen and went back into the spare room. When he reappeared he was not only dressed but he was carrying his rounders bat. Kinsella looked at me.

"Your human rights?" I asked.

"You know what he's like, don't you?" he said.

I glanced up at the kitchen clock. "Three thirty. Too early to call Commander Blackwell, tell him you dropped in."

"You're right, that's all it was. An old friend, coming to see..."

"You came because you thought she was dealing some of that heroin, to pay the bills. Wasted journey. I found it."

He smiled, almost playfully. "Where, out of interest?"

I shook my head. "You'd kick yourself if I told you."

He tried to fall back on one of his many personae, the apologetic coward who'd made mistakes out of fear for his own safety. "Alright, so I chickened out of giving evidence against..."

"Shut up! You murdered those two men..."

"Me?"

"...and you played every card in the deck, from terrified victim to bullied witness. Christ, you even had me believing Carew and Sweetman had written your statement for you."

The handcuffs slid up the down pipe, taking paint off it, as Kinsella rose from the stool he'd been sitting on. He pointed at me with his free hand, offended now. "I was right there. I saw it all."

"I believe you. You saw it because you were standing next to them." I went over to him, right into his space. "As close as we are now."

He was appalled. "Even if that was true, how could you prove such a thing?"

"I don't have to prove it; I just have to give Blackwell justification for building a case against you. The evidence is up to him, but if he thinks you're guilty he'll find it."

"And this ... justification?"

"That day at my house when Sillitoe took you through the evidence, you said you'd witnessed the murders from twenty metres away. Aaron was head and shoulders above the other two, you said. Vic was looking sprauncy, that was the word you used. And Freddie was Freddie, same old anorak, same old cords. And he hadn't shaved for a couple of days."

He shrugged. "I can't remember what I said yesterday, let alone six weeks ago..."

"That's alright, because the whole thing is on tape. Marion Bewley. Her 'career development'." He still hadn't drawn level with me. "You couldn't have seen two days' growth on his face from twenty metres away. You had to be standing next to him." I pointed two fingers at him, pistol fashion. "Bang, bang."

He sat down again, leaned back against the wall.

Grogan came over to us, rounders bat in one hand, slapping it gently in the palm of the other. "I'm going to ask Mr Hawk to go and put some clothes on now."

"No..." said Kinsella, trying to back away into the plasterwork.

"I want to know what happened to Petra Fairchild and, if you've any sense, you want to tell me."

I made my way to the doorway through to the hall.

"Don't go!" Kinsella called out.

"Can't walk around all day like this."

Grogan looked him over, then homed in on his right knee. As he raised the bat Kinsella yelled out, "She's alright! Two days after leaving your house, she disappeared."

"That's a nasty word, Liam," I said.

"Maybe she realised you weren't Clyde Barrow after all," Grogan suggested. "Where?"

"I don't know. She just ... took off."

328

I went back to the bedroom to get dressed, closed the door behind me. I heard one or two screams from the kitchen but Kinsella didn't change his story. Fairchild had just vanished.

- 33 -

I arrived back at Beech Tree to praise and blame, the former for having found Liam Kinsella, to say nothing of the heroin, the latter for having taken so long about it. Fee and Yukito were anxious to return to Tokyo but she hadn't wanted to do so without saying goodbye.

That night as I sat in the cabin, e-mailing Blackwell a receipt for a cheque from 'the safe-house contingency fund' and clearing up fifty or sixty details with Angelica Carter, Fee knocked on the door. They'd booked a taxi for eleven the next morning. Meantime she wanted me to know that she was going back with Yukito of her own free will, not because of anything I'd said, done or implied, not because of an emptiness brought on by Ellie, Jaikie and me moving on, not because of age creeping up on her, not because...

Suffice to say that she had a bagful of reasons and I listened to each one of them, nodding sincerely.

Before she went back into the house she looked at me intensely and said, "What's wrong?"

I gave her the answer I thought she expected. "I'll miss you..."

"Not that! Jesus, it's Christmas in six weeks' time. We'll be back. I meant what is wrong?"

I must have a neon forehead or something. I smiled. "Petra Fairchild, if you must know."

"Dad, if he killed her as well, go find the body. If he didn't, go find the woman herself. It'll give you something to do."

It was a great plan, I said, mocking her, and so simple to execute. Did she have any suggestion as to where I might start the search? She thought about it for a moment, then answered with her gift for spotting the elusive obvious.

"If I were in really deep shit, and assuming I was still alive, where would I go? Back home to Mum. Or, in my case, Dad."

Two days later I drove into the Fairchilds' yard in Ashendon, with that gentle swish of old tyres on new shingle. I can only say that nothing looked out of place. Why that should have made me suspicious I've no idea; my jaundiced view of human nature working overtime, I guess. There were two cars parked in the thatched carport, a His Jag and a Hers VW. Nothing else. No tyre tracks in the gravel, no sign of a hasty retreat. Or advance.

I got out and as I stood looking across at the house a man my age, only better dressed, came out through the back door with a 'who the fuck are you?' look on his face. He was tall, with collar-length white hair but a complexion like overripe fruit, bruised here, shrivelled there. A drinker's face, old before its time. His voice was smoky with a flat battery of a cough to go with it. "Morning. Can I help?"

"My name is Nathan Hawk."

"Jack Fairchild."

As we shook hands I explained that I was a friend of his daughter, that we'd brought a dishevelled young man here to have his hair cut a couple of months ago. He nodded.

"Is Grace about?" I asked.

"She's hoovering, I believe." He paused to listen. No sound. "Maybe not. Ah..."

Grace had come to the door and stepped out onto the patio. "Mr Hawk, how lovely to see you again."

She was polite smiles and gentle manners and, taking his cue from that, her husband relaxed a little. Nevertheless, we stood unnaturally still, three points of a masonic triangle, the Fairchilds waiting for me to dictate the angles.

"I need to talk to you about Petra."

She closed her eyes, maybe trying to squeeze out a tear. I wasn't sure. "I can't tell you how upset we've been by all this," she said in a small voice.

"May I come in?"

"Yes, yes, please do..."

The kitchen was the same as I remembered it: pin-neat, everything put away after use, surfaces wiped, floor swept. And just as you'd expect from any mock farmhouse there was a pleasant smell of baking in the air. I moved slowly around the room, an old trick I'd learned from yet another ancient desk sergeant. The slower you move, the more likely it is that others will stay put. By the time you reach your destination it's too late for them to stop you.

"Has she been home since ... you know?" I asked.

"Why would she have been?" said her father.

I shrugged. "Get some clothes, reassure you, borrow money, any number of things."

"No, she hasn't..."

Jack Fairchild couldn't lie to save his life, never mind his daughter's.

I'd reached the oven, picked up the mittens and put one on. They stood and watched, reacting only when I opened it, reached in and took out a tray of Danish apple bars.

"Your daughter's favourite. I got a whiff of the cinnamon out in the yard. Go and get her, Mr Fairchild."

As he passed me on his way to the hall he stopped and glared at me. "What would you have done, for your daughter?"

I shrugged. "The same. Only better."

A few moments later Petra entered the kitchen ahead of her father. She must've been behind the door, listening. She stood perfectly still and I couldn't determine her mood, if it was one of horror, surprise or fear. I settled for the last, rating it the kind which runs through you when you've done something so stupid it defies belief. It isn't the act itself which terrifies so much as the knowledge that you did it willingly and, having done it once, the chances are you'll do it again, then again...

I told her she wasn't looking too bad, given the circumstances. It was true. The clothes were fresh, the make-up reasonable, the hair immaculate. The voice was small, though, that of a girl and not the woman who'd tried putting me in my place on more than one occasion.

"I'm sorry," she whispered.

"I wonder if we'd all be better in the lounge," said Jack.

No doubt that was where the booze lived. I said I preferred kitchens and sat at the table. Petra slithered down onto the bench opposite me.

"Why are you here?" she asked.

"Worried about you."

She believed me, but when I told her Bill Grogan was also worried she laughed, then from somewhere she dredged up some grit and flung it at me. "I suppose you want to know all the torrid details, how a police officer of eight years fell prey to a con artist?"

"I don't want details, I can work them out for myself..."

"Maybe you're worried that you should've stepped in and done something about it?" said her father.

"She's thirty-two years old, for Christ's sake! She may be a child to you, but to the rest of the world she's fully grown and smart enough to be a member of SOU."

He said he'd still like to know how it had happened right under my nose, hoping perhaps that when the time came it could all be blamed on me. Petra stretched a hand out to her father and he backed off.

She spoke carefully, haltingly, but the gist of it was that she'd started off feeling sorry for Kinsella and, yes, he had a talent for getting sympathy from the most unlikely places. So, before she knew it, she was helping him, buying presents and cards for his friends, posting them off. And why not? she insisted. He was meant to be on our side but Grogan bullied him, beat him up, cuffed him to the plumbing, kept him on a rope when we went for a jog. No wonder the defeated, bullied little boy came through, bewildered, frightened, vulnerable. Scared of Grogan,

334

scared that Flaxman was out to kill him, scared of me, his reluctant host. Somewhere along the way he told her she was the only human being in the house. Then he told her he loved her.

I started drumming the table, both sets of fingers. "Then he told you he was rich?"

She nodded. "But I never believed he had money. It was a pipe dream, a way of impressing me."

"But you still fell for him..."

"I wasn't the only one he fooled. Doctor Peterson had him down as a casualty of the system; your daughter thought you'd abused his human rights. Jesus, you even pleaded his immunity to Henry Sillitoe."

"Not quite the same as falling in love with him."

"It's *exactly* the same, just taken to another level..."

"How come you're still alive, Petra?" I asked.

The idea that Kinsella might have killed her, had the chance arisen, the circumstances been different, still troubled her.

"I don't know," she said. "If we'd been on our own for longer...?"

She leaned forward on both arms and stared down at the table, took her time recounting. He'd got rid of her just an hour after leaving Beech Tree. They were four, five miles away from Ashendon. He stopped the car she'd provided him with, on a narrow, twisty lane, turned to her and told her to get out. She'd laughed, believing it was a joke, but then his whole demeanour changed, his temper flared. He screamed at her to get out of the fucking car and thank her lucky stars he didn't have time to kill her and dump the body. He pushed her against the door; she opened it, stepped out and he tore off, knocking her onto the muddy verge. She saw him brake half a mile down the road and, out of fear that he was having second thoughts, she scrambled over the gate beside her and ran off across the field. She didn't stop until she reached her parents' house.

I nodded and leaned back.

"So now you know," said her father. "She made a mistake, but she's as much a victim in all this..."

"No! She believed he had 15 million quid in the offing."

"She's just told you, it was a pipe dream."

"And who do you think will believe her? They'll prefer the version where he offered her a cut to help him escape. And she took it."

Petra sat rigid on the bench and stared at me. I half-expected a blast of invective but instead she began to melt into tears. That brought her mother back into the fray, bristling with unconditional love. She'd hardly said a word since we'd entered the house and now, with both hands on the table, she leaned into my face.

"You may have earned a few stars in the eyes of your cronies. Murder solved, drugs found, police officer tracked down? Just don't expect us to be impressed." She waited, eyes darting all over my face, and then cut me down to size. "You can go now."

"Or what? You'll call the police?" I stood up, reached into my inside pocket for an old business card, the only one I've ever been given and kept. I dropped it onto the table. "You'll have to play ball with the system, sooner or later, Petra. Get in touch with that man there. He saved me from being charged with assault, then secured my pension in the wake of my, well ... having thumped a fellow officer for being a prize twat. Tell him it was me recommended him."

I headed for the back door.

"So when?" she called after me.

"When what?"

"When will you tell Blackwell you found me?"

"Couple of years' time."

There isn't much more to say about the case, really. Fairchild got in touch with my solicitor friend, who told her to go and stay in France for a couple of weeks, get her story straight, then return and face the music. He conducted the orchestra quite brilliantly, in my opinion. She wound up doing time but not as much as we'd all expected. Furthermore she served it in a prison he approved, one where she didn't have to spend all day looking over her shoulder just because she'd once been a policewoman.

Other guilty parties were given sentences of varying lengths, thirty years being handed down for the double murder. No parole. Of the others I remember thinking they'd all be young enough to reboot their lives once they got out.

Angelica Carter told their stories extremely well, over and over again, and I admit to being irked by her laudatory prose about Tom Blackwell. She was quoted endlessly, on television and radio news, documentaries, blogs, newspapers. One sentence stood out. "The driving force behind solving this case was Commander Tom Blackwell, who carried out his search for the truth with courage and inspiration, reminding us yet again that our police service is the finest in the world."

In other words he'd got someone else to do his dirty work for him. And taken the credit.

Lightning Source UK Ltd.
Milton Keynes UK
UKOW06f1813200815

257267UK00001B/3/P